His Other Uniform (Secret Soldier Series, Book One)

Philippa Attwood

His Other Uniform, by Philippa Attwood
All rights reserved.

Cover Design: Philippa Attwood
Editor: Philippa Attwood
Cover Photo Source: Shutterstock

Follow my social media for updates, sneak peaks, information and all news regarding my books, as well as keeping up to date with me:

Twitter - @authorphilippa
Instagram - @authorphilippaattwood

Table of Contents

Dedication:

To my Nan & Grandad, Violet & John. You both left this Earth not even 48 hours apart, but never once have you been forgotten by my heart. Not even after almost five years.

Wherever you both are, I hope I've made you proud.
Love you both, so much.

Your Granddaughter x

Author's Note:

Thank you for joining me on my next literary adventure. I had a blast writing my first and debut novel, 'Solivagant', for you all. I'm so excited to bring you all this next read, which will be a part of the 'Secret Soldier' series.

Writing something so important as this which contains issues such as soldier rehabilitation, PTSD and such others is something I've been wanting to do for a while, so I hope how I've written these relevant topics has done them justice and highlights just how important they are to acknowledge and discuss.

Please don't forget to leave a rating & review on Amazon and/or Goodreads when you're done, I'd really appreciate it.

Enjoy!

~Philippa x

PROLOGUE -
Theon
(September 2014)

You would've thought I would've learned my lesson by now. When someone goes through something traumatic, utterly-dangerous and life-threateningly risky, they'd avoid putting themselves in that position again. Nope, not me. I guess you could say I'm my very own kind of special. At least, that's what I'm told.

When I announced to my dear mother at eighteen years old that I planned to join the army, you could guess what sort of response I'd get. Only, I didn't get it. Continuing to surprise me at every turn, she responded with a simple shake of her head and a gentle, defeated sigh.

"I suppose it was inevitable. You're just like your father." She'd said, a hidden smile tugging at the corner of her mouth. My father had served in the military for a number of years, right up until he was honourably discharged just before my tenth birthday, and where they'd never hidden what he'd been doing for a living from me, my mother did her best to offer other career options for me to pursue.

Despite her best efforts, there was only one thing I could see myself doing. I was going to follow in my father's footsteps, and join the army. Of course, both of my parents had insisted that I completed some sort of education first. This was a hard point to negotiate on as I had no idea what I wanted to study at college, not that there was a lack of choices at Texas A&M. No. I just had my heart set on joining the army, nothing else came close that I was passionate about carrying out as a next step.

Eventually, we all came to an agreement we were all satisfied with. I would be joining the army after my twenty-first birthday. My father wanted me to either pursue home education or work on the family ranch for those three years. I chose the ranch work. I'd always preferred manual labour, so it wasn't a hard choice. After that, I'd be free to join the army and go through the required United States Army Basic Training, also known as IET (Initial Entry Training), which all U.S Army, Army Reserve and Army National Guard go through. From there should I be lucky to pass basic training, I'd be re-routed to a specific training course more specific to what I wanted to do within the army.

Three years and many back-breaking hours working on the ranch later, my twenty-first birthday rolled around and soon after that, I signed up to join the United States Army. Just before I left, my mother threw me a going away 'party'. Though as this was Texas in the height of summer, it was more of a massive BBQ cookout than a party, which I was totally fine with, as I was more of a cookout guy than a party-mad lad. I got a fair share of teasing off my buddies for that, though I knew they didn't mean it nastily. They were good guys at heart. Guys I'd known and grown up with. I knew I'd miss their camaraderie when I went off to fight for our country, but knowing they'd be right there to welcome me home cancelled out the sadness of not having them at my side. Just.

As the cookout/party came to a close and it was time for me to leave, my parents pulled me aside before I was due to head for the airport. My mother had embraced me for longer than she's ever done before, her silence spoke all the words I knew she wanted to say but didn't. My father gave me the typical man-hug/proud father pat on the back, his eyes saying all that he wished to say but didn't, too. Neither of them were the type of parents to spill their hearts out emotionally, unlike some, to which I was thankful because if they were the crying type, I knew I'd have a harder time leaving than I was fighting secretly inside.

Shortly after this, I left for the airport. A new adventure waiting for me on the other end.

A new adventure that I had no idea what I was getting into, or in for.

All of this brings me to where I am now, four years later, gun in hand as I lead my team into the final mission of our current tour.

Thank God.

Our latest mission saw us posted to Raqqa, Syria. Fighting here began back in 2011, four years prior to now. Hard to believe something this destructive and devastating mostly to those innocent in all this, was still going on. Countless efforts have been made by other forces, groups and movements to put an end to this, all to no avail. The innocent continued to suffer and a once culturally-rich country continued to get decimated until cities, towns and homes were reduced to nothing. Mere shells and rubble of places full of former citizens.

So far, twenty or so targets had been hit by our jets trying to take out the current terror force out here. We all know who they are, no need to even say their names.   On the ground, we were the guys whose task it was to take out anyone who hadn't been taken out by the jets. Enough innocents had died, it was time to put an end to all this, and me and my squad were just the men to do it, along with all the other U.S-lead soldiers dotted around where we were needed.

Let's get this done and get home to our loved ones!

"On me! Move! Move! Move!" I gave the command for us to move, barking it into the mic attached to the helmet strapped securely onto my head and chin.

Moving into the positions we'd been brief and told to move into, all seemed to go smoothly. Out of our hiding spot and into a position where we'd be unloading our fire, I was thankful none of my men had been taken out by any sneaky snipers left laying around, somehow surviving the last bomb drop. I'd been lucky in my time as a Captain, not to lose too many men while on deployment. We all lost men at some stage, to both judgement errors and as a casualty of war due to the opposition, which made me even more thankful for the choices I made when putting this squad together. They were a crack team of skilled fighters, planners, logistics and various others who always got the job done and got us all back home in one piece. Well, almost all of us.

God damn it Harrison, why'd you have to play a hero like that?

You should be here...with us. With...me.

Thinking back to the last moments I shared with my best buddy always brought a tear to my eye. Though right now, I did not have the time to let it get to me. Not when once again, the lives of men and women were up to me to keep safe and bring home alive.

Side-glancing at my second-in-command, Sergeant Layton Reed, the man whom I'd signed up with and had been part of our former best buddy trio, I was ready to give the second command to move out and attack. 'Was', being the keyword to that sentence. The chance to give the command never arose, as the moment my mouth opened ready to breathe the word 'advance', the world as I once knew it was ripped away from me.

I knew nothing of sight, smell, sound, taste or touch. At least, not in the normal sense. All around me, all that surrounded me was not the familiar scene we'd known for weeks now. Instead, all was white. Nor was there any sound of gunfire, dropping of bombs or cries of scared, innocent children or their parents. Replaced by that was a singular shrill whistle, echoing over and over in my ears. The familiar weight of my feet firmly planted on the earth no longer existed. I was weightless. Floating. Falling.

Unlike in books or movies, my life didn't flash before my eyes. The blinding white remained a constant presence as the world carried on outside of it. Without me.

Mother...Father...I'm sorry...

I love you both...so much.

Those were my last thoughts as my once heaven-white world turned to black, passing through the grey where for the briefest of moments, I saw what I never thought I'd see in what might be my last few moments in this world. A woman. An angel, perhaps? Whoever she was, she was the most beautiful thing my eyes ever saw. Besides my own mother.

As much as I'd love to know who that woman--or angel--was, if she was real or part of the chaos my mind and body were currently caught up in, it just wasn't plausible right now. It was time to meet my maker. Or so I thought.

Just as the world seemed to close in around me just as the blackness had done before it, two words floated into the last of my earthly consciousness.

"Hold on…"
Okay…I'll hold on.
I'll…hold on.
Hold…on.
Hold…
Darkness. Nothing. Peace, at last.

CHAPTER ONE
Kenna
(Present Day - May 2019)

Hot. Sweaty. Humid.

That's how I would describe my current situation right now, standing holding a silver-platter full of hors d'oeuvres, filling in last-minute in place of my best friend, Jess, who suddenly came down with the flu. Therefore as her duty as the best friend, I offered to take her place, not fully aware of what I would be getting herself into, or how hard it would be to be a server for one evening.

Jess had called me earlier full of flu, begging for her help. That never happened unless my best friend ran out of options, so here I was. I had no desire of refusing Jess' request for help, as more often than not, Jess helped out when I had my own share dilemmas. After all, that's what best friends, who were more like sisters, did for one another. At least, it was the case for Jess and myself.

From what I had been told, albeit briefly about this evening, it was gathering of sorts for elder/senior military members who were no longer serving, but were being celebrated or remembering those they'd served with. Or something along those lines. I don't know anyone who'd served so I'm not all that clued up on the goings-on within the military world. Not anymore. Soon after arriving and dressed in the borrowed, tight-fitting all black server's uniform with white shirt and sensible shoes, I knew exactly what I had walked into.

A sign reading, 'Honouring General O'D' hung above the entrance to the building I had been given an address to follow on my GPS. So as it turned out, the evening was to honour someone. A person who I would never meet again and that was perfectly fine with me, as I wasn't the only one. Many worked these sorts of jobs, as Jess does, where they'll never meet their clients again so, it wasn't anything unique or personal to me.

As of now, I would have to guess that I was roughly halfway through the shift for the evening. Even if she couldn't check her phone to guess, I would guess it was about halfway which meant it was soon time for my allotted break time slot. That is, before I set back to work for the final stretch until quitting time.

Shifting the silver plate into my other gloved hand, I moved my neck from side to side, attempting to relieve some of the muscular pain at the base of my aching neck. After clocking off tonight, the first thing I'm going to do is head for her heavenly claw footed bathtub. Soaking away the ache in places I'm still not used to having them in.

If I ever finish up here…

As one of the partygoers removes a canapé from her tray, I offer the guest a polite smile, receiving a softly muttered 'thank you' in return, before the guest moves back to a man in uniform who she assumed was her date this evening. Lucky woman. I hadn't even been so lucky to have had a date to my high school prom, let alone stand here and dare to dream about being at the side of a man in uniform. Still, I couldn't be mad at the poor woman. They looked happy no matter how they were connected, and that's all that mattered.

In fact, it's how all the people littered around the room looked. Each of them possessed the same happy, contented looks on their faces and in how each of them stood proud. Not that I could blame them for being so. Serving in any force for the United States was something to be extremely proud of and ought to be celebrated, such as the case tonight.

Turning her attention away from the happy couple, I looked around once more at the guests dotted around the room. Several of the men, varying in age, were dressed in their respective force uniform ranging from what I knew was the army, navy, marine and a few others. All of whom looked dashing. As did the women. Never have I seen such beautiful women, again ranging in various ages, dressed up in all their finery as if they were attending a ball held by the Queen of England. Everyone here was just simply magnificent. At least that's what I thought.

Two people in particular caught my eye, stopping my gaze from roaming the crowd. One man clad in an army uniform, held gently another man's hand. The second wasn't from the army, but of a force I wasn't familiar with. Though, that was irrelevant. What wasn't irrelevant, was how it made me feel seeing two men, obviously an item, feel so comfortable with showcasing their relationship in a room full of service personnel.

Where society had made major acceptance advances in many areas of modern life, I knew all too well how in some places, homophobia was still sadly present. Or at the very least, it was still an underlying issue that needed to be stopped. I don't know why–as one of the few examples—the military was one of the places where it existed and how it came to be, which is why when I see small acts like this one before my eyes, it warms my heart more than a fire pit on a cold winter's night.

"You look like you're away with the fairies. Again." A voice said from behind me. One I knew well.

Without the need to turn my head, I could tell who the voice belonged to as its owner came to stand beside her. Maeve, one of the 'senior' servers I often worked with when filling in for Jess, stood to my right. In her late 40's, Maeve was the mother-figure to all of us 'young ones', which she often said when referring to anyone younger than herself, so not old at all. Her light brown hair was scraped back into its traditional casual 'serving bun', her go-to style when on the job.

"Hmm, not really. Just people-watching." I replied, keeping her voice low for only Maeve to hear.

"Dangerous thing to do, people-watching. Has gotten me into quite a bit of trouble over the years." A humorous tone coated Maeve's voice as she spoke.

Kenna smirked. "So I've heard."

The two of us stood in a comfortable silence for a moment until Maeve spoke up, breaking it. "Allow me." She said, taking the slightly lighter silver tray from my hand.

Opening my mouth to speak, I was cut off by the soft wave of Maeve's hand, stilling any words that were due to fly from my mouth. "Break time for you, hon. Go on, scoot! I've got this until you're back."

Not one to object against Maeve, I flashed her a thankful smile before exiting the room via the 'servers' door leading into the kitchen, grabbing the lunchbox with my name on it containing her food and drink, emerging then out onto the back part of the building. I have seen this part only once when first starting my shift earlier this evening, though it felt like forever since then and now, finally on my break.

Sitting down on a bench well-secured into a hidden alcove at the back of the building, I felt my muscles finally relax. Not having to stand up for a while was indeed a blessing I never thought I would be thankful for. How Jess did this day after day was beyond her. Though I now have a new appreciation for Jess and her work. Never again would I think it easy or not as taxing as my own.

Breaking away from the thoughts of my best friend, I opened the lunch box and began to enjoy the delicious goodies within.

#

Popping the last of her food into my mouth, I let out a sweet moans of delight. I'm not one to blow my own trumpet, but even I know when I was good at throwing ingredients together to make something pallet-dancingly delicious. Even if it was something as simple as a sandwich. Jess appreciated my culinary efforts too, on many a night when the two of us would binge-watch movies and just not have to worry about the world or what anyone thought about us, just for that night.

Jess often came round when one of us had a free night. Free from work or other commitments. Being each other's go-to person for company wasn't so bad, it paid off when either of us just wanted the instant company of another person and could immediately head on over without having to phone ahead.

Waiting back at home for her today when I would clock off from this job wouldn't be Jess, but a book I had been unable to put down since its release on April 16th. 'The Mister' by E.L.James. As a fan of her previous works, which you'd have to have been living on Mars to NOT know about, I jumped for joy when in January of this year, we were going to be blessed with a new novel by the legendary British author.

Immediately, I signed up to be notified from every social media account possible that would share any and all information about the then mystery read. I wasn't going to miss out on this for the world. Of course though, everyone went into a crazy fit about it possibly new Fifty Shades book. Thankfully, I knew better. If they'd pay as much attention to the world of E.L.James as I had, they would know that wasn't the case.

This time around, the story was based in London, instead of the U.S like her previous work. I loved London. Having been there several times for work-related trips, I'm beyond excited to read about somewhere she'd been to.

However, not everyone was as excited as I was about The Mister. Namely, critics. Of course. Immediately, I saw backlash from critics who jumped on the bandwagon to slate this read in any way possible, for any reason possible by looking at it on its own and comparing it to Fifty Shades. It was kind of sad how these people automatically went the hateful route. Passing judgement on the book for not being 'sexy' enough, being too 'tame' or 'boring', among the many unimaginative comments made about the book. No matter what Erika did when writing The Mister, critics would've viewed it the same way. If it was written more erotic than Fifty Shades, it'd be slated. If it was written as a sweet romance, comedy or any such other genre, it would've been slated. All critics do as soon as they see the name 'E.L.James', is pre-judge her work without even reading it and when they do, they go into it with a biased view.

It made my blood boil.

If I had the power to, I would get rid of all book critics altogether and let fans (who are the ones who ever matter when it comes to opinions about books) write the reviews. Critics just made things worse for potential readers, putting off people who would've given the book a read if not for their pointless review. Though I knew that the amount of hate against E.L.James and her work was small in comparison to the massively positive worldwide fan reception, I still get a bee in my bonnet with the critics and how the media portrays her.

At the end of the day, I knew I belonged in a worldwide fandom family who would always support a beloved author despite the insignificant hate, and that's all that matters.

"Are you done daydreaming? Or can someone else sit here too?" a deep voice said to me, ripping through the layers of my thoughts about all things E.L.James.

Towering above where I sat, stood a man clad in the most form-fitting tuxedo-type suit I had ever seen on a member of the opposite sex. He looked tall, though it was hard to tell from sitting down. As he waited for my response, his face, which was darkened by the night-time which surrounded them, grew equally as dark.

"I'm sorry…" I started to say, finding my voice at last. "Who exactly are you talking to? Me or a piece of trash on the street?"

The rude man in question crossed his arms over his tuxedo-clad chest, stretching the material impossibly tighter than it already was. "Oh? I thought the staff weren't supposed to talk like that to guests?"

I scoffed, "You could've fooled me. Judging by the way you look and the way you're speaking to me, I certainly wouldn't have thought of you as a guest. Guests have more respect for people than how you've treated me."

There, that told him.

"You know I can get you fired for your smart mouth talking to me like this, right?" he spoke up again, his tone cockier than before.

Whoever this guy thought he was, he wasn't going to treat me like this. Jess could've easily been sitting here tonight instead of me, and I knew my best friend well enough to solidly say that she would've walked away without standing up for herself. Not because she didn't want to, she just had her job on the line and has more than once walked away from a rude guest or employer. I however, wasn't an official employee. This wasn't my real job. He had no grounds to fire someone who didn't exist on record.

This ends right here, right now.

Thankful to have packed up all of my stuff back into my lunchbox, I grabbed my drink, which was a 'green juice' drink I had made prior to leaving for this shift tonight, and rose from my seat on the bench. "Alright, if sitting here is that important to you and that you have to insult me in order for me to move out of your royal way, here you go." Moving away from the bench, I gave him my best curtsey. Standing back up straight, I met his unreadable gaze. "I will say this though, and I'll be out of your way so your royal behind can have as much of this bench as it wants."

I closed the distance between us, leaving less than a metre to spare. "You will NOT speak to me or any other server like that again. I don't know who you are or if you're a current or past server of the military, but that still doesn't excuse your words to me tonight. Since you insist on speaking to me like I'm a piece of crap on the bottom of your over-polished shoe, and I'm a big believer in equality, I'll leave you with this." Raising my arm with the hand holding my green juice, I poured the remains of it over his head. The man's unreadable look immediately transformed into one of both shock and bemusement, clearly stunned that I had done what I had just done to him. "What the…" he began to say, interrupted by my hand which was raised to halt his words.

"Now you look like the trash you were making me feel like. Isn't equality fantastic? Enjoy the rest of your evening, sir." I ended my speech with a typical butler's bow, turning my heel and swiftly making my way back inside through the way I had come out from initially.

Once inside the kitchen, I felt the adrenaline rush through her from her confrontation with the irritatingly handsome, rude stranger just now.

Calming my breath and my heart, I knew Jess would more than likely hear about this when I got home. I knew Jess weasel it out of me somehow. At least my best friend's job was safe. Jess wouldn't be too happy with me if I had lost it.

Taking a few more moments to calm myself as best as possible, I put all thoughts out of my mind concerning the rude man. Maeve was waiting for me to come back off my break, and I had a job to do before I could head back home and to The Mister. Squaring off my shoulders and holding my head high, I left the kitchen and re-entered the main room, silently wishing I wouldn't encounter the man twice in one night.

CHAPTER TWO
Theon
Three months later - August 2019

At this time of year, the temperature really began to escalate more so than ever during the middle of the day. Even those who claimed to love the summer heat would struggle in the humidity that plagued Austin, Texas. Or anyone who wasn't used to the temperatures reached in these parts, if you were from a northern state. Thankfully, I was used to how hot things could get while working out in the midday sun. Being Texas born and bred had its occasional benefits, this being one of them.

Shutting the door on my horse's stall, having come back from checking the fences that were recently repaired, I turned to face the latest addition to the stables here on my folks' ranch. In front of me stood a two year-old rescue that had been left to roam wild after escaping from a nearby failing ranch, bobbed his head wildly as soon as he caught me staring at him.

I had been breaking in the horse slower than I had ever done before, getting it used to being around other horses, as well as being in routine and learning how to conduct itself around a working ranch and its many visitors. It wasn't an easy task, as the creature was still prone to bouts of excitement and 'zoomies', every now and then. Many a time had I come close to being bucked off, though thankfully due to sheer dumb luck, I had always managed to hang on. Just.

I was yet to name this energetically spunky individual. When the time came when a name would come to me which would appropriately suit just-so, there wasn't a shadow of a doubt in my mind that it would be a name to equally match his personality and temperament.

Approaching the unpredictable horse, I went through the unwritten routine I had used in the few times I had taken the beast outside. Thankfully, I was rewarded with no resistance from a horse whom I had hoped someday would become a good working or breeding horse. I wasn't picky. Either would do as long as he earned his keep at the ranch.

So far, so good.

Though if I was any kind of betting man, which I pride myself in being the opposite, I would hedge my bets and say I had thought that sentence a little too early.

Stepping back outside once more into the midday sun, I propped his Stetson back onto my head, shielding my face as best as I could under the wide rim. Much to my surprise, the horse stood placated at my side. Perhaps today would be a day things surprised me for the better, after all.

"Alright…" I began, slowly turning my back on the horse to get the saddle waiting on the fence nearby. If I dared trying to put this on back inside the stables, for sure I would have booked it the hell out of there, like I had done after the first time I tried getting it him. Lesson learned, never to be repeated again.

Step two, not that I listed a step one in the first place, was to place and secure the saddle.

Easy. Easy.

Saddle now in place, I stepped back to get a good look at this horse which had been successfully saddled for the first time. It truly was a magnificent sight. Though my first choice of career wasn't anything to do with horses, I couldn't lie to myself and deny that this was a pretty picture perfect specimen of a horse as ever you'd find around these parts. I silently dared any man to tell me otherwise, though I was met with as much silence as my dare was asked in.

One day, this horse would do great things. I could feel it. For now though, a simple walk around the training pen/corral would do. The training pen was as it sounded, new horses or horses that were to be trained and rehabilitated, much like the ranch's occupants, went in there before progressing onto the surrounding grasslands. Thankfully, we had plenty of such lands. Most ranches often did, it was just that us, the O'Donoghues, had slightly more than your average rancher, thanks to one of their ancestors long ago negotiating a deal with his then neighbour back in 1880-something. Since then, the land had been in our possession and passed down from father to eldest son or daughter. Now, it was my turn to look after this land.

Not that it was my decision to do so.

I didn't regret the decision to come back and help my parents run our family ranch, it was just that I wished often that it was my own choice, and not led by the hand of fate. That's all.

Favouring my good leg, I moved from his spot and carefully approached the horse once more, not wanting to spook the animal considering how surprisingly well things had gone so far. Much to my relief, it didn't spook. Not even when I rested my hand on the saddle's horn and once more favouring my good leg, used it to push my other leg over the horse, both feet now securely in the stirrups.

Well, colour me impressed. Not even a flinch from the horse now between his legs. Not one. Taking the reins in my hands and gripping them semi-tightly, a rare satisfied smile spread across my barely bearded face. If anyone were to see me now, I'm sure they would have to do a double-take to see if it really was me smiling.

I didn't smile much these days.

Still, this was one reason for me to let one slide free. I had heard of these 'miracle horses'. They were horses that made a U-turn when immediately being loved after abuse or had been rescued for the better, though I had never had one of those horses. Until now.

Thankfully, I had the hindsight to open the pen's gate before mounting the horse, lessening the risk of spooking it if there was someone on the ground below them now to do it for me. Foresight had always been one of his strong points. A good quality in a captain.

Former. Former captain.

It was hard to come to terms with what happened, as sometimes I forget that there was no current terms I could use anymore. Instead, I had to keep reminding myself that I'm now a 'former' captain. Ex. Thoughts like this often made me pause to breathe, so not to bring on something I didn't want anyone else to witness. Matters like that I liked to keep behind closed doors where I could deal with it on my own, without being under the eyes of anyone who would pity me. I didn't do pity.

Not wanting to bring on anything, I shook his head free of those thoughts, shelving them for another time. Hopefully even permanently. My focus now was on the beast underneath me, and getting him around the training pen before tackling the rest of what I had to do today.

Clicking my tongue, I eased his horse slowly but gently into the training pen, letting the horse decide whether he wanted to go left or right when inside the pen. He chose right.

Alright boy, doing well. Doing very well.

Considering my day hadn't started out all that well, what with my leg giving him some of its usual trouble, things were shaping up to be not too bad after all. I was even starting to feel glad that I had decided to roll out of bed this morning, after debating to let one of the other hands take my duties for today.

Ten minutes later, things were still going as smoothly as they were when I set out with this horse here in the training pen. The horse was nowhere near being used to or learning to take commands, but instead responded very well to what I called 'encouragements'. These were subtle nudges, rein pulls or gentle foot commands which would indicate to a horse what the rider wanted it to do. In this case, when I gently pulled the reins to the right, the horse sauntered right. If I gently tap the heel of my boot on the left side of his horse's belly, he sauntered left. Following simple, easy commands was a good sign for further progression. Eventually.

Sitting still for a moment, I let the horse take in his surroundings once more. Breaks from training, no matter how brief the 'training' was, it counted. Since I had all the time in the world if it was one of my own horses, I wasn't going to be rushing things. When I did things, you can bet your bottom dollar it was done with an abundance of time and dedication.

Boy do I have plenty of both in more than spades. I had it by the bucket full.

One thing I didn't have by the bucket full which I previously prided myself in having, was plenty of hindsight. As things were going so well, I had relaxed up far too much than I normally do. So what was about to happen next, it never even entered my mind as a possibility of happening to me. The once still horse suddenly and unpredictably became erratic, its body and legs moving in every direction as if not knowing where they wanted to go or what they should be doing.

"Woah! Woah boy, easy!" I calmly commanded, not wanting to escalate the situation any further. Though as if the last few moments were anything to go by, I should've known that the unexpected can really happen when you least expect it to.

Everything went into slow motion. I wasn't sure how I became separated from the horse, as it didn't matter to me at the moment. What I can remember, is all that came next. A series of painful events which even compared to what I had suffered in combat, were pretty painful. That's saying a lot considering I had my fair share of literal scrapes here and there.

The first thing I felt was the brutal collision of my back against the hard ground, eliciting a grunt from deep within my chest. Pain radiates through my torso like rapid gunfire. Before I had time to register this pain, I felt my body being dragged forward. Cracking open an eye, I spotted my foot caught in one of the stirrups, the horse still flailing about and me along for the ride.

Dang it.

I would've said something a lot more colourful, but there would be time for that later.

Struggling to dislodge the stirrup from the sole of my boot, I started to think if anyone had heard what was going on. I heard not one to call for help. Surely someone would have come by to help right about now.

They didn't.

Next to feel an impact was my pelvic/hip region, then with my foot finally coming loose it sent me flying into the training pen fence, sending debris flying from the collision of my body and the fence. The horse had been going with enough force to lift my body up and swing it, much to my amazement as I was no featherweight. The gunfire-like pain now spread to my midsection, meeting up with the roaring pain in my pelvis and hips, colliding together in an eye-watering symphony of pain.

Managing to open both of my eyes, sweat formed and dripped down my face like a cascading waterfall. Under the hot sun and searing pain, I could see the raised front legs of the horse ready to crash down on me if I didn't move quickly. Unfortunately, I didn't seem to be able to move from my current spot. The only thing I could do now was brace for impact. Crossing my arms across my head and closing my eyes, a series of blows landed across my body from the startled mount.

It was impossible to tell which parts of me were hit or which hurt more, as it just felt like every part of my body had been doused in gas and lit on fire, forever to burn until the allure of the other side promised to take away all of his pain and suffering. Fortunately for me, that's what appeared to be happening to him next, grinding the slow-motion reality to a grinding halt.

As the world slowly began closing in on me, only one thing passed through my mind.

Mom…Dad…I'm sorry

The familiar apology was rather a melancholy one in my mind. I had used the same apology before passing out on my last mission. Ironic, really. Very little remained of my hold on reality. Though as I closed my eyes, I swore I could hear activity going on around me, besides the lessening sounds of the horse's hooves impacting on the ground.

"Hang…there. We're…help. Don'…die…us, boss." A distant, warping voice floated around my ears.

If that's the voice of an angel, then damn.

Second to thinking about my parents, that was the last thing that floated through my mind as the last chord that linked him to earth, snapped. Eyes closed, I began to make my peace with whatever was coming my way.

CHAPTER THREE
Kenna

If there was a day that wasn't busy in the ER unit, I would start to doubt where I was working. I'd been working here for two, almost three years now, and not once on any shift I've ever worked, has been a quiet or easy-going one. Even when I was doing my residency before becoming fully qualified, I'd been put right in the deep end to sink or swim. Thankfully, I swam.

Heart Hospital of Austin provides emergency care to more than a quarter of a million citizens each year, so it was rare that a quiet night came our way when any one of us was working a shift. I can't complain, though. I'd wanted to be a nurse ever since I was a little girl, and doing what I can to save lives would always make a long or busy shift more than worthwhile. Even if one was closing in on being on-shift for just over twenty four hours.

At least in a few hours, I can finally shut my eyes for a while. Before I'm back here again. I thought, as I stretched my arms above my head, and my neck from side to side.

"Rough night?"

Turning around, I saw Melanie, another ER nurse, come into the break room. She looked about as tired as I. As we often worked parallel shifts, we knew when the other had indeed had a rough night.

I nodded, "Yeah. We lost Mr. Rodriguez last night." My voice cracked when I spoke his name. Joaquin Rodriguez was the sweetest 89-year-old man with a heart of gold. He'd served the community and had been an active member of it for his entire life, never dreaming of asking for anything in return. After a rather nasty fall in his home, he'd been admitted just over a week ago with very promising signs. No one expected him to pass away peacefully in his sleep. We'd all grown fond of him, especially when he'd recall old stories to us that never failed to make us laugh, or put a smile on our faces. It would be lonely around here without him. Even if his stay was brief.

"I'm so sorry, Kenna." Melanie's hand came to rest on my shoulder, her trusty reusable to-go cup no doubt filled with her coffee of choice in her other. She never went without one when not dealing with a patient.

Sighing, I guided us both back onto the less-than-comfy couch at the back of the room. "It happens, you know that Mel."

"Still, it's not nice when it does."

"True."

Melanie sipped her coffee, leaning back against the couch. "How many hours do you have left?"

"Thankfully just two. I'm more than ready to call it a night."

"You and me both. You're lucky though, I've got another six. Meaning, eight. An hour or two's overtime is unavoidable."

I chuckled. "I was just thinking the same thing."

Before I could respond, my pager buzzed at my hip. Alerting me that my presence was needed in one of the ER bays. "Got to run!" I leapt up, putting the trash from my snack break in the trash can.

"Go get em!" Melanie called as I dashed out of the room, heading to bay 3.

By the time I got to bay 3, there were a few other doctors and a nurse already there surrounding the male patient laid out on the stretcher bed. A movable bed should the patient need to be taken to x-ray, surgery or other such place.

"What do we have here?" I asked one of the senior doctors, Doctor Vaughn.

"27-year-old white male, fell off a horse. Possible chest, spinal and pelvic injury by the looks of the bruising on the skin. Male is unconscious and awaiting x-ray."

I flipped over the chart in my hand, details of what the senior doctor had just told me written down officially. "Stats?"

"Blood pressure slightly elevated, breathing is strained but not critical, waiting on a few more tests to come back while porters take him down for an x-ray."

I couldn't quite see the face of the male patient, as the doctors and other nurses swarmed around to get his clothing off his body, preparing him for the x-rays which will determine if there has been any internal injuries. From the list of what had happened to this poor man on his chart details, I wouldn't be surprised if there was something he'd succumbed to.

A second later, we all moved out of the way for the porters to take the unconscious man down to x-ray to check the key areas marked out to be x-rayed, which were his chest, spine and hip areas. It was best to do this while he was unconscious, as there would be less resistance and a clean and clear x-ray could be taken. We'd know in next to no time the extent of his injuries.

Until then, onto the next patient waiting in the next bay.

Around half an hour and three patients later, one with a broken leg, and two from a car accident, I was handed the results of the 27-year-old man's x-rays. Thanking the nurse who handed them to me, I headed straight for the private room the man had been placed in, where he'd be waiting for me. Probably still unconscious.

I wonder if any of his family has turned up yet. Or a girlfriend. I need to check when I've seen him.

Either way, he was now under my direct care while he was here in the ER. Since he'd been admitted into a private room in the ER unit, I assumed he'd be with us for a while. They usually were if admittance had already happened.

Rounding the corner, I realised that this man had been admitted into the now clean room of the former Mr. Rodriguez. I couldn't help but fight back the threat of tears. Knowing such a sweet, older gentleman had passed away in this very room earlier the previous day was sombre indeed. Still, it made me even more determined to take care of this next patient. He'll survive, I'll make sure of it.

Squaring off my shoulders and holding my head high, a professional touch was needed now. Tears would have to wait. Collecting myself, I raised my hand and delivered two swift, light knocks to the patient's door before entering. After all, he might still be asleep and seeing as I was the only one delivering his results, I assumed he wasn't critical. So it wasn't key that he be awake immediately.

Closing the door behind me, a faint groaning sound came from the bed, indicating that the male patient was somewhat lucid. Walking up to the bed with the x-ray results in the brown envelope ready to be clipped to the lighting board on the wall next to the bed, I wasn't nearly as ready for the surprise ready for me as I would be seeing the man's results.

No way. It…it can't be…

It was a 0.01% of a chance that any doctor or nurse would know one of the patients admitted to hospital, with an even less and perhaps zero chance of them being allowed to attend to them, as anyone connected to a patient was automatically removed from their care. Though no one was meant to know how I'd be connected to the groaning man before me, laying in the bed like he'd gone ten rounds with Muhammad Ali and lost.

It…it is. It is him!

Never in my wildest dreams did I think I'd ever cross his path again. Not after how I'd left things with him. Yet, here we are. He's a patient and by some cruel twist of fate, I'm his nurse.

I'd met this man some months ago when I'd been covering Jess' shift at the military evening. He'd been rude to who he thought was a server. Technically, I was, but only for the night. Though he wasn't meant to know that. Unable to hold back, I'd told him what for before dumping my drink on him and leaving swiftly. I had hoped he'd learned his lesson since then.

Looking at him now though, it wasn't the time or the place to be concerned about that. I had a job to do and no matter who he was, I would do it and look after him to the best of my care.

"Ngh…" he groaned again, louder this time. Each time he made a noise, the sound was louder and seemed as though he was trying to talk. A good sign.

Setting his results on the table beside his bed, I glanced briefly at the chart at the end of his bed which would give me his name.

Theon O'Donoghue

23

Since his name had been listed, a rather fittingly-attractive name for a man like him, I assume someone was here who had identified him. Or possibly, his name was on record if he'd been admitted before. He may even have given blood, who knows? Technically, I should. Glancing back at his notes, it confirmed he was indeed a blood donor. Though a family member, friend or significant other still could be in the waiting room, waiting for news.

I'll go check after I'm done here.

Putting the chart back in its holder at the end of the bed, I move swiftly to his side where I can check on his vitals, the machine carrying his heartbeat broadcasting a strong and positive beat. As I checked over the rest of his vital signs, Theon became fully conscious, latching onto my wrist with what felt like the grip of a highland barbarian. Not that I've met many of those in my lifetime.

"Pain…" he growled out through gritted teeth, evidently feeling every bit of pain his body must be experiencing.

Detaching each finger slowly from my now reddened wrist, I leaned and pressed the button which would release a small amount of painkillers into his system. That should calm him down enough to assess him consciously. Almost immediately, the painkillers seemed to somewhat calm him down. Thank goodness. He now laid back with a more relaxed expression than before, making me feel as if I'd tamed a beast not a man.

"Everything's okay, Mr O'Donoghue. You're in hospital with a few injuries. I'm your nurse, Ms Bouchard. You may call me nurse Bouchard. Now, you had some x-rays taken while you were unconscious. Let's see what your results are." I said calmly, keeping my tone professional, yet somewhat reassuring.

As much as I wanted to let this man in on who I was, my inner moral compass was telling me to save it for another time. Right now, he was just another patient, and I was his nurse.

I felt his eyes follow me as I moved around the room, once more picking up the envelope containing his x-rays. Taking the top one, I slid it onto the lightbox and turned it on. Before me was a clear shot of his chest, ribcage and spine. Already I could see the first set of problems. "It seems you've suffered multiple rib fractures. No ribs are piercing your lungs, otherwise you wouldn't be here you'd be in surgery. The broken ribs will have to be taped, of course."

How has this happened?

Swiftly I slid the next x-ray onto the light-box, this time showing his pelvis and leg joints.

Immediately, the next set of problems appeared.

"You've got some major bruising to your tailbone, and a possible hip fracture. I'm 99.9% sure about that."

Lastly, I put the final slides up side-by-side in turn, showing both his femurs, patellas, tibias, fibulas and all the bones in his feet. There was no doubt he'd been thoroughly x-rayed, none at all. I scanned all of the images before giving my verdict on the last of his multiple, and horrendous, injuries.

"From what I can see, you've got multiple breaks and fractures on both of your legs, all of varying breakages. Some are hairline, whereas others are full-blown breaks. Thankfully, there isn't any damage to your patellas. Meaning, your kneecap. It also looks like you've got minor breaks in the bones in your foot, on top of possible nerve damage. I'll have to assess you now to know the extent of what you can and can't feel on top of all your injuries. Alright?"

It was then that I turned to face him. Somewhat surprised that he hadn't interrupted me yet. Some patients did as soon as you came in the room, though thankfully, Theon had been unconscious. Now though? Now he was staring at me through a medicated haze, as if I had grown two heads.

"Mr O'Donoghue!" I commanded his name, demanding his acknowledgement of his injuries and what I had to do next. I had no time to waste. He had injuries that needed immediate attention and I had no time for his hesitancy. "Mr O'Donoghue, do you understand?"

I wasn't even remotely close to losing my cool, but I was damn near close to stepping over the line of a professional if he didn't respond to me soon. Usually, ER patients didn't take this long to respond, with most wanting to know what's going on the second they were admitted, woken up or otherwise. This one, Theon, seemed to be the first in my experience to challenge the norm.

Lucky me.

Just as I was about to address him again, his mouth opened. Hopefully, to reply to me. It was at this point though, that I couldn't anticipate what would come out of his mouth. Most certainly, I didn't expect what did in fact come out of his mouth a few seconds later.

"Y-you. It's…I-it's you! Server-girl!"

Oh great, now he remembers me.

CHAPTER FOUR
Theon

Coming round from God knows what had kept me under, was bad enough. What was worse? Coming round and recognising the nurse standing before you as the woman you were obtusely rude to months prior. I didn't catch her name those months prior to where we were now, though watching her say it through my hazy eyes, I wouldn't forget it in a million years.

Nurse Bouchard.

Bouchard.

The name sounded like a silent, passionate whisper between two long-lost lovers. It was a name that sounded as beautiful as it did both sexy and alluring. At least, it was that way to me. I wouldn't mind whispering that name a few dozen different ways, half a dozen times a night.

What in the Sam heck is wrong with me?

That's just it, I don't know what's wrong with me. The last thing I remember before waking up here to the captivating server/nurse, nurse Bouchard, was being flat on my back after being thrown from that damn ornery horse. Now? Well, now I wasn't so sure what was going on. I'm pretty sure they pumped me full of something to numb the pain. Only, it didn't seem to be wearing off at all.

Before I could speak again, nurse Bouchard turned off the light-box on the wall and faced me, her stare giving nothing away as to what was really going on inside her head. She reeked professionalism, with no trace of letting on who she knows I am. Can't help but respect that.

"Mr O'Donoghue." She repeated again to me, this time her tone laced with mild irritation. "Do you understand what I have to do?"

I can barely understand anything right now, though I wasn't about to tell her that. I wanted to know what worked with me and what didn't, and it was her job to figure it out.

"Yes."

Over the next few minutes, her gentle hands work their way over the various points of my body which she'd pointed out had been injured. Thankfully as she pointed out, nothing seemed to be permanently damaged with my ribs. Nothing that couldn't be fixed and healed over time. Nurse Bouchard was then able to confirm the tailbone bruise by ever-so-carefully moving me to see the bruise not-so-proudly adorning my skin. I wasn't going to see it, so I wasn't all that bothered about it. It was only when she moved down to my hip and pelvis, did things really take a turn for the unexpected.

"Can you feel this, Mr O'Donoghue?"

Feel what?

In order to accurately tell what was working and what wasn't, I had my eyes closed for most of this exam. Just in case my eyes would somehow tell my brain something it shouldn't. How that works I don't know, I'm no doctor.

"Aren't you already touching the next part of me?"

There was a significant pause before she replied.

"I…I am. You…um…you can't feel this?"

For this, I opened my eyes. I could see her touching the part of my hip where she said that there was a fracture. Only, I didn't feel it.

"N-no. I can't. At least, I think I can't."

Inside my chest, I could feel my heart rapidly pick up pace. As a former soldier of the U.S. Army, it was in-built in our nature to never panic in any given situation. So far, I'd managed to do just that, even during the unspeakable events which lead to my honourable discharge. This time however, fear spread throughout my body and my whole being. I already knew what the verdict would be, I've seen enough men go through the same thing while on tour. Though I never imagined it would happen to me, much less from being thrown off a horse instead of stepping on an IUD.

While stuck in my own thoughts, Nurse Bouchard had moved on with her pointless examination. I didn't even notice that she'd moved from my hips, down over both of my legs and to my feet, pausing there.

"Can you feel this?" she gently poked the end of a short wooden stick into my big toe, followed by the upper, middle and heel of both my left and right foot.

Nothing…

Inside the bed sheets, my hands balled into fists. "No." I ground out, finding it stupid to have to respond to something we both knew already.

"Thank you for your cooperation, Mr O'Donoghue. Your doctor will be in shortly to discuss the next steps with you."

I didn't know what to say. What should I say? Thank you? Okay? I wasn't a man of many words, but the few that would be appropriate here seemed to escape my lips, not making it out of my addled brain. All those months ago when I first met her, I knew what to say. Yes I was an ass, but I knew what to say. Ironic now when the tables were turned, in this case for the worse, the wise ass was silenced.

Nurse Bouchard picked up everything she'd used on me during her examination, swiftly moving over to the door to leave. As she approached it, her hand on the door handle, she paused and turned back around to me.

"For what it's worth, no matter how unprofessional this is of me, I'm sorry."

She's…she's sorry? For what? This isn't her fault.

Something in whatever expression I had on my face must've told her that I had no clue what she was on about, as she answered my unspoken thoughts. "No matter what you did to me, I never would've wished this on you." she paused, swallowing before she continued. "We'll do everything we can to help you while you're here with us, I can promise you that. I'll be back later after the doctor has seen you, after I've seen my other patients. I'm truly sorry."

With that, she left the room. All appeared to be as if she'd never been here in the first place. Just myself alone with my sombre thoughts. Only this time I was awake, my thoughts more prominent than when I'd last been semi-conscious.

On top of everything that's going on, and by no means is the cherry on the cake, I'm still dumbfounded at the turn of events that landed nurse Bouchard as my, well, nurse. I'm not a man who believes in such things as fate, so whoever was pulling this one off must be laughing at my expense right now and then some. The tables had more than turned, they'd been flipped upside down with their legs in the air.

Now my fate, again not that I believe that I have one, was left in the hands of the doctors and nurses, with just how much they'd be able to do for me. For what she can do for me.

I wasn't left alone with my thoughts for too long, before the doctor that nurse Bouchard told me was on his way, entered the room. Already, his face looked as sombre as my mood felt, knowing he had to deliver to me the news I already knew inside.

He looked to be in his early-to-mid thirties, a man who knew what he was doing. Hopefully. "Mr O'Donoghue, I'm Doctor Reynolds…" he started to say.

Does no one around here know my first name?

"Yes."

"Nurse Bouchard has informed me of her assessment of your injuries. I'm here to talk over what will happen with you next, and what your options are."

Is this guy for real?

I know what my options are! I don't have any! A fool could understand what would happen to someone like me next with the injuries I have. It was a slim-to-none chance that I would ever walk again, all thanks to that damned horse and whatever happened to have spooked it. You can bet your bottom dollar that when I get back to that ranch, someone better keep that beast out of my sight. Or else.

Never would I hurt an animal intentionally, but he and I weren't going to be bosom buddies any time soon. Someone else can break the damn thing in, I'm done.

Every word that came from Doctor Reynolds' mouth fell on my not so deaf ears. Almost. He told me what procedures I must go through in order to fix what can be fixed, and what would happen in the recovery process for each of those. The only thing that no one knew for sure, was what would happen with my legs. Doctor Reynolds quickly did his own, more thorough assessment, of just how much I could feel and move them. We quickly knew the answer. Again.

Laying my left leg down, he once more turned to look at me. "Where I can't say for sure right now, Mr O'Donoghue…" he hesitated, swallowing before he continued. "Based on your general assessment I've just conducted, I'm afraid you've got an 80-90% chance you won't walk again. I'm sorry."

For the second time today, someone was telling me that they were sorry and also for the second time today, I have no idea why. These people saw patients with more severe injuries than mine, often in way worse shapes. Hell, I've even seen it! You didn't come out of a single tour of duty without seeing someone, often a close buddy of yours, put through the wringer. Hoping and praying that they'd make it through to touch back down on American soil.

Sadly, that wasn't always the case.

Standing up, Doctor Reynolds held his hand out to me.

What, he wants to shake my hand for telling me I won't walk again?!

"I've given you some pretty heavy news today, I'll admit. On that note, I just want to say thank you for your service to our country. You'll never know truly how much we all appreciate each and every one of you men and women who give your lives so we can live ours."

Well...that was unexpected.

Now I felt like a total jerk. Hell, I am. Who could blame me though? How would anyone feel when they were told they wouldn't walk again? Devastated. I'd survived the worst that life could throw at any soldier, and I was taken down by something as simple as a horse.

"Thank you. I appreciate it. And...what you're doing for me." I managed to get out, my voice catching.

With a simple nod, Doctor Reynolds released my hand from our shake and left the room with a promise of letting my family in the waiting room in to see me soon. I had no idea anyone was waiting for me anyway.

It did beg the question though as to who had brought me here. Additionally, who was waiting for me in the waiting room? It was most likely my folks. I couldn't think of anyone else who'd be waiting there.

I could imagine them now. My mother, my dear sweet mother, would be beside herself with worry. Her eyes would be filled with tears and sorrow while my father, ever the stronger one of the two, would have his arm around her, reassuring her that everything would be alright. Even if he had no idea that things would be okay, he'd do it to put her mind at peace as best as he could as he was that kind of guy. A man I admired deeply.

Since there was nothing else for me to do now until they or whoever was waiting for me was shown in, I got as comfortable as I could and closed my eyes. Hopefully if I fell asleep, my dreams would take me off to better and brighter pastures.

Preferably, pastures that involved a certain nurse sans the drink she covered me with the last time I dreamed about her.

CHAPTER FIVE
Theon

As I'd predicted before I temporarily fell asleep, it was my folks who were waiting in the waiting room to finally see me. The ranch hand who'd found me and somehow got me to hospital was with them. Russ was his name. He'd been with us a short time, fresh from his unsuccessful counselling with a specialist who dealt with soldiers with PTSD.

After thanking him, he was more than keen to get on his way back to the ranch to work off the enormous burden he'd felt for not getting to me sooner. As he was nearby when the horse threw me, but wasn't able to reach me in time to break my fall or shield me from any of the impacts on my body. I didn't blame him though, nor did I find he had any burden, though I wasn't about to question his reasoning. If working his butt off was what it would take for him to feel better, even if he was innocent in all of this, so be it.

I was able to spend a full twenty or so minutes with my folks before I was taken away for the first of many events that would follow. Nurse Bouchard came back to assist in taking me to get my ribs taped, which was as fun as being stuck in a bag with a wild coyote. Which anyone could tell you, was not fun at all. It hurt like…well…as I imagined hell would. Or something pretty darn close to it.

From the taping, it was onto the various parts of my body that would be encased in plaster for the foreseeable future. Okay, it was more like a few months, it just felt like forever right now as I lay here as my buddy Rikuh would say, 'star-fishing after a good night's sweet lovin''. Meaning, you went at it so hard you couldn't move from this position, your lady love long gone into the night. Or morning. Whatever time of day you ended up finishing. Literally.

Somehow, I didn't seem to be able to find the usual abundance of amusement this time around. With my ribs taped and temporarily bound, both of my legs in plaster cast, which would no doubt make me walk stupider than a cat stuck with smarties tubes on its legs, and my right hand taped and bound in a temporary brace after a further assessment showed a fracture there too, I looked like I'd gone ten rounds with Genghis Khan and lost. Badly.

The only thing I hadn't been treated for, at least while awake, was the mild concussion I'd sustained from a kick to the head after I'd passed out. According to what Rikuh had said before he left. I was assessed and given meds for that before I came to, hence the delirium and confusion before spotting Nurse Bouchard at the bottom of my hospital bed.

We'd barely said two words to each other during the time we'd been in the same room. Or rather, I barely said anything to her. Why? I wasn't too sure. Just like I wasn't sure of much at the moment.

It was slightly irritating, among other things, that she was on my mind as much as she is currently. Where I wasn't a lover and a leaver of women, I had casual relationships with the promise of a good time in bed before parting. So it does beg the question once more that would not leave my head, what was it about her that kept it going back there time and again?

Who knows?

Not me.

For all I knew, she was with someone. There wasn't a chance that someone like her would be single. At best, she'd have to be engaged. And I'd have to stop thinking about her, if I had any brains between these ears of mine.

You're only thinking about her because there's nothing else TO think about.

At least, that's what I was telling myself. More like fooling myself with.

I wasn't alone with my thoughts for very much longer as a nurse, though it wasn't Nurse Bouchard, came into my room with an irritatingly happy smile on her face.

"Good morning, Mr O'Donoghue!"

Oh good God…

"What's so good about it?" I muttered, failing to see what she saw was evidently so good about it.

Thankfully, my irritable muttering fell on deaf ears and this time, they weren't my own. This nurse, who'd introduced herself as Melanie, carried on with whatever she'd come in to do, walking up to my bed and crouching down to the floor. I kept my eye on her as best as I could, considering I couldn't move my damn self from the waist down.

What on Earth is she doing down there?

"Alright, that all looks great! Bag isn't too full, so I won't change it out just yet."

Bag? What bag?

She must've sensed the silent question in my head because as she stood up, she pointed down to where she'd just been. "Your catheter bag. It was fitted while you were out of it. We change it between half and three quarters full, but yours is fine for now"

Then it dawned on me. What was left of the shred of decency I had, went as swiftly as the realisation of what she meant, came. Running a hand down my stubbled cheeks, I let out a resigned groan. The humiliation of my situation was enough, it didn't need to be spoken about.

Clearing my throat, I averted my eyes from the nurse. "Yes…well… thank you. Yes."

Swiftly she left the room, the door slightly ajar from not being closed all the way. I couldn't blame her for my embarrassment, it wouldn't be fair. Though, how would anyone feel about only realising being in such a state now, and that your privates were handled when you didn't know about it? Laying here, more than one suggestion crossed my mind. None that would lie kindly on gentle ears.

For now though, now I can only hope I can enjoy this moment's peace before God knows what happens next. Given that I couldn't do much until these casts came off, the options were more limited than they already were.

Soon enough, the sound of a soft voice ended my moment's peaceful silence. A familiar voice floated in through the barely opened door, carrying all the way to my ears. Immediately, I recognised the voice and its owner. Nurse Bouchard.

She sighed, a sorrowful noise. "I don't know Jess. I'm not sure if this is some cruel twist of fate, or if it's well…that's just it. I'm not sure what the hell it is."

You and me both.

I couldn't hear the reply on the other end from this Jess person. Then again, I don't think I needed to. It was pretty easy to surmise the topic of conversation. Me.

"You know I had no choice but to do what I did to him a few months back. He thought that he could insult someone of 'lower' status, and get away with it! I can't stand people who think themselves higher and mightier than others. Yes I know, you can't either. Though, would you have done what I did?"

I sure hope not, one drink over me was enough.

Her friend, or whoever this Jess was to her, said something that enticed a laugh from her. A laugh I could imagine seeing coming from her own two lips, instead of floating on the non-existent wind. "Yes I know. You're not a fan of the shakes I drink. That's beside the point here girlie."

Shifting as best as I could into a more comfortable position, I continued to listen to their conversation. Usually, this would be eavesdropping. But what else can I do when I can't move and she chose to hold her conversation outside of my room? She should've chosen a more private spot.

"There's not much I can do about it now, though. He's my patient and I'm his nurse, fate or no fate. I've got a job to do and that's all and exactly what I'm going to do. Nothing more, nothing less. Besides, it's highly likely that we'll see one another again after he's been discharged. Whenever that may be. I mean, what are the chances that he and I will meet twice in an unlikely manner?"

Two to one I'd say…

Something within me, as broken as I lay, told me very loudly that somehow this wouldn't be the last time I'd see this woman. Never before have I encountered someone I knew would be in my life on more than one occasion, not before Nurse Bouchard here. Still, I could think of a few other people I would be worse off with for repeated company. At least this one will be able to fix what is broken. Well, most of it, anyway.

By the sounds of it, her conversation with Jess was wrapping up.

"Mhm, definitely. It's been a long one, this shift. Over twenty-four hours. I'm clocking off soon, thank God. Just a few things to tend to before checking in on Mr O'Donoghue one last time, then I'll be off. No, silly. Not that kind of 'off'. That's your lucky department, not mine."

Oh? Now that's interesting.

"I'll see you tomorrow after my shift. Yes." She laughed once more, "I'll bring the wine you bring the ice cream and pizza. Yes, both. I'm feeling slobbish. Catch you later. Bye."

Having nothing but whatever has been fed to me through the IV drip, the promise of ice cream and pizza sounded mighty fine right about now. Even if I did have those things, I'd still need someone to feed it to me like a damned baby. No, I've had enough humiliation for one day. The drip would have to do until I get back home, where things wouldn't nearly be as damaging to my already dented pride.

Nurse Bouchard's footsteps echoed away down the corridor, fading away as she walked further and further away from my room. Clearly it wasn't time for her attention yet, which felt both a blessing and a curse at the same time. I wanted to be seen and done with so I could sleep some more, the pain was beginning to be unbearable and I didn't want to take any more medication than necessary. I hated relying on the stuff.

As a boy, I'd been prone to more than one accident that required pain meds to help cope with the healing. Much to my mother's distress, I refused them. Every time. I didn't see the point of blocking out pain, when you can embrace and better cope with it the next time something happened to you. Not even when I broke my arm, or my leg, did I cry out for painkillers. Some called me tough, ballsy even. I was neither. Still aren't.

Now is probably the one and only time I'll ever be subject to having painkillers, and that was only because the decision to do otherwise was out of my control. In fact, I had none. My hands and my life were in the hands of the nurses and doctors, and they were the ones telling me I needed these drugs.

Whatever lay ahead of me outside of his hospital when I eventually break free, I'd do it without drugs. No matter who begged and how hard. Soldiering at least prepared me to cope with that, and I'd always be that. A soldier. On or off the battlefield, a soldier was never not a soldier. You were one for life.

Time passed, and soon the barely opened door was opened all of the way, with Nurse Bouchard slipping inside. Just like she told Jess she would. Not that she knew I already knew she'd be back, despite her already having told me that she's my nurse.

"Good, you're awake. How are you feeling, Mr O'Donoghue?"

Like I've gone ten rounds fighting a bull.

I turned my eyes away from her, not trusting myself not to stare at her. "Fine."

"Not in too much pain then?"

She knew I'd be in pain, yet she still had the gall to ask me. Still, I guess it was her job to believe the patient, even if they were lying. Or in any case, go along with their lies and carry out what she intended to do no matter what answer said patient might have given. In this case, I was her patient, and I was lying.

"No. None."

"Good, I'm glad to hear it, Mr O'Donoghue."

Oh for the lord of all that's holy…I have a first name woman.

"Theon."

I turned my head back to her, my gaze meeting hers.

"Pardon?"

"Theon. My name."

Something unspoken passed between us, an understanding that she no longer had to repeatedly call me by my family name, but that I had given her permission of sorts, to use my Christian name. I didn't know if all of her patients did this, but I would. Mr O'Donoghue was my father, and I would go by my Christian name wherever and whenever possible. I had nothing against my father or his title, but I was my own man until one day, I would be in his shoes as Mr O'Donoghue.

She nodded, "Theon."

Why did that have to sound so good coming from her lips? Too good.

"Kenna."

Now it was my turn to raise a brow. "What?"

"If I am to call you, my patient, Theon. Then you are to call me, your nurse, Kenna. After all, it is my name. Also depending on how long you're with us, you might as well get used to using it as I'll be seeing you quite a bit."

You don't say…

Nothing else needed to be said from me, at least right now. All I could do was watch her as she checked my vitals, making sure everything was as it should be until she would return for her next shift. Hearing no complaints or muttered concerns, I took it that all is well.

"Alright, well, that's all from me for now. I'll be seeing you soon."

I nodded.

Clearing her throat, she continued. "Nurse Randall will be overseeing you until I'm next on my next shift. Behave for her will you?"

"Yes ma'am." I muttered.

My mutterings did not miss her ears, as she seemed to be hiding a smirk as she turned and headed for the door, grabbing its handle and opening it for her to step through.

"Rest. Sleep well, Theon."

As she stepped through the door, closing it behind her, I dropped my head back onto the pillow with a loud groan. However long I was going to be in here, it would feel ten times longer with that irritatingly captivating temptress as my nurse.

How on Earth did things come to this?

It wasn't like me to be so…distracted, by a woman and believe me, the second a lady found out you were a soldier, one of two things happened. They either were so taken with you, ever so suddenly, that they needed you in their bed instantly or else. Or, they would be so upset, having known and most likely lost someone in a conflict somewhere. The ladies in between were usually otherwise taken, in some way.

There was no other reason for it other than the fresh medication that was working its way through my system. The sneaky little siren had pressed the button for a dose to be administered, all while she was talking to me about names, knowing very well I couldn't protest while distracted.

Oh well, what's done is done.

Sleep indeed was coming my way as my lids grew heavier, and all and any thoughts of what had just occurred started to slip away. It would be best for me to let sleep take me for now, for when I awoke once more, as I would need all the wit that I had left.

If there were any left to be used, that is.

CHAPTER SIX
Theon

Two days. It had been two days since I'd woken up in this hospital bed, told that I wouldn't likely ever walk again. So much has happened in this short space of time, which ironically, also felt like the longest time in the world. Laying around doing nothing will do that to you, it'll make you feel like you've been here forever. Which is exactly how I feel right about now.

I hadn't been doing much over the last two days, nothing that would require a lot of effort and energy, that is. Mostly, I'd been lying here in my bed as a constant stream of doctors and nurses came to assess, check up and monitor me. Nurse Bouchard…Kenna…included. As of last night, she was back on the day shift with no overtime, so I'd be seeing a lot more of her. A blessing, I've come to deduce. It was far less humiliating for anything… intimate, to be dealt with by someone familiar.

My folks had come by every day so far, during the visitor's hours. As I'm in the intensive care unit, visiting times were limited each day by time and how many could visit at any one time. My mother snuck me in a drop of my favourite whiskey, Jameson's Irish Whiskey. I wasn't allowed any alcohol when on medication, so luckily I stopped taking any in the hopes of getting a sip of the good stuff. Just to take the edge off. It worked like a charm.

Thankfully, no one, not even Kenna, caught on. If they did, no one made it known to me that they knew.

One good thing did come out of all of this if anything. Food. I'd been on a liquid diet through the IV since waking up but the good news is, if I was able to keep on track as per the request of the doctor, I'd move back onto solids within the week.

Oh the irony. A fully grown man progressing back onto solids like a baby. Well, at least I'm alive. Wouldn't have been eating anything if it had turned out any differently.

Additionally, every other test and examination that the doctor first initially told me I'd need to have done, I have done. The only things that were left now was to wait out the injuries that would heal on their own, learn to use my wheelchair once I've got my arms back, and cope with life as a paraplegic. Something that would take forever and a day to even begin to wrap my mind around, let alone accept it.

If I could be honest about one thing, it would be that I'm counting down the days until I'm sprang from this place. Yes, I didn't know how many days I'm going to be here, but that's not stopping me from counting down the hours, minutes, and seconds. I just don't do hospitals. Period.

Over the years, I've lost countless friends, buddies, and brothers in arms inside a place that's supposed to heal and help people live again. No. Every time I've stepped inside some sort of hospital, besides the times I've had to get something wrapped or cast, someone close to me has passed on. At least this time it's only me inside, and I know I'm going to survive. Hell, I've been to Syria. If I can survive the madness out there, I can survive an Austin hospital. I hope.

A knock at the door pulled me out of my thoughts. A second later, Kenna stepped through.

Of course it's her. Who else would it be?

Today, her hair was put up with some kind of ribbon, which was wrapped around the semi-casual bun at the back of her head. So far, I've only ever noticed a plain band of sorts keeping her long tresses of hair at bay. Only a few cascaded down both sides of her face, touching the line of her jaw. Any man would kill to see how far those locks would fall down, should that ribbon be removed. Not this man, though. This man was far from tempted. At least that's what I told myself anyway.

"Good morning, Mr O'...Theon." She corrected herself, "How are you this morning?"

Fine and dandy, thanks for asking.

I told her the same thing I've said to everyone these past few days.

"Great." They all knew it was a lie, but at the same time they've come to not expect anything else from me. I've accepted my new future as less than human, human being than most and that's that. No one here could magically help me walk again, so they've come to accept my gruffness as a response to my situation. Hell, anyone would react the same way, I'd expect.

"I've come with good news for you."

That was not something I was expecting to hear. Not so soon, anyway. "Oh?"

"You'll be able to leave at the end of the week. Friday night if not early Saturday morning, if all goes well and stays as it should."

Finally.

This news, although somewhat premature, was welcome and very much music to my ears. Where I didn't expect to hear these sweet words for at least another week, maybe more, they were more than welcome. Soon, I'll be back in my own home, in my own bed and doing things as much in my way as possible. Given the circumstances. My mother was bound to hover and fuss over me for a while, but I'd happily make do with that over being pent up in here for any longer than I have to be.

Still, I can't fault that the doctors and nurses here have been anything but the best in treating me. Doing all they can to make me as comfortable as possible. They respected my wishes to go as med-free as I could, while also giving me all the treatments and procedures that thankfully, my insurance more than covered. Not everyone got the same treatment as I did here, and I was lucky that I was able to thank them. Or will thank them, come the time it comes for me to be discharged.

"Theon? Did you hear what I said?"

No, not a single word.

I nodded, "Yes. Yes, thank you. That's good news. Great news."

"Excellent. Doctor Balt will be with you shortly to provide you with all the necessary care information you'll need to pass on to your carer."

"What?"

She looked at me as if I'd grown two heads. "A carer, Theon. You won't be able to look after yourself for at least the next 6-8 weeks, not with those arms in casts. We understand that you live in a house on your family's property, at least that's what your mother told one of the nurses at the desk. Arrangements of course are up to you and your folks, but you're only being released under the understanding that you've got someone to care for you." she paused. "If this isn't the case, you'll be stuck here until someone can be found."

I wasn't sure if she was telling me, or threatening me. Probably a bit of both. The humiliation level kicked up a notch at the thought of me, a man in his mid-twenties being cared for by a 'carer'. It might be my folks, namely my mother, though it was still demoralising in a way to have it said aloud.

"No." I cleared my throat, shifting slightly in the bed. "That won't be a problem." I knew I came across a little gruff, again, I just couldn't help it. Finally I would be out of this place and back in a place of better comfort. A place where I can lament on my situation without being asked if I was alright, every five minutes and believe me, it was literally that.

Kenna shuffled her feet a little, clutching the clipboard she was carrying close to her ample chest. If she had something to say, she should just come out and say it. I hate people who hesitated. Though I had a feeling, I wouldn't hate anything this woman would do. Not after her caring after me.

A moment later, she spoke.

"This might be bordering on inappropriate, but I just have to say it."

Go on.

"Before you were in this room, I tended to an elderly gentleman who was very sweet. He became a firm favourite of ours before he sadly passed away. If I had to say, he was the best patient I've ever had the pleasure of treating since I became a fully qualified nurse and started a position here." She paused again, collecting herself before she continued. "When you were first admitted, I didn't know that you wouldn't walk out of here. Literally. I had no idea how bad your injuries were but like that elderly gentleman, I was determined to do my best for the time that you were in my care. Despite your demeanour at times, it's been a pleasure to try and do all I can to help and aid you, no matter if it made a difference or not. We may have gotten off on the wrong foot a few months back, and I know we haven't exactly been the best of friends now, but it's going to be sad to see you go."

All the power of speech failed me at that moment. It seems to be happening a lot more these days. What would someone say to that? Especially when they weren't expecting to hear something so heartfelt. Raw. Honest. I guess I should try and at least be decent to her in the remaining days I was here for. It wouldn't be fair to treat her, or anyone, any other way after such a touching speech for someone such as myself who's not good at words. Heartfelt words, at least.

"I…um…uh…Thank you. You've been…exceptional. I couldn't have asked for better care."

Her smile almost melted the ice around my heart. Almost. I had a feeling this woman could melt the heart of the devil if she tried.

"You're welcome. I'll leave you to get some rest, and I'll come back and check on you later. Okay?"

"Yes. Thank you."

Leaving me with nothing but her smile and my own thoughts, Kenna left the room with an added spring in her step. A spring I'd just put there. You're in far too over your own head, boy.

Too damn far.

Come this weekend, Friday or Saturday when I'd be discharged, I'd bid farewell to the bewitching Kenna and the rest of the hospital staff. Waving by to temptation that came into my room several times a day.

This is exactly why I don't get entangled with women, not emotionally. Before leaving the army unwillingly, I had nothing to promise a woman other than the prospect that I might not make it home after I'd said I'd be back. Now? Now it was much the same. I still had nothing to offer a woman other than the ranch I worked on, and a life of working the land and yet somehow, throwing into the mix that I couldn't any longer walk lowered that prospect even still.

At least whoever got this bed next would be subject to Kenna's deserving professional care and attention, and I would go home to where things were less complicated and just the way I liked them.

That was however, what I kept telling myself. Knowing that it was the furthest from the truth that both my head, and now my heart, were screaming out.

Much to my amazement, Friday soon came around amidst a million things that continued to go on around me in the ward. Today was the day. I would be a free man come the time I was collected by whoever was coming to take me back to my family's ranch. It wasn't known to me who it would be, though it didn't matter. Getting out of here was key and was the only thing I was concerned with. If someone had a horse and cart to take me home in, I'd take it.

All of the belongings that had been salvaged from the day of my admittance had been packed nicely, by Kenna, into a plastic zip lock bag that I could take home with me. With help, I'd been changed into clothes that Rikuh had dropped off for me at one point during the week while I was taking a snooze. Everything was ready to go. Well, almost everything.

A knock came from the door and Kenna poked her head in, her infectious smile on her face as she came all the way into my room. "Ready, Mr O'Donoghue?"

"What happened to my name?"

"Well, the last time I checked, that is your name."

I rolled my eyes.

"You know what I mean. What's with the formalities?

Kenna walked up close to the wheelchair I'd been assisted into by one of the new male nurses in the ward. "All part of the departure service."

"I see." I muttered, trying to hide the smirk forming at the corner of my mouth.

Secretly, I'd been dreading this moment. Where I wasn't a man of many words, I always hated having to say goodbye. To anyone. Especially when it came to saying goodbye to my folks when I was out on another deployment, which was a crippler for the both of us. Thankfully, neither of us would be going through that ever again.

As the week went on, I could see Kenna getting quieter and quieter as she to no doubt, wasn't looking forward to this moment. Made obvious by the speech that still stuck prominently in my brain.

"So...are you?"

I looked at her. "Hm?"

"Your ride is here. To take you home. Someone by the name of Brett Neil. Claims to be your best buddy bringing you home on behalf of your folks, saving them from coming all this way."

I smirked. Of course it would be Brett. No one else would go to hell and back, even in a small way, for my folks than he would. He'd done so ever since they'd taken him in at an early age after losing his folks in a barn fire. Since then, he'd been my best friend and closest thing to a brother as I'd get.

He was going to have a fun time loading me into his truck while my arms stuck out in these casts, as if I was permanently asking for a hug. It was going to be amusing, at least. Something to add a little humour into all of this, which I welcomed greatly.

"Yes, I'm ready."

"Then let's get you going!" she said, her voice chipper as ever. With just a slight hint of sadness tinging her words.

Plastic bag secured safely on my lap, Kenna expertly pushed the wheelchair out of the room and into the corridor. I suppose she's done this dozens of times. Still, I'm no lightweight and adding in the weight of the casts, her strength was mighty impressive.

I tried not to stare at the other patients as we passed each room leading down the corridor, but my eyes did wander into a few of them. Some looked to be in a worse state than I was, to which I quickly said a silent prayer for their recovery, counting my blessings that I was at least leaving here with my life. The fate of humankind was fickle, so I could only hope these men and women left with their lives like I.

A few turns here and there, and we arrived at the nurse's station where I could see Brett waiting for us. Leaning his right arm on the countertop, waiting for us to arrive.

"Hey!" I called out as Kenna pulled me to a stop, putting the break on the wheelchair.

Brett turned around, immediately looking to where he'd assumed I'd be. Only to find that I wasn't standing. A moment later he looked down, meeting my eyes with a hint of regret in his own. "Hey. I..."

If I could hold up a hand to stop him, I would. Instead, I interrupted what he was about to say. "Don't, it's okay. Well, it's not. You know what I mean."

He stuffed his hands into his pockets, his shoulders slumping slightly. "Y-yeah."

"Mr O'Neil, thank you for coming. Are his papers all in order? Signed for discharge?"

Brett nodded, brightening at the sound of Kenna's voice as she addressed him. "Yes ma'am. All signed, sealed and safely stored." He gave his hand a pat inside his right pocket, where I assumed the paperwork laid.

"Great! Let's get Mr O'Donoghue out to your vehicle so you can both be on your way."

Kenna had us down the hall, into and out of the elevator and into the main entrance lobby in no time at all. Shortly after which, we pulled up next to Brett's truck. A huge Ford F150.

I'm going to enjoy this.

Expecting to feel Brett's hands around my upper body, imagine my surprise when instead a pair of strong, capable, female hands embraced me instead.

"What are you doing?" I asked.

"Helping you into the truck. Hospital policy. We're liable if anything happens to you on hospital grounds, so we have to help those incapacitated into vehicles."

I see.

"And you can do that, can you?"

Kenna gave a little grunt as she worked her arms under my armpits, raising me out of the wheelchair a fraction. "Never underestimate a nurse determined to do her job."

I nodded. "Noted."

Between them, Brett and Kenna somehow managed to get me, my casts and my dead legs into Brett's truck. I was nothing short of amazed, considering the job they had set ahead of them when we'd first exited the hospital entrance.

"There, all settled." Kenna huffed, stepping away from the open passenger door. "You're good to go."

Brett swiftly moved around the back of the truck, hopping up into the front of the truck beside me, belting himself into the driver's seat. "Thank you ma'am, we appreciate it."

She flashed us her smile once more before closing the door, the window open so we could communicate at least until we pulled away.

"Drive safe now. Wouldn't want either of you to end up back here again any time soon."

"Not that I have much left to break." I muttered.

At my muttering, her melodic laugh rang out once more. "True."

The truck's engine kicked into life, a loud beast it was. You could hear the damn thing coming from another state. Brett turned to me, "Ready to blow this popsicle stand?"

Instead of answering him, I turned my head to meet Kenna's eyes which never left me since I was seated in the truck. "Thank you, for everything." I meant it. I was truly grateful.

Not sure if I was seeing things or not, but I'm pretty sure that her eyes were watering up at my words. She must've known I mean them too.

You're getting sappy, boy.

"You're welcome. Goodbye, Theon."

With that, she quickly departed back inside the hospital, leaving me no time to give a reply. A good thing, considering I don't do goodbyes. Turning back to Brett, I gave him the nod, giving the okay to take us home.

Skilfully, Brett pulled out from where he'd parked and started us on our journey home. Though just before we left the hospital parking lot, I took one last look at the place through the rear-view mirror.

Goodbye, Kenna, and thank you.

CHAPTER SEVEN
Kenna

Pulling up at the hospital in my allocated parking spot, I killed the car engine. It has been one week since I'd bid farewell to Theon and his best friend Brett, who'd taken him from her care and back to wherever he happened to live. The irritating thing about it all? I've not been able to stop thinking about him, Theon, that is, whenever I've had a spare moment to think.

If I wasn't occupied on any one task, he is where my mind would immediately go.

Gosh darn it.

I've never in my life had a problem keeping my mind off a man before. Not that there's been that many in my life to get my mind off, but still. There had to be something about this man, something that I'm clearly missing, which kept sending my mind back to him. If only I could think just what it was, it would be a lot easier to put it, and him, behind me. Sadly, I'm not that smart. Despite being a nurse, when it came to people, I always missed the obvious.

Jess though, now she was as sharp as a tack. I'd like to think that's why we make such a good team. She's forever pointing out the things I miss, and vice versa. Where I miss the obvious, she doesn't. And where she misses the hidden things, I don't. We'd make a good crime-fighting team, if either one of us were remotely qualified or liked that line of work. Sadly, that's not the case.

For the next week though, it was just me. Jess had been called out of state for a family thing up in North Carolina, her home state. So, I was flying solo, so to speak. The offer was on the table for me to go with her, though she'd insisted I'd lose the time I'd saved off work if something more important came up in the future. Yes, I saw her point, but it would've been nice to get a mini-break away from all the chaos. Away from Theon.

Ugh!

Which is why I'm here at the hospital on my day off, to give me something to do to get my mind off that man. Yes, I'm only picking up something from my locker, but maybe I'll hang around and chat with anyone in the break room for a little bit. Anything to keep me occupied until I absolutely had to leave.

Letting out the breath that had been building up inside me, I grabbed my phone, my ID and my locker key, I got out of my car, locking it behind me with the key as I strode towards the staff entrance.

An hour and a half later, I found myself climbing back into my car. Much to my relief, there were a few other nurses in the break room when I got there, after filtering through my locker, who were more than happy to chat to me until they headed back for their shifts. Neither of them were regulars that I saw on a daily basis, but we'd passed in the halls on occasion.

It was only after leaving the break room before heading on out here, that I had no idea what to do with the rest of my time or the rest of the day, for that matter. With Jess out of state and all of my other go-to friends busy with work, it didn't exactly leave me with many fun options to do things on my own. Nothing I hadn't done hundreds of times over anyway.

I didn't have to wait long for a suggestion to make itself clear. Loudly, at that. My stomach made itself known. Clearly, that's what I'd be doing next. Feeding it. No complaints here, I'm more than happy to let it have its own way. Food and I were best friends, second to Jess and I. Which is exactly why I had to spend 4-5 days a week after work in the gym to work off my excess food consumption.

Wasting no time, I turned the key in my car and proceeded to make my way out of the hospital parking lot, heading towards my favourite sandwich-come-coffee place in downtown Austin.

Less than twenty minutes later, I pulled up outside the self-same sandwich-come-coffee bar, even though I don't drink coffee, eager to quell the hunger brewing deep within my stomach. Stepping inside, the same familiar, delicious smell met me as the door closed behind my back. This was probably the reason why I, and so many others, kept coming back. They suckered us in with their delicious smells which left us even more hungry to come back, than when we first came in.

Leary, whose real name is Alondra, a mutual friend of Jess and myself who we'd met during college, gives me a cheery wave as I move out of the bar's doorway. Whenever I come by, she's the one I always find who's on shift. I don't think I've ever seen her take a break or a day off in the last four years she's been working, not once. Then again, that's why she fits in with Jess and I so well. We're not so much the three musketeers, but more like the three workaholics. None of us really take a day off if we have to, as us girls have got to earn our coin.

"I'll bring your usual over in a minute! I'm on break in 5!" Leary calls out to me, mindful of the customer she's currently handing change back to.

Waving my hand in confirmation, I head on over to my usual booth spot which is by sheer luck, currently free for me to slide into. I wasn't left waiting long when five minutes later, Leary joined me on the other side of the cozy booth, sliding my usual steak and cheese sandwich with English breakfast tea in front of me.

"Phew! I swear they're all coming in at this time to spite me."

"Oh I'm sure they do." I laughed, picking up my sandwich. "They must wake up in the morning thinking, 'Oh I'm going to go in around midday, with everyone else, just to spite Leary'".

She rolled her eyes, shaking her head at my failed attempt at being funny. "Har-de-har. Mock me all you like, but you have the same thing do you not?"

Taking a bite out of my sandwich, I nodded. "Yup."

Leary brought out her own homemade lunch from her pocket, which was nothing more than a basic square sandwich she'd made at home that morning, I'm assuming.

"No Jess today?"

I shook my head, "Not today. She's out of state for some family thing up in North Carolina. Something about her brother Ronan, or for Ronan, I'm not sure. She didn't really explain it in detail before she was gone and out the door."

Leary pouted, setting her unwrapped sandwich on the table top.

"Bummer. I really wanted to speak to her about something. Though I guess that explains why she's not been answering my texts, if she's been travelling."

Jess very rarely travelled and used her phone unless absolutely necessary, so this was every bit the possibility. Unlike me, I tend to use my phone and battery pack to occupy my time if I didn't have a good book in my hands.

"What did you want to speak to her about?"

At this, Leary looked at me. "Oh, nothing important. I just wanted to ask if she could cover me this Saturday, but I guess I won't get a hold of her if she's out of state. How long is she gone for?"

"A week."

In all but a few bites, Leary had finished half of her measly sandwich. "Double drat."

"Why would you need her to cover for you?"

This time instead of replying, Leary seemed…hesitant. As if she didn't know how, or didn't even want to say. At least, not out in public. No way was I going to force her to say something she didn't want to, not even to me as close as the three of us were. We never forced one another to do something we really didn't want to say.

A whisper of a sigh escaped Leary's lips, a moment before she surprised me by coming out with what she wanted to say.

"It's my yearly physical. For…you know. I went with the yearly choice instead of three or five. I'm okay going on my own, I just need someone to cover for me so I can attend the appointment."

Back in college, Leary had a cervical cancer scare. Well, it wasn't really her scare, but it scared her nonetheless. All three of us go for regular cervical screenings and have done since the recommended age for all young women to start having them. Though one year back in college, Leary got a call from the hospital to say she'd had a positive result from her latest screening. Understandably, this set her more than over the edge and as a result, she's super aware of her health and every last thing that could be wrong.

Upon going to the hospital with Jess and I at her side and one examination later, she was given the all clear. Of course this confused us all, as Leary had told us she'd been called in due to a positive result. As it turned out, the hospital had a mix-up of colossal proportions, putting Leary's name on another woman's results by mistake.

How this could happen when we're in such a time where mistakes like these don't happen, thanks to advances in technology lessening human error, was beyond any of us. We were just glad that Leary wasn't suffering from cervical cancer, while also feeling for the woman who was told she was clear but would soon, and unfortunately, be told otherwise.

After this mix-up, Leary was compensated for her unnecessary suffering and the case was dropped. If only could be the same for her emotional health. That wasn't something that could be fixed as easily as being compensated. So now every year, she went back for a check just to be on the safe side. Even though there's no chance of her getting another, genuine, positive result. She does it as a reassurance thing, rather than out of paranoia. I'd do the same in her shoes, if it had happened to me.

"Want me to see if I can switch shifts so I can cover you?"

Leary shook her head, knowing immediately I'd offer. "No need. I've got one of the other girls on standby if I couldn't reach Jess. Thanks for the offer though."

"You know I'd do anything for you two."

Her smile told me all I needed to hear. She knew very well I would. So would they.

Before either of us could speak again, a shout for Leary came from somewhere out the back behind the counter, eliciting a sigh from her once more.

"Guess that's my break over early. Catch you soon?"

Standing up, I embraced Leary in my arms, bringing her close to me before stepping back. "Of course! I'll see you after you're done on Saturday, come to mine."

With another shout from the back and a nod from my dear friend, she swiftly departed my company, leaving me as alone as I was when I first came in no more than fifteen minutes ago.

Everyone seemed to have something going on in their lives to pull them every which way, as did I but a week ago.

I wonder how he's doing now...

Just as I was about to both mentally and physically shake my head free of the thoughts of Theon O'Donoghue, a figure crossed to the left of my vision, coming to a stop at my side.

Looking up, a woman in her mid-to-late fifties, carrying her own lunch looked down at me with a sincere, yet apologetic expression on her face. "I'm so sorry to bother you, but is anyone sitting with you?"

"O-oh, no. No. Please, have a seat." I gesture with my free hand, offering the kind-looking woman the vacant space Leary had but a moment ago left.

"Thank you so much!"

Even if I wanted to, I don't think I could've refused her a seat opposite me. Whereas I'm a person who likes her personal space as much as the next, you'd have to be someone really up their own behind morally, to refuse such a simple request. After all, wouldn't we want to be treated in kind if we were the ones asking to sit down? Of course.

Once seated, the middle-aged woman set a tray laden with sandwiches on her side of the table. Enough to me which looks as if they could feed an army.

"I won't take up too much of your personal space, I just need to get these packed away where I can actually move." The woman laughed, the sound almost an angelic one. "No room to swing a cat up there."

Looking at the counter where orders were placed and collected, I could easily see what she meant. Maybe Leary was right, perhaps people were here to spite her and keep her busy after all.

Ignoring her comment about space, I waved my hand dismissively. "You're not in my way at all, I'm not staying long myself."

"Oh, busy day ahead?"

I shook my head, "Not really. Well, not unless you count me, my movie collection and an unhealthy amount of popcorn as a busy day."

This earned me a laugh. Clearly she too must have had several days where you couldn't think of anything else better to do on your day off, than to do something so completely and utterly as cliché as watch Netflix and eat food you normally wouldn't do. A woman after my own heart.

She continued to move the various sandwiches around, sorting them out and carefully starting to load them into a cooled bag. "I take it you don't get many days off, by the sounds of it."

"Not many, no. Not that I'd take them. I'm a bit of a workaholic."

The middle-aged woman, whose name I've still yet to learn, looked up to meet my eyes. "Aren't we all?" she smiled, "What is it that you do dear?"

I shrugged, "I'm an ER nurse."

You would think I'd have told her that she'd been so lucky as to have won the lottery, simply by telling her what I do for a living, because that's exactly how I would describe the glow on her face. If people thought that pregnant women glow, they've got nothing on how illuminated this woman was before me.

"That so? My word! It's as if God himself has been listening to my very prayers!"

Well, isn't that kind of what he does anyway?

I still didn't know what it was that was making her say this, though I'm sure I was about to find out. Not before long, her hands left the sandwiches in the cooled bag and gently clasped over my own. Good thing I'm not iffy about being touched, like someone I once knew. You touch her for even a single second and she'd have her antibacterial gel out before you can say 'germs'.

"Listen, dear. I'm probably coming across as a bit of a fuddy-duddy right now. Or at least, very strange. But I need to ask you something very important."

O…okay then.

I still don't see what's so special about me, that I have to be the one to help this woman.

What do I possess that no one else does, just because I'm a nurse?

Before I could deliberate further, the woman continued.

"I was just about to head on over to the hospital to enquire about hiring a nurse to come and help me with my son. See, he got himself a little bit hurt not too long ago, and we thought we'd be able to help him when he came back to our ranch. Sadly, we underestimated just how stubborn he really is. Now, at least. He never used to be. He won't let us help with the more… delicate, of things. We're running out of options and this is the last thing besides doing all that we can do as his folks, to help him on the road to recovery. His condition is a little, how to put it…prideful, somewhat. There's not much we can do about helping him back one hundred percent the man he was before the accident, but we've been trying to adapt and it's knocking his pride a little bit." She paused, gripping my hands a little as if to steady herself. "What I'm trying to say is…we need to hire a nurse to come live at our ranch for the duration of our son's recovery process, at least until he's able to live a mostly independent life without needing assistance. Would the hospital you're working at be willing to lend your services to us, to help our son?"

Well, that was a verbal info dump if ever I heard one.

I've had my fair share of people ask me things before, various requests of all kinds, though I'd never had one like this from a stranger in the middle of a sandwich bar. I could be anyone, yet she was willing to just ask and risk it for the love of her son. Mother's love is a powerful thing, as it is with my mother and me. I know how much she'd do and how far she'd go for me, it looks like this woman and she are one and the same.

Our hospital, like most within the rest of America, did run some sort of programme which allowed a qualified male or female nurse to go and assist a patient if they truly needed it. By the sounds of it even though I haven't heard the whole story, this woman's son sounded like he was one of those who did.

I didn't need to think long to make my decision on what to do, it was a pretty sure-fire thing as soon as she stopped speaking as to what I would do. Nothing within me as I am as a person, or who I was as a nurse, could refuse a person in need. Even if it was under the most unlikely of circumstances that something like this would come my way. In the hospital or out on the street, my answer would remain the same.

Her hopeful eyes stayed firm on my face, waiting for my answer. I wasn't going to make her wait any longer.

"I would love to help out you and your son. I'm honoured that you feel you can trust me to do this as I know in times like today, it's not easy to trust someone you haven't met." Moving my hands out of hers, I now took up the position of being the one to hold hers in mine, giving back to her a reassuring squeeze. "There's a lot to get done before we can make it official, though if you have time now, I'll be more than happy to head on over to the hospital to get the process started with you."

Sitting here with this woman's hands in mine, I have no regrets or bad feeling in my gut. In fact, it felt like my gut was doing cheers of its own, telling me that this was meant to be. Not being a believer in fate, I'm guessing this is what it would feel like to someone who does.

Agreed on our next move, we stand to leave the sandwich bar and take my car back on over to the hospital. Making out way out I give a parting wave to Leary, who returns in kind as the door closed slowly behind our backs. Hopefully I'll still be able to see her this Saturday, given the turn of events within the last half an hour.

Putting the cooled bag in the trunk of my car, I helped the woman inside before sliding into the driver's seat, belting myself inside and turning the engine on. Gripping the wheel ready to get going, I turned to my passenger.

"Ready?"

She nodded. "Yes dear. Though I feel we've missed something rather important."

We?

"Oh?"

Genuinely, I had no idea what this would be. After a day of surprises, well, one big one, I wouldn't be surprised if I was missing something.

"My name, dear." The woman clarified, smiling kindly. "It's nice to meet you, officially. I'm Mara, short for Tamara."

Oh yes! Names. Damn.

Turning to face the woman now officially known as Mara, I held out my hand which was soon filled with hers once more. "Kenna. Kenna Bouchard. My patients call me Nurse Bouchard." Which they did, aside from one. Sliding my hand from hers after our shake, I flashed her my hospital ID which had been left to rest on my dashboard. "Just in case you were having any doubts."

Mara shook her head, "Never for a second. Hopefully soon, you'll be my son's nurse. Temporary, of course."

"Yes, hopefully so."

Late introductions out of the way, we made our way across town, heading once more to the hospital.

CHAPTER EIGHT
Theon

If I could describe this past week in a nutshell, it would be something as close to hell as a human being could imagine, having not actually been there before. Unless you'd served in a war-torn country fighting for someone's liberation and freedom, then you'd come pretty darn close.

In every which way humanly conceivable, my life has presented me with more challenges than I'd ever imagined once I'd been released from hospital, and into the care of my folks. Eating and drinking was a challenge. Getting myself dressed was a challenge. Going to the bathroom, yes you guessed it, another challenge. That and more in fact, wasn't actually attainable unless I had assistance, utterly humiliating and degrading as I'd imagined them to be when I was laying in that hospital bed considering it all.

Of course, I couldn't pin any of this on my folks. They weren't the ones who were making me feel that way. If anything, they were going above and beyond as they'd always done to help me. But still, I knew seeing their only son reduced to the state I currently find myself in, was less anything less than emotionally painful for them. Literally for me. Everything I did even in the smallest sense was painful. Though no matter how much pain it would mean for me, I still refused to take those god awful meds issued as I was discharged.

No. Thank. You.

On top of everything else, I was just plain irritated. No longer was I able to get up in the morning of my own free will and go about my day doing what I wanted, at my own speed, and as I liked. No longer was I able to pick and choose what chores or activities I could do to occupy my time and to help out the other men and women on the ranch. No longer was I able to be the man I was before. I was now at the mercy of reduced activity and irritating idleness, at least for the next several weeks until all of my casts came off.

Even then, I was still restricted. No matter how much time passed and various casts would come off, it still wouldn't grant me back the use of my formerly strong and sturdy legs. Legs which had carried me miles through war zones, missions and tours. Those legs were long gone. Metaphorically speaking. All these legs could do now was sit motionless, doing nothing at all no matter how much my mind willed them to move. They hadn't moved an inch. Not one single ounce of a feeling coursed through them, none at all.

Why I even tried was beyond me. It was a fool's hope they'd work again.

If my former commander before I was made captain could see me now, he'd whip my ass to hell and back for giving up so quickly. No one was allowed to give up when they were under his command, not for anything. But he wasn't here, not anymore.

The memory of his passing haunted us all, as it hadn't been a kind or easy one. A mission had gone wrong and he'd paid the ultimate price for it. A price several of us wished we'd paid in his place, knowing that would never be and no matter how much we wished it were so, it wouldn't bring him back. All that was left was the memory of what once was, and the family that he'd left behind. His wife was a strong woman who was taking great care of their two kids, kids who I had the pleasure of seeing regularly on the ranch as they'd been here ever since I got off my last tour.

Captain Harrison O'Toole's wife, Sandra, had taken up a teaching position here on the ranch after a call was put out for a kid's horse-riding teacher was posted. Our last 'teacher' left for maternity leave and after having her baby boy, informed us that she'd decided to stay at home as a stay-at-home mother. Fair enough, as it was her decision to make, though it did leave us short one teacher and after one call to Sandra, the position was quickly filled once more.

I'd promised Captain O'Toole that I'd look after his family if anything were to ever happen to him, and I was going to keep that promise no matter what. Looking after them long-distance was starting to prove a bit difficult, so when I called to offer her the job along with housing at one of the ranch-homes on our family's property, Sandra was only too happy to help and to move closer to people who considered her and her kids, kin.

"You look like you're deep in thought there, son."

I looked up to catch my father, former General Aidan O'Donoghue of the United States Army, enter through the porch doors. Thanks to my current condition, he'd volunteered to step in for me. Secretly, I knew he was doing it because he knew I'd never be able to do half of the chores ever again, though he'd never admit it. Though with this being a rehab ranch, there would be things I could do, sans use of my legs, in the future. Those days though, were a long way away.

I nodded, "Yeah. Yeah I guess I was."

Not one to beat about the bush, he stepped up to me where I'd been placed on the couch, and clapped his hand firmly on my shoulder. "Well don't linger there too long, son. You hear? You got to live in the here and now, not stuck in your own head."

Like I hadn't heard that enough since I got back from my last tour.

My father had many mottos, saying and such other expressions of the like, something which made him both wise and dominant during his forty-year stint in the U.S. Army. No one questioned him and no one messed with him. Despite that, he was still one of the most highly respected generals there's ever been, so there has to be something said for why he conducted himself the way he did.

Though it must be said, if any of his former army buddies saw him with my mother on one of their weekly dates, romantic dinners or witnessed the acts of affection dotted here and there throughout the day, they'd see him as less of a bulldog, and more of the sappy puppy dog he is under his tough exterior.

"Any idea where my wife is?" he said on his way to the kitchen, opening the fridge to get an ice-cold bottle of water.

"I think she said something about a sandwich bar. I wasn't really listening."

Leaning his back against the countertop, my father took a long gulp from his water bottle before softly shaking his head. "I don't know why she goes into downtown Austin to get something we can make here."

"Maybe because it's the best sandwich place in the state, and secretly you love their food but don't want to show your excitement about something as simple as a sandwich?" I smirked.

This earned me his famous eye squint, the expression that was a tell-tale sign you were right without him verbally confirming it. "Watch your sass mouth there, son."

Hmph, hardly. You know I'm right, old man.

Our conversation was interrupted by the infernal alarm set on both of our phones, one which heralded the unfortunate next attempt at giving me my medication. Setting down his bottle, my father snoozed both of the alarms and looked at me with as much determination as I once saw on my own face, once upon a time.

Crossing his arms, he looked down at me. "Is it worth me even trying?"

I couldn't meet his eye. He knew the answer. Nothing anyone would ever try would convince me to take medication. I dealt with things better when I was aware of what I was going through, pain included. Not when I'm mended out of my head and not aware of what day it is or when I last ate. No thank you.

"Listen…" I began to say, but my father quickly cut me off with one swift movement of his hand, telling me to zip it quick.

"I know what you're going to say, what you always say these days, but it's time to hear me out for once soldier."

I'm not a soldier anymore, father.

"Last night for the first time in a hell of a long time, your mother cried half of the night in my arms. We know this has been more than rough on you son, but imagine seeing the one person you love whom you gave life to, subjecting themselves to such pain and you're powerless to convince them otherwise. A parent, as you might know someday, will go to hell and back for their child no matter how old they get. But when that child, albeit a grown one, puts themselves through the very hell their own mother would walk through, it wears at you after a while. We know nothing will convince you to abandon your own morals and beliefs, as I wouldn't expect you to ask me to abandon my own, but think of your mother for once in all of this. If for just today, take those damn pills and let her sleep for one night, knowing her baby boy is alright."

Unable to do otherwise, I met my father's eyes, stunned speechless at what had just been laid at my ears. Neither one of us was overly sentimental when it came to such matters, so for him to say something so heartfelt and not be directed at my mother, well, it was a real eye-opener.

A fool would have a hard time denying he was right. Today, I wouldn't be that fool.

With a sigh and the closing of my eyes, I gave a slow nod. "No need to say anymore, father. I'll take them."

If he was shocked that I'd agreed to take the damn medication, he sure as hell didn't show it. It was the line about my mother giving me life that really did it, convincing me to do it for her at least for today. If I had a son or daughter, there's no denying I'd do anything for him or her.

After all, she'd done so much for me since the day I was born, they both have, so giving her this one thing wasn't going to take away what I believed in. Not one bit.

"You'll have to get them for me though. I can't." I grumbled.

Soon, I'd swallowed the damn meds and had been left in a comfortable as possible position, in front of the TV playing some god-awful daytime talk show. There were side effects of my medication, but sadly drowsiness wasn't one of them. Something I could do with right now to put me out of my misery of listening to middle-aged women dribble on about some issue or rather that I didn't really care about, unable to change the channel to something less painful.

My father had long since departed to go off and do God-knows what. I'd be able to think clearly about what it would be right about now, though rather unfortunately that was one of the side-effects of my medication which seemed to be kicking in quicker today. Forgetfulness.

Left with nothing but the sound of the TV and my own bleak thoughts, I closed my eyes once more, hoping to settle for a bit and try to enjoy what was left of the peace of the day. A rather optimistic notion as sooner than expected, the peace of the moment was broken by the sound of the front door of my folks' house opening and closing.

"I'm back!" my mother's voice called out, making me open my eyes.

The medication was more than doing its job in however much time had passed since my father left, and my mother's return. Time between the two events was lost to me while my eyes were closed. However long that was. Yet another side-effect, a minor one, granted. Loss of understanding of date and time. I'm sure there was an official name or term for it, though truth be told I really didn't care. Soon enough I'd be rid of it by the time I'd be due my next set of meds later tonight.

Sounds of footsteps filled the audible silence in this part of the house, getting closer and closer with each step. Expecting it to be my mother, whose voice called out moments ago, I spoke up.

"Get the sandwiches okay Ma? I'm starving."

Even more so, thanks to the pills…

No answer met my question. Instead, all I heard was the softest of gasps sounding nothing like my mother's usual gasp.

I called out again, "Ma?"

Turning as best as I could given the limited mobility of my casts and dead legs combined, I wasn't prepared to see who was standing just inside the room across from where I currently sat.

What in the merry hell is SHE doing here?!

I'd call it a while back that I had a feeling the hospital wouldn't be the last time I would see her, but I never imagined that the next time would be here in the main house on my family ranch. Passing each other if I ever went back into downtown Austin? Yes. But this? Never in a million years.

Looking equally as shocked on the outside as I felt on the inside, stood none other than Nurse Kenna Bouchard in all her casual, non-uniformed glory.

Well, well, well.

This was going to be interesting.

How she came to be standing before me would no doubt be made clear to me soon. Right now however, I was enjoying the look on her face as it conveyed what her mind was clearly thinking as it went through all the possibilities, solutions and reasons for how to deal with seeing me again in such an…intimate setting. I was no mind reader, but it was plain as the nose on her face that this was what was going on inside that pretty little head of hers.

No way was I going to let on how equally stunned and surprised I was, as I was too well-trained for that. Not even under interrogation would I let it slip. Even though that wasn't the case here. So I might as well have my fun and put her out of her misery at the same time, killing two birds with one stone and all that.

I smirked, fighting off the effects of my medication to appear somewhat normal. "Nurse…Kenna. What a surprise to see you here."

"Theon O'Donoghue, you be kind to Miss Kenna now do you hear me?" my mother called from the hallway, appearing with her arms laden with sandwiches, cutting me off before I could even begin my teasing.

How the hell does she still do that?

She's psychic, I swear!

Psychic abilities aside, I answered her question with a grunt. It was one thing to bring Kenna here without prior warning, but to bring her here and show me up for not even being one bit disrespectful to her? No, I wasn't going to rise to that. Better to keep my mouth shut and say nothing than to say something to actually put my foot in it.

Kenna still stood in the same place when I'd first originally spotted her, though this time her expression had shifted to something more neutral, as if her guard was back up and her composure regained. My mother had set the sandwiches down on the kitchen island counter, dropping the cooled bag to her feet. "Where's your father?"

I turned my head to the back doors, "I think he went that way, I'm not sure."

Grabbing two sandwiches and another set of bottled water, she swiftly made her way outside to locate my father. The two of them usually ate together every day no matter what one of them was doing, something I found admirable about their relationship. They always made time for one another after all these years.

Something I'll never have.

No one would want me as I am now, and I wouldn't give anyone anything less than a whole man.

An uncomfortable silence descended over the two of us as I continued to sit here, not willing to be the first to break it, and Kenna continuing to stand uncomfortably over by the doorway. If one of us didn't speak soon, I don't think I could honestly take that level of awkwardness on top of what has already mounted.

Clearing my throat, I looked back at her with the most deadpan expression I could muster. "Sit down. Please." I ask her kindly as possible.

Snapping out of her own thoughts, Kenna casually makes her way over to the other couch opposite where I sat, lowering herself onto it with all the grace only a princess would be jealous of. Who knew that busy, organised, put-together Nurse Kenna Bouchard was graceful? Guess life is full of little surprises after all.

I don't know what my mother was thinking by bringing her, so I sure as hell didn't know what she was thinking about leaving me here all alone with her. I was rather hoping she'd explain after she'd set the sandwiches down, but of course she went in search of my father so that but the kibosh on that.

Soon though, I had my answer when Kenna cleared her throat which grabbed my full attention.

"Listen, I bet you're just as surprised as I am to see me…each other, again. How this happened…well…it's bizarre to say the least. So how about this, I explain what went down so hopefully the rod that's inserted someplace out of sight inside of you, can be removed and we can act like decent, civil human beings to one another. Does that sound good?"

Sounds stupendous…

Truly, I wanted this over as much as she did. I gave her the nod to continue.

Kenna took a breath before she continued, flexing her hands open and closed on top of her knees, her legs tucked close to the couch. "Right… well…okay." She cleared her throat. "I was at the sandwich bar minding my own business, when after saying goodbye to my friend, your mother approached my table. I thought she was just going to sit and sort the food she'd bought into her bag, but we got talking. As strangers do sometimes. We're not all antisocial. Anyway, while we were talking, your mother asked me what I did for a living and naturally, I told her. I didn't see any reason not to, as I was thinking I wouldn't see her again. That's where things get a bit… well, you know…"

"No, I don't." I shook my head. "That's why you're explaining it to me." I grumbled.

"R-right! Yes. Well, according to your mother on our talk on the way to the hospital after I'd agreed to help, I…"

I raised my casted right hand, halting her mid-speech. "Woah, woah, woah. Why was she in your car with you?"

Kenna squinted her eyes at me in the most frustratingly adorable glare I've ever seen from a woman. "I'm trying to get there, where you wanted me to get to, if you'd just let me explain."

Fair point. Not that I'd admit it.

Holding up both of my casted hands in surrender, she continued.

"I agreed to give her my help as in the bar, she pleaded to me just how much her son meant to her and her husband. No one would do that so openly in public, where dozens of ears could overhear, if they weren't truly seeking their last resort option. Getting back to where I was, on the way to the hospital we spoke a little more in-depth about what she was looking for out of hiring a nurse for at-home care, initially telling me more about the patient's needs and requirements. As it was my day off, I wasn't on-duty to handle her request while off the clock, so I took her into the hospital for her to fill out what paperwork could be completed without my needing to be there, with the rest waiting for me to sign and complete the other necessary steps the next time I'm on shift. Tomorrow, actually."

So far, not too bad.

"Keep going." I said politely, not wanting to upset her again.

"I waited for your mother out in the hospital parking lot while she got the necessary paperwork done, and I drove her back to where she'd parked her car before coming into the sandwich bar."

"That's it?"

Kenna nodded. "That's it. She didn't tell me the name of the patient I might be looking after for the next several weeks, mainly because I'm guessing there was a possibility I'd know who you were and immediately refuse. Though I don't see how that would be, since your mother didn't know me or what I do for a living, before she approached me."

I scoffed, "Never underestimate my mother. The woman is too damn psychic for her own good."

I swear I caught the faintest hint of a smirk tugging at the corner of Kenna's mouth, though she hid it well.

There were a million and one plot-holes in this story, several things that have yet to be clarified but if truth be told, I was too weary and too tired to begin asking those questions right now. What stunned me the most was that my mother, my own mother, had gone and asked a random stranger for such a request behind my back without consulting me and possibly my father too. Thinking back on what Kenna had said, it sounded to me like it was done so I couldn't object, knowing very much so that I couldn't say something after an arrangement had been put in place. As I wasn't in a position physically to undo it.

It was just a matter of how to phrase a 'no thank you' in just the right way that won't be too much of a blow. To either of them. I fully understood where my mother was coming from, and why she wanted to do this, but I didn't need help. I was fine with how I was coping with things. The last thing I wanted was someone to assist me, humiliating me further and seeing me when I'm even less than when I was at my worst.

Thanks, but no thanks.

I must've been silent and thinking about things inside my own head for longer than I thought, as when I went to offer up my gentle rejection of this situation, Kenna was ready and waiting to interject. "I know what you're going to say, but don't even bother. This is outside of your control, the paperwork is signed and I'm all ready to start on Monday, after I move my stuff this Sunday."

Surely I misheard her. It sounded as if she said she was moving in. Here. With my folks. With me.

No, absolutely not!

"Listen, Kenna. I…"

"Are more than happy to accept my help and your mother's intervention? Good! That's what I thought." She beamed, getting to her feet once more. Steadier than when she'd fist come in.

I shook my head, shifting my upper half to face her better. "N-no! I…"

"Am so thankful that I'm here? You know what? So am I! I think we're going to get along just great and you're going to be back to your normal self in no time."

I wouldn't be so sure of that just yet, woman.

You'll never get me to walk again.

No one will.

There isn't going to be anything else either one of us can say that would change the outcome of my mother's actions, nor would there be anything I could say to possibly deter Kenna from caring for me. At least, not today anyway. Plans started flowing into my head just as they did when I was back leading my men on tour, plans that I intended to put to good use when she was as good as moved in. I'll have her mind changed in no time. Soon she'll be back on her way to the hospital, and I can get on with this dismal existence that would be my life now.

For now, it was Kenna 1, me 0. Though I thoroughly intended to change that statistic. Dramatically.

Acting as if I was resigned to my fate, I dropped my head, my chin touching the fabric of my shirt. "Alright, alright. You don't have to say anymore. I'll accept, but on one condition."

"Which is?" Kenna replied, sounding surprised.

Looking up, I met her eyes. "If you're to be my personal carer… nurse…whatever your role title is, it's to be in my own home in my own space. If I'm not going to be under my mother's eyes then we'll be doing this in my place. Deal?"

Kenna walked right on up to me as if she had just won against a lion in an arena. Only, she was coming across more as the lion, who was proudly looking down at her prey who was finally under her paw. She slid her hand into mine, shaking my hand as best as my limited movement would allow her. "Deal."

Game on, Miss Bouchard. Game on.

CHAPTER NINE
Theon

After watching the taillights of Kenna's car pull away from the main house and down the long, dirt road leading to the ranch entrance, I could only but imagine now how it would be between us now she'd be moving in with me. Well, for as long as she can take my resistance. The plan was very much still in place to get her out as soon as possible.

It wasn't that I had anything against her personally, as I would still be doing this if it was any other nurse coming to 'assist' me at home. Admittedly though, it's been difficult to do basic things even someone restricted could do, so I might keep her around until I have full use of my arms again. Then I'll make things a bit more difficult. We'll see.

Around half an hour or so after watching Kenna leave, my mother re-entered through the porch back doors. A somewhat sheepish look on her face. I knew she was gauging how I looked right now in order to say the right thing. Something that won't set me off. "Did Ms Bouchard...Kenna, leave?"

I nodded, "She did. Half an hour ago."

"You seem...fine. Did everything um...go okay? With Kenna."

For a moment, I did consider stringing it out a little longer, teasing her into thinking that something did go down. The moment didn't last long, as I remembered even though my dear mother was a sweet-tempered, kind, compassionate woman, she could also lay down a verbal whoopin' when she wanted to so, best to avoid it. Even at my age. You're never too old to receive a what for from your mother.

I shrugged, "I am fine. All things considered." I said, looking down at my casted and bandaged body.

"You know what I mean." She crossed her arms, stopping in front of me. "So, nothing happened between the two of you?"

Oh, something happened alright.

Shifting into a more comfortable position, which would probably last for all of five minutes before finding another, I faced my mother. "Nothing other than her telling me what's really going on here. By that I mean the truth, mother."

Uncrossing her arms, she let out a soft sigh. "I was doing the best thing I could think of for you, Theon. You might be and have been an adult for many years, but when it comes to your own wellbeing you seem to forget that fact. Sometimes you just need a little nudge in the right direction for your eyes to be opened to what you really need."

"So you think that Kenna is the right direction for me? To heal me?"

She nodded, "I do. You'll see for yourself in no time."

I wouldn't be too sure about that, mother.

"Maybe." I smirked inwardly. "Although, we've come to one arrangement as a condition for this whole thing going down behind my back."

"Which is?" she said, her brow arching in obvious curiosity.

Inclining my neck, I gutted my chin in the general direction where my house was located, elsewhere on the family ranch spread. "She's going to be living with me. At my place. Alone." I searched her face for any sort of reaction to what I'd just announced. A moment later, I got one.

If my mother's jaw got any lower, it would soon end up on the floor. "Did I just hear you right?"

"You did." I nodded. "I don't see the issue. You wanted me to have a nurse to assist me. I didn't. I could've sent her away and refused all help while she was here, but I didn't. I see this as the best of both worlds. Sort of. While I'm still not happy about having help, I know it'll give you peace of mind I'm not stuck in bed, or on my back like a turtle."

Unable to hide back a laugh, I watched it break free on her face, making me chuckle along. Just a little bit.

"Wouldn't want that now, would we?"

"No ma'am."

Walking up to me, she planted a tender kiss on my forehead. "I'm glad to hear it. At the end of the day, I still see the little boy you once were and it makes me want to protect you from everything. I see that same little boy in your eyes and no matter what you say, I will always move heaven and earth for that boy and for the man you are today. That's a parent's love, Theon. And I'll always love you."

With that, she flashed me a brief smile and I swear I could see her eyes tearing up a little bit. Damn if that didn't make me swallow back my words, I don't know what else would. Wiping my own damp eyes, I watched her retreating form as best as I could until she'd vanished through the doorway, heading God knows where in another part of the house.

I don't know how she did it, but somehow my mother always managed not to guilt trip me out, but instead to dig deep inside my emotionless shell to reach the all-feeling heart I once wore on my sleeve. The woman was indeed a wonder. A wonder I was proud no matter what, to call my mother.

The rest of the day went as slowly as it had begun, leading me to consume several hours of dreary, degrading reality TV before someone finally came in and changed over to something more to my taste.

Eventually, after dinner, visits from a few of the ranch residents and a late-night gift basket from our elderly neighbour, Clara, I was more than ready for my now less-than-comfortable bed. Without the use of my legs, and the added limited movement of all of my casts, it was a hell of a lot harder to find a comfortable sleeping position. Even after a week of practise, I was more than ready for my now less-than-comfortable bed.

At least it's a good thing I mostly sleep on my back...

Settling down as best as I could for the night, I closed my eyes. Sure as eggs are eggs as was the case for the last week, my dreams would be filled with nothing but Nurse Kenna Bouchard and all of the insane, unreachable, unattainable desires my subconscious teased me with.

If only I was the man I was before my accident. He would've happily submitted to those hidden desires. No questions asked. But I'm not that man. Not now, not ever.

With that depressing thought, I let the darkness and medication both take me into the darkness once more.

As I predicted, I didn't sleep well last night. Between the usual PTSD nightmares I'd long since been diagnosed with, the medication making my dreams go haywire and the thoughts of Kenna floating around, I'd spent most of the night awake fighting sleep. No wonder I wasn't a morning person anymore.

It didn't stop my body waking up at 6:00AM though. No matter how much I tried to get back to sleep, the moment that I was awake, I knew I was awake for good. It was the same reason I always volunteered for a morning shift on tour, or an early morning mission whenever one took place. Having grown up on a ranch, I was more suited for rising early and getting things done. Unlike a few other men in my squad who moaned like a bunch of teenage boys as soon as the sun came up. They were soon whipped into shape. I saw to that personally.

Somehow as I slept, the sheets had become somewhat tangled up around my body. Halfway tucked under me, wrapped around my lower half, I resembled something on a Japanese sushi board than a human in a bed.

"Need some help there?" a familiar voice called from my bedroom doorway.

Looking up, I was surprised to see this person standing there. Blinking a few times, I made sure if who I was seeing was who I was really seeing, and that I wasn't dreaming her up. Highly unlikely given the fact I'd been awake for a good half an hour, but still. Best to make twice as sure.

"What are you doing here?" I asked, confused.

Kenna closed the door behind her, stepping inside the room a little further. "Did you forget our arrangement already, Mr O'Donoghue?"

Oh, it's back to that, is it?

"No. No I haven't." I cleared my throat, "I just thought the arrangement was to meet at my house. Last time I checked, this was my folks' place."

Technically, no arrangements had been made last night, only the agreement to do this thing at my place. Secretly, I hoped that between last night and this morning, all would've been forgotten about. Clearly with Kenna's watchful eye on me in this room, that wasn't the case.

Looking at her now, standing there with her arms crossed over her ample chest, I saw the physical representation of the look of sheer determination. Whatever she'd come in here to do, other than help with my bedsheets, she looked determined to see it through.

"Yes, yes it is. And since we didn't come to an arrangement last night, I thought it best to come bright and early to get you moved back into your place so we can get this thing started. No time like the present."

Let a man have his coffee first at least. Christ, woman.

I suppose she has a point. The sooner we can get back to my place, the sooner I can show her how much of a mistake it will be to look after me, and she can get back to looking after patients at her hospital who actually need her help.

"Now, let's get you untangled from those sheets shall we? Then we can get you in the bathroom, changed and fed."

This was definitely going to be more humiliating than I thought. I knew very well what she meant by that, as it was simple enough. Though it didn't stop it from sounding like I was a damn baby, who'd woken from a night's sleep and needed tending to. On the upside, at least I hadn't gone to the bathroom in my sleep. That would be a whole new level of humiliation I'd never recover from.

Grabbing gently under both of my arms, Kenna moved with stunning speed and strength to prop me up somewhat, in order to get access to the sheets that had become tangled. In no time at all, she'd got the sheets untangled and folded down to the bottom of the bed that would've impressed any drill sergeant training new men and women. I was certainly impressed, even as ex-army.

Perhaps all the time spent in the hospital tending to patients also covered turning down beds. After all like soldiers, nurses had to cover many bases within their job role. Including menial work from time to time.

Watching her while she was doing her thing gave me time to assess my own…situation. It was no mystery what happened to most of us males in the morning, but it wasn't something I was prepared for her to see just yet. If it happened in the hospital, then I wasn't aware of it and nor would I want to be. Looking down at myself, I was relieved to see that I was still very much 'out of commission'.

Crisis avoided. For now.

Putting her hands on her hips, Kenna faced where I'd been propped with the pillows behind my back at the head of the bed frame. "Ready for part two?"

"As ready as I'll ever be." I grumbled. Once I was in the bathroom, I was doing it solo. At least, that was the plan.

Without the need of assistance, Kenna expertly placed me into the wheelchair that we'd acquired once arriving back here in order to help me around. Getting around wasn't so bad in this thing, given the fact that I had my arms sticking out and my legs like sausage dogs in smarties tubes. Also factoring in that this place wasn't exactly built for disabled movement and access, getting around wasn't as bad as it would be in a modern downtown Austin home. In a modern home, things were too damn small and I'd have no chance of even basic mobility. At least when we'd be back at my place, we'd have even more room and what wasn't adapted for disabled access, could be adapted to do so.

Wheeling me into the bathroom, Kenna put the break on the wheelchair as soon as she'd shut the door behind her, giving us privacy from anyone possibly walking by.

"What are you doing?" I questioned, my brows furrowing.

"I thought we'd been through this already." Kenna stated, sounding as if she thought I'd already forgotten from the bedroom to here. "We're getting you sorted in here, then into some new clothes and some breakfast inside of you."

If we were about to do what I think we were about to do, then it was a massive 'hello no' from me. I'd managed once seated, to do things on my own with a bit of wiggling and shuffling to get my pants down, and that's what I'd do now. She didn't need to help me with anything more than that.

I cleared my throat, "You can just, um…put me on…you know. I can do the rest from there. Thank you."

When Kenna made no effort to leave the room, I addressed her again. "You can go after you've um…helped me. If you don't mind."

Nothing. No reply. There's no mistaking that she's heard me so, why isn't she at least responding?

Looking up, my eyes caught hers in the mirror in front of us on the far bathroom wall. Her look was not one of amusement. In fact, she looked as less amused as a human could possibly look.

"Are you serious? You've gone all shy on me all of a sudden? My God!" she sighed, shifting her weight onto her right foot, her left hand going to her hip. "Do you realise the things I've seen in my line of work? The things I've had to do? I imagine as a former soldier, something similar to what you've had to see. Going shy on me in the bathroom is nothing that's going to deter me from doing what I've come here to do. Now either you buck up and just let me get on with it, or I can arrange for another catheter for you to use instead. Your pick."

I didn't need a mirror to know that my eyes widened at the mere suggestion of another one of those devil devices.

Pride, prepare to be swallowed.

With a sigh, I nodded to her. "Just make it quick. Please." I added with a whisper.

Not wasting any time, with my consent Kenna swiftly and once more with expert ability, lifted me under my arms and manoeuvred me onto the toilet. The lid is already open for ease of access.

Remembering that this was all for my own benefit, it took everything I had to keep my eyes closed and to not meet Kenna's eye. Giving my consent was more than enough, we didn't need to be doing this while looking at one another.

It was only when seated did I realise that in the haste to get me situated, we'd forgotten something really rather important. I still had my pyjama pants on and over my casts. No way would I be able to go with these things still on me. Not without lowering my already rock-bottom pride in the process.

Clearly, Kenna realised the dilemma at the same time as I. She looked up to meet my now open eyes, searching my face once more for unspoken permission to rectify the situation.

"Yes." I said, my breath barely a whisper. "Do it, but please leave the room once you have. I'll call you when I'm…when I'm done." I pleaded, hoping she'll comply.

A moment later, she gave her nod in response and proceeded to shimmy down my pyjama pants until they were at my knees. Thankfully during all of this, her eyes remained fixated on my clothed chest, sparing me what would be the final nail in the humiliation coffin. Swiftly after making sure I was able to do what I needed to do, Kenna left the bathroom with the closing of the door behind her back.

Leaning my head back and letting out a long-awaited trapped breath escape my lips, I prayed for a swift recovery and the use of my arms back so I wouldn't have to go through this more than I have to.

At least, it won't get any worse than this.

Little did I know, I would someday soon be eating those very words.

Bathroom, dressing and breakfast took care of and with my father's help, Kenna and I were now en route to my place a short distance away. I was surprised to find her car was big enough for me and a few of my things from my folks' house, as I was expecting a smaller car than the Volvo we were currently in.

Someone at least had the sense to suggest using it, as it was a more manageable height to get me in and out of, than the truck in which I'd first been brought home in. That said, I was just glad to be getting out of the hospital, it didn't matter what I was brought home in. I would've happily sat in a tank, should one have shown up.

Watching Kenna drive in the front seat gave me time to observe her without coming across as some sort of creeper. Given the nature of my incapacitation, I found myself 'people watching' more than I've ever done. Out in the field, you had to watch people. The way they moved, spoke, even the way they did nothing at all. You had to know how to read people from the top of their heads to the tips of their toes. Sometimes, it proved pivotal between a matter of life and death.

Times I care not to linger on too often.

Kenna once again had her hair up. Not in a nurse-style bun I've only seen her sport, but the kind of messy, on-the-top-of-the-head kind of thing often done in a hurry. Done in quickness and ease. If she didn't have it up and if I was a bettin' man, I'd say those lovely locks would reach down to her butt at least. She didn't strike me as the kind of girl who'd opt for the shorter do.

I also noticed that unlike other women I've been close enough to observe, Kenna didn't wear nail polish or have long-ish nails. My guess is as a nurse, it wouldn't be practical to have nails long enough to scratch a man's back. To some, without this small decoration of the hands a woman might appear a plain Jane. To me, Kenna carried an air of grace and dignity about her. Simple suited her. Though spare a man his heart beating out of his chest when she did make herself up nice, as I'm sure many a man would need CPR.

Not this man, though. Certainly not with Kenna. Nor any other woman.

Pushing those unwanted thoughts aside, I fixed my attention once more upon the woman in question. I noticed from the moment my eyes opened and set upon her, that she wasn't like any other woman I've taken the time to really look over. Even in hospital uniform and with me under the influence of high-strength medication.

Today, Kenna's body would be considered 'plus size' or even 'curvy', simply because she was not a size 0 and without an ounce of fat on her. Any real man, or woman, wouldn't see such God-awful labels if they truly cared about the object of their desire. Since when did the size of a person mattered compared to the size of their heart? Even a stone cold, heartless monster such as myself could understand that. If we were truly living in an age where those in many a community were being accepted in areas, where once they were previously subject to segregation and hate, why were we still stuck in the past by body-shaming women who weren't 'model quality'?

Sadly, this didn't only apply to women. Though they were subject to it more so than anyone born or identifying as male. Many friends of mine in the past, especially in high school and college, were subject to body-shaming simply because they weren't tall and muscle-bound. The most used and commonly known stereotype of a southern boy, falling under the 'cowboy' category. I've passed many a girl up simply because of how they've treated one of my friends whilst I was around. If they couldn't treat all men equally and respect them for how they looked, they weren't worth my time.

The self-same scenario worked the other way around too, of course. If any man I knew treated any woman with any less respect just because she might be bigger, curvier or any such other aspect because she wasn't a stick, I sure made it known to them that they didn't deserve the love of any woman.

"We're here." Kenna's voice called out, breaking through my deep thoughts. Thinking about such things distracted me from our journey, missing the fact that we'd come to a stop in front of my place.

Such thoughts can wait till another time.

Looking past Kenna's head and out of the front windscreen of her car, I could see the figure of Russ, one of our ranch hands, leaning back against the railing of my front porch. Evidently, he was here to help me since my father had business to take care of on the ranch.

Russ had been working on my family's ranch for as long as I can remember. Having served with my father in the army, he came to us when he was done with his service and was a staple on the scene ever since. Things wouldn't be the same around here if Russ wasn't about. I certainly wouldn't know what to do without him when an extra hand was needed.

The door opened beside me, and his rugged face appeared in the opening.

"Jesus son, I go away for a week and you look like a cat with smarties tubes stuck on its legs."

Exactly what I was thinking...

This is what Russ did though. Any time a man, or woman, was in something very deep, he'd try to insert a bit of humour. Even if the situation someone was in was a bad one. Like me. He meant well and this was his way of coping with what he was seeing. I wasn't going to stop that.

"Har-de-har, smart ass." I joked, "Stop yer yappin' and help me inside, will ye?"

Russ smirked, "I always did like it when you get mad, Theon. Brings out your inner Irishman."

Kenna came around the corner of the car, stepping beside Russ. "You're Irish? Other than your last name?"

Was now really the best time for a lesson into my family's ancestry? That stuff could wait until I was at least somewhat comfortable in my own home.

"Later, Kenna. I just want to get inside for now."

She shrugged, nonplussed. "Fair enough. Let's get on with it, then."

Between them, Russ and Kenna managed to get me inside and laid onto an inflated double bed that had been set up, by Russ, for me to lay on. Since my place was two-stories, it looks like I'd be occupying the downstairs for a while.

Laid out on my back looking up at the wooden ceiling, this was probably the most comfortable I've been for a whole week. Given that there's no wall or anything to put me at an awkward angle.

Around me, Kenna and Russ continued to flit back and forth, ferrying in all my belongings from her car until the last item had been brought in. I turned my head to look at the two of them over by the door.

"Thank you so much for your help, Russ. We both really appreciate it. It was nice meeting you too." Kenna smiled, sliding her hand into Russ', giving it a firm shake.

My brow arched, "I can speak for myself, you know."

At this, Kenna rolled her eyes. "Ignore Mr. Grumpy. We had a bit of a bumpy start to our day earlier this morning."

Sweet Lord Jesus Christ! Russ did NOT need to know about that, and I most certainly didn't need a reminder of it any time soon.

I cleared my throat, "Yes, well. She's right. Thanks buddy, appreciate it."

After shaking her hand, Russ watched our exchange with a smirk. He knew something had gone down, though he was being wise not to ask. At least not in front of Kenna.

"No problem." He clapped his hands together, "Now, most of the things have been adapted in your house for you both to use with ease. After all, we did have a week and quite a few of the guys were more than keen to help you out. The only thing that's left to do is fit the stairlift. The guy we contacted is on vacation until next week."

Fantastic.

After a few more exchanged thanks and promises to call for help if we needed it, Russ departed, leaving us alone once more.

With the closing of the front door, I found myself at a bit of a loss as to what to do next. Considering my options were limited, it didn't leave me with much. Normally I'd show a guest around, perhaps even show them to their room. Now? Now all I can do is lay here like a useless lemon in a fruit bowl.

Before I could suggest something, the scraping of suitcase wheels on my flooring interrupted my thoughts. Kenna moved what I assumed to be her suitcase, over to the L-shaped couch next to the blow up bed which I currently occupied. Usually my coffee table would reside here not too far from the couch, but far enough from the fireplace.

Where did that go? Where'd they put it?

It didn't really matter where they'd put the coffee table. What did matter was what Kenna was up to with her case.

"What are you doing?"

"Well, since you can't get up the stairs until next week, I'm going to take up residence on your couch where I can be close to assist you and jump to your aid if you need me during the night." She said, plopping down in the corner of the couch. "Problem?"

I shook my head. It was a smart idea, no doubt. I just thought I'd have some privacy now that I was back in my own home. Under my own roof.

One thing was for sure. I was slowly but surely starting to learn that when it came to whatever this was between us now, Kenna and I, nothing was ever going to go the way I thought they would. And that the unexpected was very much going to be exactly the opposite.

"No, not at all."

My mind was now alive and whirring with all of the possible scenarios that my subconscious had been plaguing me with all week. Those all seemed impossible while I was apart from Kenna, my mind unable to stop thinking about her when it had free rein while I was asleep. Now that I was in her company again, those scenarios seemed less of a subconscious fantasy, and more of an undeniable and inescapable reality.

These next weeks were going to be interesting.

Understatement of the year, Theon. Understatement. Of. The. Year.

CHAPTER TEN
Kenna

If you had told me that one week ago, I was going to accept a stranger's plea for help in the name of her son, and that I'd move into said son's home to take care of him, I'd have said you were mad. Insane. As it turned out, I was the insane one for even considering, then accepting the proposal.

Day one pretty much set the tone for the week that would follow. I thought that at least back in his own home, Theon would be much more agreeable and cooperative. I was wrong. So, so wrong. Every suggestion I made, he objected. Every time I tried to help him, he waved me off. Nothing I did, or tried to do, was ever received well.

Not even when I was on shift at the hospital did I ever get this from my worst patients and believe me, there's been some real doozies here and there. Theon was truly proving to be one of a kind, and not in a good way.

He proved that this morning when he did his best to refuse profusely about returning to the hospital for his weekly appointment. It was mandatory for some patients to have follow-up appointments to check and assess the progress of their recovery, not that it stopped Theon from trying to worm his way out of going, using every trick in the book.

Eventually, he gave in. Much to my relief.

At least today while we were here at the hospital, Russ was overseeing the installation of the stairlift which would allow Theon to have access to the second floor of his house. Not to mention I'd be able to sleep in one of the guest rooms, away from Theon's godforsaken snoring. Honest to God, I thought it was thunder when I first heard it.

Plus I'm sure he'll be glad to have some personal space and time away from me, too. I can't blame him for wanting that. It'll be nice for me also, during the times I don't need to attend to him.

A girl has needs. Needs that a stranger shouldn't be privy to watching when he doesn't know her that well.

Not that he's ever going to get that opportunity...

Speaking of Theon, I couldn't help but wonder how he was getting on upstairs. Since I wasn't technically assigned to hospital work at the moment, the doctors who saw to him when he'd first been admitted were currently assessing his progress now. If there was any to be found.

We hadn't done much physical therapy back at his home since I'd moved in. Nothing that would be classed as worthwhile, anyway. He'd allow me to manipulate his calves, ankles and lower thighs for all of five, maybe ten minutes, before complaining that it wasn't going to work. Bargaining that he'd take his medication if I'd leave him alone for that day. That went on for a whole week.

Eventually, he'd crack and allow me to do what I'd been hired to do as his temporary live-at-home nurse. I just hoped that day was sooner rather than later.

I'd be notified when I was to collect him so for now, the hospital café, and it's less than comfortable seats, was where I'd be 'confined' to. With its bland, hospital-grade white walls and less than comforting posters about this disease and that disease, condition or illness and how to avoid/treat them, it didn't leave much to entertain me with. Thankfully, thinking back on this last week, minus Theon's lack of progress, would do perfectly.

As promised, I'd met up with Leary after her yearly screening. I'd managed to use my free time when I wasn't caring for Theon, to slip out and spend some time with her. Her results came back that same day and thankfully, she was cancer-free. Not that she was at risk, but I could see the heavy weight lift from her shoulders and even I felt relieved for her.

We made plans to meet up in a few weeks' time when she had some time off. Long overdue, if you ask me. Hopefully Jess will be back from her trip by then, so we'd go and do something as a threesome. She'd extended her trip by a week, not really giving a reason as to why, so hopefully she'd be able to make it out if she didn't have to work overtime.

Though as much as I miss her, I wouldn't want her to come out if she really didn't want to, or couldn't. I wouldn't be that cruel of a friend. Anyone who forced someone to do something they really didn't want to do, sure wouldn't like it if the tables were turned and it was they who were being forced.

I'd also managed to speak to my parents a few times this last week, which was a novelty. Since moving out of state to Arkansas, the opportunity wasn't there to speak as frequently as we did before. They'd decided they wanted a new start someplace, well, new. Nowhere near ready to retire or slow it down, they'd both decided to try their hand at what they've always wanted to do. So, my mother picked up her long-awaited dream of becoming a romance writer, finding a good starting place and a small following of her work. While my father became a coach for a local 'rugby' team. Rugby being the English, and rather more "manly", less-padded version of American Football. He'd always liked and admired the sport and the way the Brits played, so taking up a position for a 16-21 group and helping young men and women learn and play the sport was right up his alley.

I'd been to several games with him as a child and into my teenage years, though he could never quite convince me to play the sport. Instead, I tended to well, tend, to those who'd been injured in any way. If you could count bandages and ice packs as 'tending', that is.

We'd agreed while on Skype, that I'd come and stay with them in Arkansas for Christmas this year. Never having spent Christmas outside of Texas, this was something I was really looking forward to. Yet somehow, I'd still miss the fact that for the first time ever, my Christmas wouldn't be in Texas. I'm a complex creature. No shock there.

Much to my delight, they'd also offered a free bed and a Christmas to remember to both Jess and Leary if neither of them had plans. Which was more than kind of them to do. Considering I was and am an only child, they'd always opened up their home to any friends of mine who needed a meal, or a bed, or even an ear if they didn't have that in their own lives. For this I admired them more than I already did. I always count my blessings for how lucky I am that they were given to me as my parents.

Someday, I hope to be just like them where I'm in a place to do such a thing. Well, better than the small spare room in my apartment I always keep open for anyone who needs it anyway. A double-bed is something I'd definitely invest in for them, should I ever move to a bigger apartment someday.

Sitting here, eating my way through a series of none-too-delightfully-edible food and drink, thinking about this and that, enough time had passed until the buzzing in my pocket alerted me that Theon must be done with his appointment. Pulling my phone out of my pocket, the text indeed waiting for me was from my colleague informing me that I could come and collect Theon.

There was no indication from the text about how well it had gone, though I'm sure I'd soon find out either from the doctor in question, or the look on Theon's face. Which was usually a big indicator of what was going on inside his head, not that he knew. It was amusing to watch the man who thought he wore an iron mask, leak more than he was aware of. Most of the time.

With my butt aching from all the sitting in the not-so-comfortable chair, I tossed my trash into the bin and headed on over to the elevator, which took me up to the floor I'd dropped Theon off on. Soon, my answer to my earlier inner question became clear. The look on Theon's face, although meaning anything from sad, upset, to angry as hell, told me that it hadn't gone the way he was hoping it would.

Oh dear.

I came to a stop just in front of Theon and his attending doctor.

"Is everything alright here? Is he all done?"

The doctor, whose name-tag read 'Dr N.R. Taura', looked up from whatever he was writing on his clipboard, standing behind where Theon sat miserably in his wheelchair. Doctor Taura's face brightened into a smile when I approached. "Ah, Nurse Bouchard. There you are. Yes, he's all done and all yours."

Well, that's debatable.

I nodded, "Thank you, doctor. How did he do?"

Standing there, I could feel a lower set of eyes burning into the side of my head. If I was a betting woman, I'd say those eyes were telling me to 'get the hell on with it and get us out of here'.

"As well as can be expected, all things considered. Not much improvement from his discharge assessment, and still no feeling in his lower limbs from below the waist. How are the at home exercises coming along?"

Before we came, I had a feeling this would come up. A sigh slipped past my lips a moment before I replied, "Could be better. I'm going to introduce a few new exercises into the routine before next week's appointment. Hopefully they'll show a slight improvement."

Doctor Taura nodded, seeming placated after jotting it down on his clipboard, closing it a moment later. "Excellent, sounds good. Well then I don't see any reason to keep you both any longer." He smiled. "Take care and I'll see you both next week."

Bidding the doctor farewell, I wasted no time in getting both of us out of there and into my car. Truthfully, I didn't want to be there any longer than Theon felt was necessary either. I know my patients and their limitations, and he was close to his. Any longer in there and he'd refuse to go back again.

Driving away from the hospital and into town, I decided a change of scenery and something new was in order. As far as I know before I arrived, the week after Theon had been released from hospital he hadn't gone anywhere, including the week I'd been at his side. It was time he got out there a bit more. Mingling with the rest of society.

As I was about to broach the subject, Theon spoke up. "Don't even think about it. I know what you're up to."

Rumbled.

Damn, he's too smart for his own good.

Turning right at a junction, I kept my eyes straight ahead. Though out of the corner of my eye I could see Theon staring out of his own window, not taking his eyes off the downtown scenery rolling by.

"What? I'm not up to anything."

Theon scoffed, not buying my words one bit. "I'm disabled, not an idiot. I've taken the route from the hospital back to my place enough times to know that back there at the junction, you should've turned left. Not right. Whatever you've got planned, don't bother." He turned to look at me now, "Take me home."

What, no 'please'?

Of course not.

For a moment I debated on playing dumb, pretending not to know what he knew was the truth. If I did that, then I'd probably lose the only winning 'card', as it were. He'd stop taking his medication willingly, and I'd be left with more knotted muscles in my neck and shoulders than I already have. I don't want to add any more.

Reluctantly, I pulled my car over into an empty spot outside a strip of stores, flopping back into my seat after killing the engine.

"You got me."

"Wasn't exactly hard." Theon muttered, averting his eyes.

Usually, I consider myself a very patient woman. Now though? That hardened patience was starting to thin. Obviously whatever had gone down with Theon at his appointment, had set him in such a mood that would make a hedgehog run away at the prickliness he was displaying. Part of me... correction, most of me wanted to know what that was and by God I will find out somehow. It was just a matter of time.

For now, I think a sprinkling of negotiating is called for.

"While waiting for you, I ate some of that awful cafeteria food. So, being the thoughtful person that I am, I was going to treat us both to a nice lunch out. Someplace nice."

"Public, you mean."

I nodded, "Yes. Public. You say that word as if it's something vile."

"It is. Now."

His short responses were telling me all that I needed to know. Aside from the obvious verbal confirmation of his reluctance and dislike of being out in the public eye. Still, I pressed on.

"Why is that?"

Buttons were once more being pressed here, I knew that. No matter, it wasn't going to stop me no matter what the consequence of said button-pushing would be.

The knuckles of Theon's right hand turned white from the intense gripping he was doing, the armrest of the passenger seat straining under the immense strength he still possessed in his muscular hand.

"You...you don't understand."

Turning in my seat, I faced him straight-on. "Then make me. You'll be surprised at the results."

"Will I really?" his tone dripped with sarcasm.

If only more people in this world were just simply honest and truthful with one another, a compromise or understanding would be reached much quicker. No one would have to suffer before having a happy ending.

"I promise you, yes. Tell me what's going on in your head and I'll listen to you. That's all. No hidden agenda, no compromise or trickery. Believe me, none of them have gotten me anywhere so far, have they?" I mused.

A hint of a smile crossed Theon's face as a chuckle bubbled within his built chest, his hand relaxing on the armrest. "No, no I suppose it hasn't."

Well that's somewhat of a progression. At last!

"Well then, what say I take us away from here and head on over to somewhere more private?" I suggested, hoping he'd agree.

Theon turned his head at last, to meet my gaze. His eyes had softened from the once hard, guarded look he'd sported when I'd first pulled over. Now they were much gentler, more relieved. "How private?"

Clearly he still doubted me somewhat. All the more chance to prove him wrong and that he can in fact, trust me. Starting up the car again, I flicked on my right turn signal and flashed him a look. "You'll just have to trust me on this."

With no objection coming from his mouth, I seized the opportunity to merge back into the traffic, heading towards the spot I know Theon would appreciate for what would hopefully be the talk of the century. At least, when it came to him.

Less than half an hour later and very little conversation to pass the time, I finally pulled the car up to the spot I thought of bringing Theon to. Killing the engine, I removed my seatbelt and grabbed my bag from the backseat. "Ready?"

"I guess."

"Good!"

On the way over here, I didn't give much detail to Theon about just where we were going. Using his imagination to wonder about it was bound to take his mind, temporarily, off of whatever was burdening him. Hopefully making him more open to talk about it after being distracted and somewhat calmed. Though it wouldn't take a genius, or rather, would need one, to put two and two together.

Much like any other ranch in Texas, this one once led to a grand main house previously owned by my father's parents. My grandparents. The house had sadly perished a few years back when a storm, with a tornado following close behind, destroyed it. Luckily, neither I nor my parents lived in the house at that time. Unluckily, we'd all lose every last physical memory of my grandparents as it all went up in the tornado, forever scattered and lost across the surrounding land. Though I'd never actually lived on this ranch, it was still a huge blow, literally, to lose everything all in one go.

All that was left of this once thriving, familial home, was what I was bringing Theon here today to see and hopefully, he won't shoot me down at the idea that had formed in my head. As it might come across as somewhat bizarre, yet childish.

Making short work of getting Theon into the wheelchair I now kept in the back of my car, I shifted the bag onto my shoulder and began to push him towards the destination I had in mind.

"I can push myself, you know."

I shook my head. "Not right now. You don't know where you're going. I do."

"You do know I have experience navigating around terrains of all kinds, right?" he pressed, arms crossed across his chest in mild annoyance.

Oh?

"You like to hike?"

Another laugh-of-sorts broke free from Theon, a laugh that was growing on me. It was a deep, comforting rumble that would soothe you at night after you'd had a bad dream, and he'd tell you a joke to cheer you up.

"Yeah, something like that."

"The answer is still no. Besides, we're almost there."

The final destination wasn't far from where I parked my car, having been designed to be a place away from home, while still within walking distance of the former main ranch house. A few moments later as we rounded the last bend on the gravel path, it came into view. Nostalgia hit me thick and fast as my eyes looked it up and down.

"Um…I think you made a wrong turn back there…wherever you meant to go." Theon piped up.

Oh I haven't, not in the slightest.

It was time to pull the metaphorical, non-existent wool from off his eyes, letting it fall to the ground. "We're exactly where I meant to go."

"We're at a treehouse. A huge one, at that."

We most certainly were.

"Yep. Well done. You get a sticker when we get back home later!" I smirked, pushing Theon's wheelchair to the base of the tree.

"How in the sweet Lord Jesus do you plan on getting me up there? I'm not going into that treehouse!"

Putting my bag on his lap, I came around to his front and placed my hands on my wide hips. "Oh you'll see and yes you are. You agreed to this and I took you away from the public eye. Now sit back and watch this."

Theon scoffed, "As opposed to what? Doing cartwheels for laughs?"

Now that would be something I'd pay to see.

Hopefully I will, should he walk again someday.

For now, I'm settling with getting him up in that treehouse, and getting his tight lips to do some major talking.

CHAPTER ELEVEN
Theon

For as long as I'd known Kenna this last week, on top of when we'd met at the hospital, she continued to be a constant source of surprise. Never failing to pull rabbit after rabbit out of her non-existent magic hat.

So far, she'd managed to convince me to do what little exercises I could while still casted every which way, and to take my medication without refusal. Considering I'm as stubborn as an ox at times, this was some feat. And not because she was a woman. There was just something about her. She made you do the impossible, all with charming you with her words as her weapon. Nothing else.

To top it all off, she'd managed to surprise me once more, making it three for three, by getting me up into this goddamned treehouse I never knew she had access too. Why would I? In a way, I wish someone had been standing by to record the whole thing, because it sure was something truly to marvel at.

Pulling at a rope which partially dangled from one of the many sturdy branches, a thicker, more durable one came with it. Using said thicker, durable rope, Kenna fashioned a makeshift hoist to pull me up inside. She didn't strike me as the sort of person who knew how to do such a thing. It was some proper *Fifty Shades of Grey* stuff right there.

Yes, I've read it. Okay?

Some guys do like it, funnily enough.

With an amazing feat of strength, she hoisted me up into the air and to the already opened treehouse door. Once I was level, I was able to shimmy inside with the one part of me that wasn't casted. My butt.

Naturally, if I had the use of my arms I would've at least pulled myself, and my useless lower half, inside. But, I had to make do and make do I did.

A few moments later, Kenna joined me inside. She'd climbed up the traditional treehouse 'ladder', casually slinging her bag inside before climbing in, which nearly clocked me in the head if I hadn't moved in time. I didn't need another injury.

"Phew!" Kenna exclaimed, flopping on her back the moment she was able to do so. "Now that was a workout! Do you realise how heavy you are?"

Of course I knew how heavy I was! I'm over six foot and built like a brick house. You had to be somewhat…okay, a lot, physically built for life in the army. "I used to workout a lot. Not to mention work on the ranch used to keep me pretty busy and in shape."

Not anymore.

If I had to say, I swore a faint blush crossed her cheeks as the remained laying there, her eyes cast up to the ceiling of the treehouse.

Interesting…

"Well…yes…I suppose. Yes."

I couldn't help but find it amusing that the unflappable Kenna, seemed to be somewhat…well…flapped. Flustered.

She continued to lay there now that both of us were stuck here for a while. I'd shimmied my butt back against the wall of the treehouse, feeling much like an abandoned doll whose limbs were permanently fixed until next played with. Not that Kenna would be playing with me. No. That was never going to happen.

Shaking my head, I forced the thoughts far from my mind and into the restricted section of my brain.

Seeing as I had nothing else to do while Kenna was laying there without a care in the world, my eyes wandered and cast over the inside of this rather adult-looking treehouse. This wasn't your run-of-the-mill generic treehouse. No. Whoever designed and built this obviously intended for it to be used beyond childhood years.

It was fashioned out of your typically-used treehouse wood, strong and sturdy to withstand both time and weather. The wood is a rich, dark colour, rather than the lighter woods I've seen other tree houses made with. I could see the appeal, as to me it was more of a log-cabin sort of construct. Love me a good log cabin. Unlike most treehouses however, this one did come with windows, instead of window-shaped holes. Again, interesting choice. At least the dark frames matched the wood used to make this treehouse. Other than that, the inside was pretty basic. A few beanbags, cushions, rugs and seating were casually spread around to give occupants the option of sitting in more than one spot.

Over in the corner connected to a pipe leading up and out of the treehouse, was a log fire. Small enough to warm the place, but not big enough to be a fire hazard. From the outside before coming up, the tree had been clearly cut away especially for this purpose. Although I did not see a 'chimney' from where we've been, I'm sure that there was one.

"Alright then!" Kenna exclaimed, springing up from her starfish position, coming to a stop in front of me with her legs crossed after shutting the door to the outside world. "Are you ready?"

I kind of hoped she'd forgotten about this…

I wasn't looking forward to spilling my guts. Not yet.

Thinking about it though, it was a pretty far-fetched idea that she'd forget to get me to talk in the first place. After all, that is why she got me up here. Bringing me up here would be pretty pointless if not for getting me to talk. I'd probably wonder why the hell a grown man was joining a grown woman in a treehouse. Kenna's, most likely.

"This your place?" I said, gesturing my head towards the other side of the treehouse.

She nodded. "Yes."

Despite her confirmation, there was a hint of sadness in her voice.

"I've never been in one before."

"WHAT?!" she grabbed both of my casted wrists, looking at me with a genuinely shocked expression. It was almost as if she didn't believe me. "Tell me that's a lie! Every kid has been in a treehouse."

I shook my head, "Nope, not a lie. Not this kid. Well, former kid."

"You poor thing!"

Smirking, I shook my head at her sweet-as-hell outburst. "Not really. I just had no desire to climb a tree, potentially breaking something in the process if I fell off. Kind of ironic looking at me now. Maybe I should've stayed away from horses and climbed trees instead."

This earned a laugh from Kenna, a sound I was scarily looking forward to and loving to hear.

"Well, you've made up for that now."

"Yeah, not by my own will if you remember."

"Which brings me to why I bought you here. We're going to talk about what happened back there in town. Don't even try to get out of it, I'm not allowing it!" she said, wiggling her pointer finger in my general direction.

I blinked, "How would I do that exactly? Climb down the rope? Jump out of the window and hope for the best?"

Kenna rolled her eyes, "Smart ass. You know what I mean! There's nothing you can do to worm your way out of this so, go ahead. Start talking."

Trying to not let my annoyance at her persistence show, I figured I might as well get this over and done with. With that look of stubbornness on her face, I have no doubt she was a woman of her word. She'd stop me if I even thought about getting out of this. I was a mouse at the mercy of her cat-like tenacity.

With a sigh, I began. "It's no secret that since my accident I've been a little…closed off."

Kenna nodded, but didn't speak. I continued.

"I'm used to going around the ranch, and town, with no problem. I was able to get into my truck whenever I wanted, drive and get out again. Never needing help with anything because, who would when you could use your own two legs? One day, I'm working on this horse that needs 'breaking'. Basically, training and taming. It all seems to be going well, the horse suspiciously allowing me to saddle, rein and mount her."

I paused, remembering the speedy series of events that two weeks ago, changed my life forever. It was almost too painful to think about, now that I had more enough time on my hands to do so.

Taking a deep breath once more, I pushed on. "Then…she bucks me off. Normally it wouldn't be much of an issue, every cowboy or rancher falls off of a horse now and then. Only, not when your foot gets caught in the stirrup."

Kenna blinked, "Oh, is that what happened? I didn't know the full story."

I nodded, "Yeah. I don't know how or why my foot got caught, but I wasn't exactly concerned with the 'how' at the time. I was more preoccupied with getting it unstuck and away from that damned horse."

"But…you didn't?"

No. No I did not.

If there was even the slightest possibility of that, I wouldn't have ended up in the hospital.

"Correct. When I eventually did get free, I was thrown onto the fence which winded the hell out of me. It was then that the damned horse decided that it was fun to stop, kick and generally maim me. It kicked my head, chest, ribs, legs and God knows what else. After the kick in the head, it's all a bit… fuzzy."

Kenna had moved into a more comfortable position whilst I spoke, exchanging the wood floor for a comfortable bean bag. She motioned with her right hand for me to continue on with my story.

Shifting what little I could into a new position, I did just that. "Turns out when I landed on the fence, I landed right at the base of my spine. At least, that's what the doctor surmised from one of the x-rays. Factoring in all of the other injuries…well…you know what happened."

"So, you don't want to go into public for fear of what? Shame? Pride?"

If it were only that simple.

I wasn't going to tell her the whole truth. Not yet. There was no great hurry, nor need, to tell her about my Army past. Though I am surprised that she didn't already find it out from my file at the hospital, as I'm sure I heard that doctors and nurses somehow knew everything. Background included. Still, I'm relieved she was still naïve to the horrors that lay there. No one, not even her as my personal at-home care nurse, needed to be privy to that sordid information anytime soon.

"You wouldn't understand."

"That's why we're here. Make me understand, Theon. Let me listen to whatever and however you want to explain this to me." Kenna pleaded, her hands gripping the beanbag in frustration.

Deep down I knew she was right. Again. I guess it wasn't that she wouldn't understand, but more like I don't want to add to the weaknesses, faults and lowliness that I now possessed by recalling how I felt about what people saw and thought about me. What I knew they were thinking without saying the words to my face. The looks of shame, pity, false empathy on the first day after I was released from the hospital by everyone who saw me or came to visit me, firmly planted my reasoning for not going out in public ever again.

That part, I knew she wouldn't understand one hundred percent. Yes she may be sympathetic and genuinely so, though it wasn't her physically living each day with the pain, the hushed words, the words that would forever go unsaid and the many, many looks from men, women and children of all ages as to why a grown man was casted and in a wheelchair. Only those who were able to deduct what happened for themselves, the ones who were smart enough or knew the injuries of the trade as it were, didn't bother to stare. Their refusal to even look at me after it clicked spoke volumes.

Those were the ones that hurt most of all. People who'd know me my whole life, turning away because I was now of no use to anyone. Not even myself. It was as if I'd gone from being everyone's go-to handyman, friend and fellow townsperson to folklore legend. 'The Man Who Fell From Grace'.

One who kept falling since.

"Theon."

A voice called out to me, seeming as if it was somewhat in the distance.

"Theon."

The voice called again. This time sounding louder. Closer.

"THEON!"

When the name called louder than ever, it wasn't on its own. Something pushed at my non-casted shoulder. Something...real? Was it flesh? It sure felt warm, exactly like flesh. Its warmth and force snapped my eyes up to see Kenna much closer to me than she'd been five minutes ago.

"You've been zoned out for a good few minutes there. Are you alright?"

I blinked.

Had I really?

Thinking back to the last few moments, it occurred to me that what I had thought about was simply just that. Thoughts. None of those words escaped my lips as I thought they had done. Like I wanted them to, in order to appease this stunning creature in front of me.

Blinking again, I realised what I once more realised where my mind had just gone.

Stop. Thinking. About. Her!

At least in *that* way!

My mind was a mess, and that was no mistake. If I wasn't even capable of realising what I was thinking, and that I wasn't physically saying those words, how in God's name did I ever consider the chances of possibly being able to walk again? Or at least, gain some semblance of feeling back in my useless, pointless legs.

I brought my gaze back to Kenna's, hoping to fix this as best as I could.

"Um...yes, sorry. I did. Lack of sleep, I guess. Can't focus as much."

"Understandable. You're not the only one." she sighed, sitting back in the beanbag.

What? She hasn't been sleeping well either?

"What's bothering you?"

She smirked, shaking her head knowingly. "I know what you're up to. I warned you not to try and worm your way out of this did I not? You're not distracting me, mister. You're talking and you're talking about you. Nothing else. We're not moving from this treehouse until you do."

Damn and blast.

Well, I gave it a shot. No one can say I didn't give it my best to divert this topic.

With a resounding sigh, I began to talk. "I've been useful pretty much all of my life, as either my folks will tell you. From an early age before I could work on the ranch, I followed my father and any of the hands around, 'helping' in any way I could, learning what I could. Then when I became old enough to work on the ranch, I did just that before I went off and join—" I paused, clearing my throat. "College. Going off to college. After college I got the job of my dreams, thanks to said degree."

It killed me to lie. Especially to Kenna. Showing me nothing but kindness and sheer determination in my care, she didn't deserve to be lied to.

Still, I was already in too deep with this. There's no going back.

"Then what?" she asked, her tone curious.

"Then, I came home. To help my folks out with the ranch. That is, before they turned it over to me to make it into what it is today. A rehabilitation ranch."

I'd never discussed this with her before, as it was too close to the truth to what I once was. That said, I don't plan on revealing more than I have to about the why's about how the place came about.

"So, how does all that link to not wanting to be seen in public?"

"My point really is, I've never not been useful. I've always had a purpose, a cause or something that gave me reason to feel like I'm helping or making a difference. If anyone needs hay bailing, I'm there. Cattle moving? You got it, I'm there. Assisting in the birth of a new foal? You get the picture.

Right from an early age till as of two weeks ago, I've always been doing something, somewhere. A rancher needs his legs in order to do a good, hard, honest day's work. Without them, he, or she, is nothing." I frowned.

"The same would go for arms but thankfully, I'll be able to use those when I get these damn casts off."

And I'm countin' down the days till that happens.

Being a nurse, I'm hoping Kenna will see just how important it is to me, as her own job is very demanding. Judging by the look on her face, seeing both sorrow and sympathy, I'm bettin' she does.

"Okay. I think I understand now. Everyone in town has seen you your whole life, right?"

I nodded. "Yes."

"They're bound to talk, gossip and generally pass comments about you and how you are now after what happened to you. Correct?"

I nodded again, appearing to confirm her deductions. "Yes, they will. Most certainly."

"Why do you think you wouldn't be able to handle that? You've put up with me being very demanding when clearly it goes against everything you believe in. You've gone along with it because you know it's for your own good. That and it gets me to lay off you for a bit." She smirked, shifting positions once more on the beanbag.

Because I've been in war zones. I've led men and women into battles and on missions.

I was someone's captain. I lost my best friend and promised on his battlefield deathbed, that I would look after and find a certain someone. I didn't. *I'm nothing but a failure. I failed Anderson.* Nothing will change that. Nothing. Not while I can't walk.

The army gave me a sense of pride and belonging that this town never has, other than the real truth that on the odd occasion, I was called up to do the things I'd listed to Kenna. I knew it was what I wanted to do right from an early age because my father was who I looked up to growing up. I wanted to be just like him.

Now I'll never get the chance. Being honourably discharged put an end to all of that. The horse throwing me was just the real cherry topper to it all. Adding to the shame of forever being compared to my father and how I'd never reach his level of notoriety, I'd now earn a new badge of shame for allowing a horse to kibosh my chances of walking again. Beaten by a beast instead of battle.

When I came back into town, you can bet your bottom dollar I was the talk of it. I didn't have a choice. People talked whether I kindly asked them not to or not. It happened. At the time, I was dealing with my own demons. Not that it mattered to some. They still came with what they thought were words of comfort and with good intentions, but it wouldn't stop what had happened or bring back those that I'd lost on that last tour. Words wouldn't help stop the nightmares that were keeping me anchored in the darkness at night, or wide awake dripping with sweat and fear. Nor would they stop the PTSD attacks I hid from everyone, my folks included. Anything that remotely sounded like it could come from a war zone had the potential to set me off. Crowds included. That is why I don't want to go into the public eye. Not yet.

That and all that now came with me was my burden to carry and mine alone to do it. My folks, Kenna, nor anyone else would have to deal with the shell of a man I am now. A broken man. A fallen soldier. If I had to keep up the pretence of being afraid because of pride and stubbornness, so be it. Because for as long as Kenna was my home care nurse, she'd never know my secret shame.

Until she leaves my company, I would remain a secret soldier.

CHAPTER TWELVE
Kenna

Getting Theon up here had worked better than I thought it would. Ever since I've been coming up here, this treehouse has always worked in making people talk. I don't know how, but it did. Grandpa said it was a 'magic treehouse', as whenever he was in the doghouse with grand-mamma when the two were alive, they'd come up here and talk. Things always worked out after doing so. I'd like to think that's what happened here today.

If only Theon didn't hide everything from me. Then it would be a complete success.

In the end when he agreed to talk, I'd just sat here and listened. There was nothing else I intended to do. No hidden agendas. The only thing I wasn't able to work out, was the story between the words coming out of his mouth. There was something else he wanted to keep from me, a secret. I could hear the words unspoken, though they were somewhat muffled.

Not answering my question confirmed my earlier thoughts on why he didn't want to go into public just yet. Even if he didn't say them to me. Pride and stubbornness combined was a powerful deterrent, it seems.

We all had secrets. Something we didn't want one or more people to know. Theon however, well from those unspoken words I could tell his secret was a big one. Based on how much effort he was putting into the story to placate me. Effort that didn't go unappreciated.

Enough had been said for today. At least for now. He's said more than enough for me to work with, and there would always be another day and chance to poke him for more information. Time to shift things around a bit.

On cue, my stomach rumbled loudly.

"Well, I don't know about you, but I'm hungry. We've been up here a while. It's time we both got something inside of us."

Theon's eyes practically lit up at the prospect and promise of food.

After all, as the saying goes, 'A way to a man's heart is through his stomach'.

"Sounds good." He grunted, seeming somewhat in discomfort at having to sit like that for so long.

Wasting no time, I got the two of us down from the treehouse. This time, my limbs did protest at the heaving of such a weight on the end of the sturdy rope. Theon was no lightweight in his own right, but add in the weight of all the casts on his body, I'm sure that weight almost but doubled. Good thing I work out, or else this wouldn't have.

Back in the safe confines of my car, I bucked myself in before turning to Theon. "So, what do you fancy eating?"

Theon shrugged, waving his right hand that stuck out from inside his cast. "As long as it's greasy and somewhat unhealthy, I'm not too bothered."

I smirked, "You know I'm a nurse, right? I'm not supposed to authorise indulgences."

"Somehow, I don't think you're anything like any other nurse, Kenna."
He practically purred, his eyes twinkling with mirth.

"No, no I'm not."

Dangerous ground Kenna. Dangerous ground you're stepping on, girl.

An hour or so later, we were back at the 'Big Boo-T' ranch. The name never fails to make me smirk every time I pass under the huge, dark wood sign at the bottom of the ranch drive. I'd asked Theon around mid-week as to the name's origin. Apparently, it was somewhat of an unwritten tradition for some ranching families around here, to name their ranches like that. Not dirty, but hinting at humour.

It was Theon's decision to keep the name when he changed this place into a ranch-come-rehabilitation place. Though I'd yet to ask how that came to be, as whenever I broached the subject with him, he closed up tighter than a clam with a zip.

"So, did you figure out what you wanted to eat?" I said, settling Theon into the large armchair in his living room.

"I thought it was your stomach that was hungry, not mine?"

Rolling my eyes, I got his next round of medication ready before I ordered the food for us. "You were the one who said it sounded good when I offered to get something, so don't pin this all on me, mister."

Not waiting for a response from Mr. Sarcastic, I grabbed the phone from its dock on the small table to the side of the living room, making my way through to his kitchen to place the call. I decided to get some Japanese food, since the noodles and such would be easier for Theon to eat. He'd be able to eat something he liked, while maintaining a sense of dignity. Something that was a big deal to him.

It would be to me also, if I were in his position.

Keeping myself busy, it wasn't too much longer until the doorbell went, alerting us that our food was here.

"I'd offer to get the door but…I can't be asked." Theon quipped as I passed, grabbing my purse from my bag.

Lately, he'd become quite the comedian when referring to things he couldn't do. Gone was the grumpiness and anger. I noticed the change within the last few days, actually. Nothing in particular had happened that would possibly flip the switch from grumpy to well…whatever he was now. At least, nothing I could think of. Though it was a small, but positively plausible spark, which could possibly mean he might be willing to work with me to get him walking again.

A girl could hope.

Greeting the delivery man at the door, I handed over the necessary money, plus tip, closing the door behind me after exchanging pleasant goodbyes. Balancing the drinks and carrier bag in both hands, I looked over at Theon. "Want to eat there, or at the kitchen table?"

"Here, please. For once, I feel somewhat comfortable."

"Great!" I said, probably a little too enthusiastically. Judging by the raised brow on Theon's face, I'd say that was the case.

I made short work of setting things out between us on the coffee table in the living room, the quiet, gentle hum of the TV in the background providing a stable ambiance for our meal. Theon would still need me to feed him myself, as his arms were still bound in casts, keeping them spread out wide apart. He didn't seem to mind as much when I treated it as if I were feeding a lover, rather than as he put it, 'a cripple'.

Not that I'd had the opportunity to actually feed any of my previous boyfriends.

Wait…what?!

I knew what I'd thought the moment that it slipped out of my subconscious, and into the dangerous, carefree part of my brain. The part that had no control or parental locks, nor blockers to save me from thinking about these kinds of things. Theon things, to be exact.

Apparently, my brain decided to forgo all necessary security measures by letting that not-so-little nugget of information through.

It's been a hell of a long time since I've had a boyfriend. Well, one worth shouting home about who lasted longer than three months, anyway. Oh I didn't kick them out at that mark, no. They each just decided that it wasn't going to work, one way or another for whatever reason they could come up with. Sure, they appeared to be genuinely apologetic, but I knew the truth. None of them wanted to tell me the truth or make things messy when ending it.

Military men will do that. At least, the ones I've dated have. I know all military men aren't like them, but I wasn't allowing myself to get involved or infatuated with one any time soon. Nope. Not a chance.

Still, none of that, or them, explained my mental slip up. Theon even in his incapacitated state, far outshone any of those guys, both in personality and outward looks. Yet at the same time, he was nowhere near them in how close they were to me physically. He was…is…my patient, and I'm his nurse. Though that didn't stop my man-starved mind and body thinking up things I shouldn't, all when I'm alone at night in my room. Here, in Theon's house.

I'm just glad it stayed in my mind, instead of coming out of my mouth…

That…well…that would've landed me in something I knew I'd have one hell of a hard time digging my way out of. Sans or with dignity.

"Kenna?"

Snapping my eyes up to Theon's voice breaking me out of my reverie, I suddenly realised I might not have been as lucky as I thought. Maybe it did come out of my mouth too. Oh good God.

"Y-yes?"

"You've been holding those noodles on that fork there for about five minutes now, staring off into space. I'm kind of getting hungry again, watching them hover in front of my face while your mind wanders off elsewhere." He smirked, "May I have them now, please?"

"Huh? Oh! Damn, sorry!" I quickly and carefully placed the now colder noodles at his lips, watching him draw them into his mouth as if he hadn't been fed for a week.

And he wouldn't have been, if I had hung back any longer.

Thankfully, he didn't seem to catch on as to why I'd spent so long caught up in my own thoughts. If he did, he's keeping it very well hidden and much to himself. Then again, that's Theon all over. If his cards were any closer to his chest, he'd surely become one with them.

We ate the rest of our food in a comfortable peace. Not quite silent, but passing the occasional 'thank you' and such other comments without the former awkwardness of previous mealtimes. After finishing our food, I cleared everything away and helped Theon take his medication which surprisingly, he takes once more without protest, sending him into slumber soon after.

Positioning his casted body in a comfortable position on the couch, I cover him with a blanket before stepping out the back onto the porch for some much needed air. Spending time in the treehouse earlier made me realise just how much I miss being able to spend time outdoors, enjoying the day and the fresh air that Texas provides. Being a nurse doesn't open up for a lot of time out in the open. Unless you happen to pass by an accident in the street and administer basic first aid, that is.

Been there, done that.

It had been an experience and a half, to say the least. Of course I was glad to help, and the man did survive the impromptu car collision, it was the public that put me off. Some would stay back and watch from afar, others would try and 'help'. Not really being of any help at all, with more often than not being more in the way of me trying to administer aid to the patient. They only mean well, I know. It's just awkward to ask them to move out of the way in a pleasant way, trying your best not to let the frustration show.

Taking a deep breath I let the memory go, sinking down into one of the comfortable rocking chairs on the back porch looking over the sprawling lands of Theon's property, letting my eyes fall to a close.

The sound of an approaching engine pulled me out of my impromptu nap. Normally I don't let myself fall asleep during the middle of the day when I have things to do around here, but I didn't sleep well last night and it must've caught up to me while out here relaxing.

Careful not to wake the still sleeping Theon, I made my way silently through the house in time to see a familiar pickup park next to my car. If I remember correctly, this was a man named Brett. The gentleman who came to collect Theon when he was discharged from the hospital not too long ago. We hadn't really spoken a lot during the transition from the hospital to Brett's truck, so I guess we'd get that chance now.

"Howdy there!"

People really still say that?

I guess they do.

Stopping on the top step of the porch, I wrapped my arms around myself. "Hi."

Brett sauntered to a stop at the bottom of the steps, leaning his left arm on the wooden railing. "I don't suppose you remember who I am, do you?" he smiled. It was a kind smile. Friendly. No hint of cockiness whatsoever.

"Actually, I do. Sort of." I laughed. "I can't quite remember your last name, Brett."

Taking his dark brown Stetson from atop his head, Brett let it rest against his chest as he addressed me. "Allow me to re-introduce myself. The name's Brett O'Neil. To some I'm known as Brett O'Donoghue."

Huh...

"I thought Theon was an only child?"

Brett nodded, "He is, but there's a story attached. Quite a long one."

Things just got a bit more interesting around here. I suppose it won't hurt to do a bit of harmless digging while the subject in question isn't conscious to object to it. What harm could come from it?

"Why don't you join me out on the back porch for a cup of sweet tea while you explain? You can also explain why you're here too, while you're at it."

"Alrighty then! Sounds good!" Brett hopped to it, darting back to his truck to retrieve something before joining me out on the back porch where I'd grabbed some sweet tea from the fridge. Setting it out on the table between the rocking chairs, Brett emerged through the door. "Where can I put this?" he said, holding up the box in his hands.

I turned, eyeing the large-ish box. "What's inside?"

"Mara did a care package for Theon. Food, essentials etc...you know, mother things." He said, a hint of sadness coating his words.

Note to self, don't mention mothers around Brett. Something's not quite right there.

"Oh that's so thoughtful! I'll phone the main house later and thank her. Put it on the kitchen table and I'll put it away shortly."

Not wasting any time, Brett did just that and joined me shortly in the other rocking chair, setting his work-hardened body into it. "I can't stay long, unfortunately. I was hoping I would catch boyo when he was awake but alas, it doesn't look like I did."

I laughed, shaking my head. "No, sorry. That would be my fault. I gave him his medication a half an hour ago. Always knocks him out. High dosage."

"That bad, huh?"

I knew exactly what he meant. The extent of Theon's injuries brought him more than anyone's fair share of pain. Times that by ten and you've got a good idea of how much medication would be needed, and it's a no brainer that anyone would be knocked out by its dosage. Even a man as built as Theon O'Donoghue.

"Yeah, it's that bad. I can't tell you everything because of that pesky patient confidentiality thing..."

86

Brett chuckled and I continued, "Though I'm sure it wouldn't take much working out from what he's told you."

Most of the people working back at the main house/area of the ranch had heard about it. After all, some of them even witnessed it happening. Brett would surely know, being closest to Theon. Something I learned from Theon earlier this week. He'd talked about how his best buddy, Brett, wasn't able to come by these last few weeks, as he was overseeing a deal at a ranch two hours away for some horses that they couldn't take care of anymore. They'll be coming to the Big Boo-T ranch to live out their lives as therapy horses, once taken care of and settled in.

Truth be told, I was expecting Brett to come around at some stage. Though I had hoped he'd call first. That way, Theon would be awake and the two would be able to hold an actual conversation, without me acting as a human notepad. I know Theon values privacy, so having me relay messages sometimes can get a bit...awkward.

"Nope, not much at all." Brett mused, picking up his glass of sweet tea, draining a decent amount from the glass.

"So..." I clapped my hands together, turning to face Brett. "You were going to explain why you were sometimes called 'O'Donoghue' so, spill!"

Chuckling, he set his glass down and leaned back, hands resting behind his head. "So I did. Well, to cut a long story short...I was metaphorically 'adopted' into Theon's family when I was young. My folks both died in a barn fire, which I don't remember, so I grew up with him and his folks. Those who don't know the story often thought we were brothers. Never thought to change my name officially to it, so I just let them think I was an O'Donoghue."

Huh...not what I was expecting. Then again, what was I expecting to hear?

I could tell that there was more to this story, a hell of a lot more. But I wasn't the one for Brett to open up about it. She just hasn't come along yet.

"Why haven't you? Changed your name to theirs, I mean."

Brett shrugged, "I guess...well...it would be dishonourable to my folks' memory, even if I was too young to really remember who they were. What they were like. If I took a part of them away from me, the only part of them that was left, they'd be gone completely. Even if they'd always be here because I simply exist. I mean, how many people were orphaned and kept their name too? Dozens, I suppose. Each has their reason for changing, or not changing, their name. I'm just another who resides with the latter."

It just occurred to me that despite not knowing Brett well enough to know who he really is, it's obvious that he's a complete one-eighty to who Theon is. Where Theon is closed off, reserved and private, Brett appears to be at ease with telling people anything. He's open, deep and so not private.

Yet, I still find myself gravitating more towards the one man I shouldn't be even thinking about gravitating towards right now. Brett...well...he seemed like the kind of guy every girl wishes would be her best guy friend. Or at best, a close friend. Perhaps even an older brother. That's to me at least, the kind of vibe I'm getting from him, and it's only our second time meeting one another.

I nod, fully understanding where he's coming from. "Makes sense. I'd do the same if I was you...probably."

"Probably?"

"Both of my folks are alive. In a different state, but alive. I can't imagine a life without them, so I can't say for sure what I'd do if I had been in your shoes instead of mine."

It was then that Brett broke the heaviness of the conversation by letting out a laugh deep from his chest, "I suppose you've got a point there." he paused, standing up and stretching. "Well, it was nice talkin' to you, but I've got to get back. There's a lot more I have to do now that sonny boy in there has decided to become the ranch's hermit."

"I wasn't aware that there was much one could do on a working ranch with their limbs fully casted. Or without the use of their legs." I pointed out. Feeling slightly defensive in Theon's stead.

Brett turned around and faced me, his brow arched. "Oh ho?" he smirked, clearly catching my intent woven into my words. "I didn't mean it in a nasty way, not at all. It's just...even though this isn't what he wanted to do with his life, he's made something of it and has always been around to be a helping hand, lending himself and his skills to anyone who needed it. Even if they didn't physically ask, he'd be there. He's thrown so much of his time and effort into this rehab ranch, it's just strange to see, or rather not see, his face around the place anymore. The guys and girls miss him. They miss his words of enthusiasm and encouragement. Generally everything about him, really. He truly is the heart and soul of the place, even if he doesn't see himself as such." He sighed, "Imagine taking the heart, the very core reason something exists, away. Everything either falls apart, or isn't the same anymore. That's how it's going with the ranch. Everyone's doing their best in his absence, they really are. But in the end, none of us are close to being a replacement for Theon. Not even close."

Hearing Brett talk about Theon and the ranch with such passion almost made me want to muck in and help out myself. Though as he said, no matter how many people would pitch in to help, none would be a replacement for the man who's the heart of the whole thing. I had to agree with that, even if I didn't know the ranch as well as either of them.

Standing up, I joined Brett on his feet and put my hands on my hips. "That's exactly why I'm here, and what I aim to do. I might not guarantee that he'll be able to walk again, but that doesn't mean I won't exhaust all options by trying anyway. Even if at best I can get him back to as close as he was to his former self, wheelchair included, then that's what I'll do. He may not be able to do everything he was able to do before, but I'll try my damnedest to make it work with how he is now. I'll adapt what I need to adapt, change what I need to change. If there's a way to make it work with the man he is now, for him to put as much pride and heart into the people here, I'll find it."

Half of me expected Brett to speak up after my speech. That half was wrong. What he did next I did not expect. His hand clapped my back so hard that if I wasn't grabbing the porch railing, I would've fallen face first into the grass below.

"Now I have no doubt he's in good hands."

Wait...he had doubts before now? Charming.

Not knowing how to reply without sounding snippy, I simply nodded. At this non-verbal exchange, Brett took it as a cue for him to take his leave and get back to work. Pausing only at the door to turn back and face me, "I knew you'd be the one to bring out the soldier in him again. We need our captain back."

Feeling as if ice cold water had been thrown down my spine, I froze. "W-what?"

"You didn't know?" Brett said, cocking his head slightly to one side.

"K-know what?" I stammered, dreading the words that I knew would next come out of his mouth.

"Theon was a captain in the United States Army. He was honourably discharged when a mission officially ended his career. I thought you knew..." Brett's voice trailed off as my mind took over, his words sounding like I was underwater hearing him speak above the surface.

Theon...a captain...

Former army...United States Army...

Mission ended his...his career...

How I could've missed this, I had no idea. How I went so long without one single person mentioning this to me, I didn't know. What I did know however, was that this was happening to me all over again. I was slowly falling for a man, albeit untouchable while he's my patient, who was a military man. Former or current it didn't matter. Military was military.

My mind started piecing everything together since the moment that Theon and I met once more at the hospital after he was brought in, flooding through my mind now that the damn had been burst that was keeping it all at bay. Things that didn't make sense, no longer not made sense. It was all becoming a bit too much for my mind to deal with all at once.

The very last thing I heard before everything went to black, was Brett calling my name from what sounded like a million miles away.

No...not again.

I can't go through this again.
Theon…why?

CHAPTER THIRTEEN
Theon

I don't know what the hell went down between Brett and Kenna a few weeks ago when he dropped by, but she hasn't been the same since then. Gone is the happy, optimistic, very friendly nurse who entered my home three weeks ago. She's been replaced by the most professional version of herself that I've ever seen, including when I was in hospital. I don't like it.

As much as I'm surprised to be admitting it, I was getting used to her and all of her little quirks she didn't think I noticed. Well, what else was I to do? Being casted from head to toe, almost, didn't leave much for me to do. Physically, anyway. In my mind while I've got all the time in the world to think, I've been doing all the things I wish I could do right now. Perhaps someday, I might actually do them again for real.

We'd gone about these last two weeks much as we'd done any other. Once a week I was taken back to the hospital for an assessment. Then we'd come home and Kenna would work her magic with the limited physio we could do until my casts come off. After, she'd give me my medication and I'd conk out for an hour or two.

I'd learned that while I was out, Kenna would seize the opportunity to make the most of the time. Often she would go up to the main house, returning care packages my mother would make for me. For us. What she did up there, I don't know. It really wasn't my business what she did with her time when she wasn't caring for me, though I'd be lying if I said I wasn't curious about what she was doing. Or rather, who she was spending her time with.

Not that it was my business. It just…rankles me not knowing. If there's one thing I hate, it's not knowing something. Probably why I was made a Captain. I was always on the ball and I knew everything there was to know, with as much as I was allowed to know. I made sure of it.

Brett had stopped by more often these last few weeks, now that his negotiation for the horses had been completed and they delivered to the main ranch barn. He too seemed different, much like Kenna. I couldn't quite put my finger on it as to why the two of them were acting the way they were, but I'm sure I'll find out as after all, the truth always finds a way of making itself known one way or another. Somehow.

It always has done, in the past.

Not wanting to press the subject with either of them, I kept my mouth shut and my eyes wide open, ready to spot the moment in which was right for me to strike. Or to see what the hell was bothering them. Either way, it was all a waiting game and one that I was more than happy to participate in as after all, the waiting game was my job not too long ago. Not many people would think that a good portion of a soldier's job was waiting, with what is seen in the media. We're seen to be mostly shooting at things, going into war-torn areas and carrying out missions. What they don't see is the endless hours of planning, negotiating and delegation, which all require patience and waiting.

One thing I was done waiting for, was for Kenna to show up. We've been home a few hours from my latest hospital appointment which told me that finally, I could get my casts off and bones re-x-rayed next week. Then, she vanished. Poof! Gone. Nowhere to be seen or heard of. More so heard of, since I can't really get up off this bed on my own. Next week maybe, since we went through the option of upper body physio to allow me to move around using my healed arms when the time comes.

Thankfully, Kenna wasn't there when we had that discussion. We discussed the training routine I went through for and during the army, and how we could adapt that or bring in an army physio to assist in my further recovery sans casts. I think if Kenna had been there, she'd be even more frosty towards me than she is now, if she knew the truth. Thank God she'll never get the chance.

"Hello? Anyone home?" a voice called out from somewhere downstairs. I instantly recognised it as my father's.

"Up here!" I called back, hearing booted feet come closer a moment later.

I wonder what brings him here.

As far as I was aware, he wasn't due for a visit. Not that I'm not happy to see him anytime, anyplace, it's just that he normally calls first or makes his visit known. Like myself, he's never one to make unexpected arrivals if helped.

A second later, my father's form filled then came through the doorway, coming to a stop at the foot of the bed. He removed the Stetson from his head as he always did, before addressing me. "Son."

Such a formal greeting would seem odd to anyone outside of the family, but not to me. He always greeted me this way. Well, almost always. Before my honourable discharge, he'd call me 'soldier' in his dominant, commanding voice. Though it was always meant with love, I could tell. Since coming home, I was now 'son'. Theon Brin O'Donoghue when I was really deep in something I couldn't dig myself out of.

"What brings you here?" I asked politely.

"You might've noticed Kenna hasn't been around much after she dropped you off earlier today, that is."

I nodded. "Yeah."

"She's up at the main house. I'm here to fetch you to take you there."

Come again?

I'd barely gone anywhere since being discharged from the hospital, including the time I spent at my folks' place before insisting on being in my own home. None of the men or women on the ranch needed to see me like this, it wouldn't help them with their own individual recoveries. In fact, I'm pretty darn sure that it would set some of them back.

"No." I outright refused, a bold and daring move in front of someone like my father. No one said no to him. Ever.

As his back started to straighten, I knew I was already in the doghouse. More fool me for thinking I could just slip that into the conversation, hoping for the best. Guess there are some things that even at my age I'll never learn.

"I'm sorry to inform you, son, that you don't have a choice in this matter. I've left your mother holding down the fort which she's very much capable of doing, so I could come and get you. It's more than time to come out of your stupor or…" he waved his hand about, "…whatever it is you call this you're going through by hiding out here. Everyone agrees with your mother and I and I for one won't allow you to do this to yourself for a moment longer. You're coming with me, and that's final."

Easy for him to say. He wasn't the one lying on his back, on a bed with his father looking down on him, making him feel like a little boy all over again.

Having broken plenty of bones during my childhood at the ranch, it became a routine for him to carry me up the stairs to bed each night. That is, when he wasn't out on a deployment. If he was, then it would be my dear mother who would do the duty. It did get a bit tricky when I got a little older, what with all the gangly limbs, though by then I'd managed to scoot myself up the stairs and into my room. Of course, I didn't need carrying if it was a broken arm but as luck would have it, more than not it was one of my legs.

"Pa…it's not that I don't want to go back out there. I just…can't. Coming back from Syria was one thing, I could at least stand with the men and women as equals, to help them mend. To be one of them. Being there meant something to me because I was able to join in, be a part of the team. It meant that even though I'd left the army albeit not on my terms, I had a team again. I was their pseudo captain. Now? What sort of a captain could I be now? Hm? A captain that would not be able to do a single thing for his men and women. A captain who can't even move his legs and stand before them. No. I…I can't…" I couldn't complete the sentence. The words just caught there, trapped and never meant to be uttered.

It looks like my father was also having the same trouble finding his words. Or rather, the right ones to say. He's a passionate man, is my father. Passionate about his family, the causes he supports and of course, passionate about the army we both served in. The one place he faltered in, was words. Specifically, sentimental words. Words of authority he could do, however.

What felt like an eternity since I finished speaking, my father finally piped up. "Theon Aiden O'Donoghue…" he began, arms behind his back like the proud general he once was. "Did I, or did I not, support your decision to go into the army?"

"Yes sir, you did." I nodded.

"We made a deal, and you know that when an O'Donoghue be they man or woman makes a deal, we stick to it. No hidden agendas. You worked your way to where you wanted to be, and your mother and I respected your decision and let you spread your war wings. You came home more a man than you left, and you're most certainly still that same man today. Falling from a horse…hell son, that doesn't take any part of who you were away. Look at me, I've been to so many war zones, been on dozens of deployments and earned as many battle scars to boot. Am I any less of a man because of what's happened to me? No. Besides, what is a man? The measure of medals on his chest? The size of his heart? Or what he does or doesn't have between his legs? There's no such image, or description of what makes a man, a man. Son, we're all equal, at the end of the day. Think about those who come back with no legs at all. They have no choice but to get back up again. So I'll tell you one more time my boy, you're coming with me and we're going to the main ranch house to bring you back into the fold. Do you accept the mission, soldier?"

If that was my father's version of sentimentality, then he did a damn good job of it. I'm not a crying man, not by any means. Though I was coming pretty close to it with those words hitting me what I've heard some people say, 'right in the feels'. Which I'm guessing means something along the lines of, hitting me right in the heart. Or something like that.

Swallowing back the massive lump that had formed in my throat, I nodded. Lifting my head up off the pillow as best as I could, I met his gaze. "Yes, sir. I…I accept the mission." As much as I wanted to salute him, I couldn't make it happen. My casted arm, one of two, kept my right hand firmly away from my body. "Uh…sir…I'd salute you right now but…" I wiggled my hand, emphasising my point.

Rolling his eyes, my father slipped his Stetson back on his head. "Let's just get you up and out of here."

Yes sir!

In no time at all, my father had me out of my room, down into his truck and off to the main house. Damn, the man never messed around doing anything. Not even shifting his stocky son and his casts around. It just goes to show that age really is just a number, and he's not even in his golden years yet. Not even close.

Though as we drove closer and closer to the main house, those thoughts were far from my mind at what I noticed. Or rather, didn't. Usually on any given day, men and women milled about doing various things around the ranch and surrounding buildings. Not today. Nobody was cutting the grass, painting fences or even generally walking about. I couldn't even hear anything but the noise of the animals through the half open passenger window.

Something is definitely not right...

"Um...did something happen here?" I asked, gingerly.

"Not sure." My father replied, killing the engine as he brought the truck to a stop in his usual parking space. "Let's go see what's what?"

I blinked, "We?"

He turned to look at me, one of his brows already raised. "Yes, we. We did talk about this already back at your place, did we not?"

"Fine, fine." I surrendered

Transferred into the world's most uncomfortable wheelchair, I began being wheeled not up to the house where I was expecting us to go, but instead we were going around the back, heading towards the main barn and stables.

"Are we going the right way?"

"We are if you want to see what's going on."

He knows something. He definitely knows something.

At least someone had the sense to pave over the gravel path that once took us this way, which was a plus. It would've made for a very uncomfortable journey in this chair, on top of the already uncomfortable one I'm having. Thank God I'm only a week away from getting these damn casts off, then I can go back to a more human-like sitting position. Even if my legs won't work, they'll be sitting normally.

"Look, can't you just tell me wha—" before I could finish, I could see what I was evidently brought here to see, as we turned the corner into the back courtyard. What must be close to one hundred faces turned to look at us, including some of my closest friends who didn't work on the ranch, but obviously all of whom were here for my sake. All stood in neat rows and standing at attention, just like any army battalion would.

As the wheelchair came to a stop and its break put on, I watched as my father walked around it, heading over to and joining my mother's side. He slipped an arm around her waist and stood proudly at her side, as her husband and her general. Russ too, stood equally proud at their side. The only person I wasn't seeing among the sea of faces, was Kenna. Part of me was disappointed, admittedly. Most of me was still wondering where the hell she was, even though it wasn't my business.

Just as I was about to ask what the hell was going on, John, our longest ranch resident, stepped out of the line and approached me. He came to a halt just in front of me, holding his Stetson by the rim between his fingers. I would say he looked almost somewhat nervous, but that wasn't John. He'd come a long way since being on the ranch, a hell of a long way. It had been an honour to watch his slow, steady progress.

"I bet you're wondering what's going on here, huh?"

I smirked, "It did cross my mind, yes."

John hesitated a little before continuing, "Well, you see...it's like this. We all agreed that we're grateful for you in converting your ranch to help us, in various ways, when we came home from our deployments. Without this place, none of us would know where we'd be right about now. For once in our lives, we looked forward to waking up in the morning, knowing that we'd be working right alongside someone such as yourself. So imagine our heartache when one day after being thrown from that horse, you locked yourself away and we lost the engine to our built back together machine."

A lump started forming in my throat as he spoke, inadvertently making me swallow back the words fighting to break free. John pressed on.

"I and several others wanted to come and confront you about this, on many occasions. But we held back, no matter how much we wanted to speak to you."

"Why?" I choked out, my voice barely a whisper.

"Respect, boss. Respect. You wanted to hide away and we respected your choice, as much as we all disagreed with it. You've been through war zones as have we all, so we thought after being thrown from something like a horse, you'd be back on your feet, so to speak, in no time at all." He shifted feet before carrying on, "When we learned that you'd never walk again, or even try to, that's when we went to work. Day after day we spent our free time thinking up ways to bring you back into the fold. Eventually, we came up with this." He gestured to all the men and women standing to attention. "An ambush."

An ambush. Of course.

It was a clever move in anyone's book. My mouth began to curl upwards at both corners, and I wasn't going to fight it one bit. Only these men and women would execute a military strategy of sorts, ambushing me when I wasn't able to make a hasty escape, presenting themselves as if I really was their captain. Rather than just their boss and host.

Looking at them all, many of them sported smirks of their own. Others just stood there with their chests proudly protruding. Most nodded in agreement with the words coming out of John's mouth, waiting on what I'd say or do next. Casting my eyes over to my mother and father, they were indeed doing the same. Looking on with expectant expressions.

John's words in all truth, cut me right to the bone. Deeper, if possible. Yes, I decided to stay inside and hide away, thinking it was the best thing to do. To save all the men and women from looking at their 'captain', like they'd look on a fallen soldier. Literally. I should've known that they weren't like that, not in the slightest. There was a reason each and every one of them were here today standing before me. Each possessed only the best of characters, morals, judgement and impeccable high quality camaraderie. We were all long lost brothers and sisters, and we held one another up no matter how far or deep we fell. I should've known they'd do that for me in return. I was a fool to think otherwise.

Seeing them all here truly has opened my eyes. They'd stayed closed, much to my own doing, for far too long. Time to open them up, and get these guys fired up again. They'd see what a real captain could do.

Sitting up as best as I could, I met John's awaiting gaze. "Fall in." I commanded.

Immediately and without question, he did just that. A slight smile fighting to tug at the corner of his mouth as he realised what I was doing. "Squad, attention!"

Those on both two and one legs immediately stood to attention, while those bound to wheelchairs did their best to sit up to attention. Very admirable.

"I'm aware that I haven't exactly been as present as I should've been lately, to which I apologise to each and every one of you." I said, addressing them all. "I'm not so lowly as to not admit it publicly to you all. In fact, I'll say it over and over if need be. Now, it's been made known to me that my troops need me. It seems they miss their captain. I'm here to announce to you today, that your captain intends to return to work alongside you, sooner than he gave credit for."

A collective murmur moved along the lines, processing my words.

"On one condition." I said, raising my voice. All murmuring immediately ceased. "I return when I get these damn casts off, and I can get myself around in a better wheelchair than this god-awful contraption."

This earned me a respectful laugh.

Yeah, yeah. I'd be laughing too.

"Now…Now If you want your captain to come back to be at your side, each and every one of you will get your butts back to work and keep those heads of yours, down. I don't want any slackers in my unit, and that's an order." I smirked. "Squad, dismissed!"

I watched as they broke formation, fleeing in all directions to get back to their respective works. A good thing too, considering I had tears forming in my eyes that were soon bound to break free. I'm surprised they didn't during my address, though I'm glad of it.

Only my mother and father remained in place after most of the people had filtered out of the courtyard, walking up to me when there was enough room to do so. "Oh Theon, that was wonderful!" my mother said, planting a gentle kiss on my forehead.

Oh mother…

"Thank you."

Clearing his throat next to my mother, I turned my gaze to my father. Pride silently oozed out of every fibre of his being, even if he was never going to admit it. "Worth coming out of your cave for, son?"

I nodded. "Yes. Yes it was."

He was right. Oh so right. I wasn't even going to contest it for arguments sake, it simply would be as pointless as a space hopper on the interstate.

"Good." He nodded. "Now, I've got work of my own to be getting on with, as does your mother." He gave her hand a squeeze.

"Right. Well, I'll just stay out here for a bit. If you two don't mind, that is."

My mother shook her head, the smile still on her face from when she first walked up to me moments ago. "Not at all, Theon. Be out here as long as you need. Just get someone to push you to the ramp for dinner, you're having it with us tonight."

"Yes ma'am."

With that, my father kissed her on the cheek before striding off towards the stables, evidently to saddle up and head off to where he needed to be. My mother gave me one last smile before she too headed off towards her own destination, the main house. Leaving me sitting here under the early afternoon sun, listening to the sounds of the ranch I'd expected to hear when first arriving here.

This is how it should be. This feels right.

For the first time in a hell of a long time, there was a shred of hope and optimism on the horizon. One I'd never envisaged seeing or clinging onto. But cling onto it, I would. Hard.

Even if I was never going to walk again, I had to do something. Too far into my own thoughts had I gone, I wasn't even able to see what I would be able to do, both for myself and the others on the ranch. Not any longer. For what little I would be able to do, I'd do it and be the captain I knew deep down these hard workers deserve.

Happiness and contentment though as any soldier knew, was always brief and fleeting. You learned to take the good moments when they came, frequent or fleeting. Given my past luck with how fleeting those moments were, I should've known my moment on cloud nine just now would join those fleeting moments. Never expecting to see what I would see next.

Movement out of the corner of my eye drew my attention to the main barn not too far away. Immediately, two figures emerged. Two very familiar figures. Kenna and Brett emerged from the open barn doors, laughing like two old friends spending time catching up with one another.

What on Earth…

My blood began to boil at the scene before me. Straw littered Kenna's hair, sticking in and out of it many times. The same went for Brett, though his count was lesser than hers. Both of their clothes appeared to be somewhat dusty, as if they'd been rolling about like a pair of dogs in mud. Or rather, rolling around of a completely different kind.

It became clear as day as to where Kenna had been all this time now. She'd been with Brett, my best friend, doing a hell of a lot more than simply mucking out the horses or bailing hay. How the two of them didn't hear a speck of what had just gone down, I don't know. Actually, I did. They had been too busy seeing each other to be aware of anything else.

I was more than aware that Kenna was a free woman and not one I was able to touch right now, but that didn't matter. The fact that she'd gone behind my back when she's supposed to be assisting me with my best friend doing such ludicrous things, was good enough reason for me to be seething at both of them. You never stabbed a man in the back, ever. Not when he's like a brother to you or when he can't get back up again as easily as another man with able legs would.

Though I should've expected something like this a hell of a lot sooner. After all, what could a man like me offer a woman like Kenna Bouchard? Nothing near as much as what Brett could offer, apparently.

Well, let them reap what they both had literally just sown.

My mind was more made up than it's ever been. Not only would I become a captain that the people deserve, but it'd do it a hell of a lot quicker so I could be rid of Nurse Kenna Bouchard. I'd deal with Brett when I had my strength back.

The two were too busy caught up in cleaning one another off to even begin noticing that I was sitting here watching them. Taking that as my cue, I motioned with my head to one of the lingering ranch hands, telling him to wheel me over to the ramp at the main house. Once inside after thanking the man, whose name I'd come to learn was Lark, my anger blossomed tenfold.

I was right to believe what I'd always believed in all along, right up until the moment that Kenna took me to the treehouse for our 'talk'. No one, at least like her, would ever learn to love a cripple. We were half men, broken men. Men who would always come in second to men like my so-called best friend, Brett.

Two can play at this game and when I play, I play to win. Soon you'll be running for the hills, back to your cozy hospital tending to patients whose hearts you won't ever dream of stomping all over.

Game on Kenna Bouchard. Game. On.

CHAPTER FOURTEEN
Kenna

"Phew! Thanks for your help today, Brett! I don't know what I would have done without you." I smiled, stopping in the doorway to the barn. For a while now when I had the odd moment of time to myself where I wasn't caring for Theon, I'd come up here to work on something secret. A surprise. At least it started out that way when I first thought about it. Now...well... now it was more of a distraction from what Brett revealed the other day to me about Theon.

Much to my embarrassment, I'd fainted right into Brett's arms. I wouldn't have done it if he wasn't there to catch me. Mind you, I wouldn't have fainted at the news if it wasn't for him in the first place. He'd carried me up to my room and waited with me until I'd woken up, which thankfully wasn't too long after. Not being a fainter it was fair to say that I was more than embarrassed, on top of it happening in front of Theon's best friend.

It didn't seem to bother him though, not one bit. Taking it all in his stride, he handed me a glass of water, made sure I was good to go and went on his way. Back to wherever he'd come from before turning up.

God that man will make a woman happy someday. Not this woman, though. Brett would still feel like a big brother would a year or ten from now. A brother I've always wished I could have. After having me, my parents weren't able to have another child. The why of it is still a mystery to me, and was their business. I don't know why they just didn't adopt a child, but again, it's a mystery I have no business in.

"Oh, you've got some straw in your hair. Actually, a lot." Brett laughed, pulling me out of my own thoughts. "Here, let me get that for you."

A few moments later, my hair was more or less straw-free. Which is more than I can say for Brett in general. "You might want to focus some attention on yourself there. I think you're more straw than man."

"Huh?" Brett blinked, looking down at himself. "Oh!" Laughing it off, he brushed a few strands off. "I guess I'll go get myself cleaned up before starting on the late afternoon chores."

I crossed my arms, "Why don't you get one of the lovely female ranch hands to do it for you, hm?"

I'd yet to see Brett with a woman in my time on the ranch, even if the two of us didn't mingle as much I did with Theon or his parents. I saw him wandering around the ranch when he'd come here from being on his own, and he'd always commit one hundred percent of his time to the chores and tasks that needed doing. He didn't go out on a Friday or Saturday night, never had a date or brought anyone to the ranch for some downtime.

Then again, so many people came and went that I probably would've missed another face among the many on any given day. Still, it'd be nice to see him with someone even if it didn't last. Everyone deserves to be happy and in the short time that I've come to somewhat know Theon's best friend, he deserved it too.

Brett shrugged, flicking off a few strands of straw from his shoulders. "Nah. I'm good at doing it myself."

"Someday, Brett Neil, someone will come along and blow your socks off."

"Hmph. Wrong damn thing to be blowing..." he muttered. *Typical.*

"Yes that too, I suppose. Mark my words though, it'll happen. Maybe not now or next week, but I'll be cashing in when it does."

Brett blinked, visibly confused. "Cashing in? I wasn't aware we'd even agreed or made a bet."

I smirked, "Oh we haven't. I just...have a feeling, that's all."

"Right, well...okay."

Odd... I've never seen Brett so...flustered? I kind of feel bad now...

Deciding to put the poor man out of his misery, I decided to let the subject go. For now. "Go on, I'll let you go. Thanks again for helping me, I really appreciate it. I don't think Theon would exactly approve, but I know he'd be surprised.

"That's for sure." Brett chuckled. "Speaking of the devil, I think he just went into the main house. Better go see how the ol' boy is doing."

"Alright, I'll do that."

Embracing in a quick farewell hug, I watched Brett until he'd departed from my sight. Turning around and heading and heading towards the main house which he said he'd seen Theon just go on into.

Deep down, I knew that Theon in his entire being would not be happy with what Brett and I have been doing. In fact, I'm sure as hell he'd morally disagree. What I do though, is my decision. I'm still his nurse, at least for the next week or so, which is what matters most here. What I did outside of caring for him was my own business.

If that's the case, then why do I feel so...guilty, keeping it from him?

I knew the answer, of course. It's the same answer whenever I had to keep anything from anyone. I had a damn overactive conscience. Even if the thing I was keeping from a person was something good, I didn't last long before I confessed out of sheer excitement. Or in this case, guilt. Not that I'd be confessing it to Theon yet. No way.

It was only a matter of time before the truth about my surprise came out. Though when it did, I'm hoping...no...I know I'll be ready to confess it all to him. Every last word. Till then, I'd just keep on at it until things were as perfect as they could be.

Closing the back door behind me, I stepped into the living space of the main house, fully expecting to see Theon somewhere inside. Especially since Brett said not too long ago, that he'd seen him head on inside here.

"Hello?" I called out, alerting anyone in the house of my presence.

"Is that you Kenna?" a light-toned voice replied which sounded much like Mara, Theon's mother.

A second later, she appeared from the hallway. "I thought I heard you. You got the message about dinner?"

"Dinner? No, sorry. I didn't."

"Oh, well, not a problem. I told Theon to tell you when he came in."

I shook my head, "I haven't seen him. I came in to find him, actually."

"Hm. Well I'm sure he's in his old room. I thought I heard voices assuming it was the two of you. He must've got someone else to take him in there. Anyway, the message he would've told you, is that the two of you are welcome to join us for dinner tonight. Seeing as you're both here."

It would be nice not to cook for a change…

"Lovely! Thank you. I'll go tell Theon we're staying for dinner."

"It's at seven, if you want to stay with him for a while. The poor boy's lonely but doesn't like to say anything."

I nodded, taking her up on her offer.

Theon was indeed as she said. Of course being his mother, she'd know that better than anyone else. Though I suspect he hadn't always been this way. Something had changed him and I know it wasn't being thrown from the horse that had done it. Still, whatever it is, is his story to tell. If he ever found my ears worthy of hearing it.

Seven o'clock eventually rolled around, and so did the frostiest dinner I've ever been to. Correction, everyone else around the table was more than cordial and perfectly normal. It didn't take much working out to realise who was the sour grape among the bunch. Theon was practically seething as he sat there, no matter how much he tried containing it.

He seemed somewhat normal as I entered his room earlier. As soon as he realised it was me and not his mother or father, he changed. I didn't dare ask him what I did wrong, not with his mother so close in the living space. Since then, it's been puzzling the hell out of me as to what I could've done since leaving the house this morning. Maybe it was just that. Maybe he didn't like the fact that I came here without him. Who knows?

Definitely asking him when we're back at his place.

Wrapping up the dinner an hour or so later with help from his father, I got Theon into my car. Slowly we made our way back to his place. Dark had just begun to fall, casting the most glorious colours across the sky, blessing us with a beautiful sunset I wish I had my phone out to capture. Still, nothing I couldn't capture and remember in my mind without it.

The entire ride home, if I could even call it that right now, was filled with nothing but silence. Maybe if I had offered up something as a topic of conversation, we would've said something to one another. It was just…too awkward, to even do that. Thus, we rode in silence. There wasn't anything either of us planned or particularly wanted to do when we got back, aside from giving Theon his medication, so it looked like I was in for a long night's worth of nothing. Literally.

Once inside and fed his medicine, Theon had to break his silence temporarily to ask to be taken straight to his room. Shortly, he would be able to do this himself when his arm casts come off, with him being given the all clear to begin using them again. I don't see why he wouldn't, as he seemed to be in peak physical shape to me. All the ranch work must've been heavier than I thought to give him a body which I've been privy to these last few weeks.

With as much silence as within the car on the way home, Theon was transported upstairs and laid on his bed where he'd been for the last two hours. At least where he'd remain, until such a time I'd have to assist him in the bathroom to…you know. Even as a nurse there were things that I was less looking forward to than others, with that being one of them. A person's toilet activities and habits were their own private affairs. Though sometimes, they did need help in the form of a catheter. Or assisted expulsion of bodily waste. Either way, it was one of those grin-and-bear-it times for me. Best to get it done and out of the way than to think about it too much.

Thankfully, stinky and unpleasant thoughts were henceforth halted by the blessed interruption from my cell phone. Lighting up the darkened room, I looked over to the bedside table to see an incoming FaceTime video request from Jess.

Oh thank you sweet Lord!

Grabbing my phone, I tapped the green 'answer' button as fast as I could, setting down the phone against the bedside lamp so I could be hands-free. A second later, my friend's familiar and lovely face filled the screen.

"Hey you!" Jess beamed, waving excitedly at the camera.

"Hey! To what do I owe this pleasure?"

I wasn't expecting Jess' call tonight. Or anyone's, really. Not that I had a schedule for anyone to call me, but Jess and I usually made sure the other was ready or able to take a video call.

"I figured you wouldn't be able to meet this Saturday, what with the ranch and you having a busy week. You'd need some downtime and not with us. A nice bath and a book."

"You know me too well. Those psychic skills of yours are still as scarily sharp as ever!"

Jess laughed, "Don't you forget it either. Besides, I had an ulterior motive for calling."

"Oh?"

"Mhm." Jess' blonde-haired head bounced, her excitement bluntly evident. Leaning slightly to the right, she pulled the 'ulterior motive' into screenshot with her.

"Laney!"

"Hi hi!" she waved back at me, sitting beside Jess on her bed in her bedroom.

On top of not expecting to hear from Jess tonight, I was now twice as surprised to see both her and Laney in the same room without being told first. They knew my preference for being well-prepared, though this was one of those times they knew they'd get away without doing it.

"Wow, two of you for the price of one! I truly don't deserve such an honour."

"That's true." Laney laughed, sipping at a bottle of water.

"Hey!" I couldn't help but laugh with her. It's been a long ass day, and I'm long overdue a good laugh with my two best friends.

"So, how's life treating you there? That patient of yours giving you any trouble?" Jess asked.

How to answer that…

For the most part, Theon had been cordial. Especially as the days passed. Today however, I wasn't too sure. Something had to have happened to make him recoil back into who he was when I first arrived, though I was still clueless as to what. Probably will always be, too.

I sighed, "Mostly good. The people here are really nice. Theon, my patient, his parents are outstanding. Everyone on the ranch, worker and otherwise pull their weight and I must say, I've even mucked in a time or two when I'm technically not on the clock."

When I didn't get a response from either Jess or Laney, I looked up from my clasped hands. Both of them were staring at me, wide-eyed, as if I'd grown two heads.

Eventually, Laney spoke up. "You? Muck in? Did someone pour something into your drink or something?"

"Laney, you forget I practically grew up on my grandparents' ranch when I wasn't with my parents. I did more than just sit about. Well, when I was allowed to that is. Grandpa would only let me really muck out the stalls and such when I was tall enough to see over them. That took a while." I laughed, scratching the back of my neck. "I was a slow-grower."

"I'd forgotten about that…" she trailed off.

Clearing her throat, Jess took back control of the conversation. "So, tell us more about your patient. What you're legally allowed to tell us, you know, non-patient confidentiality."

"Well, he's like an onion. There are many layers to him, with some being thicker and tougher than others. Under it all, I can tell that there's one hell of a human being underneath. He just needs a little help and a nudge in the right direction to bring it out. He wasn't exactly kind to me, or anyone, come to think of it, at first, but there's been an improvement lately. I don't know if I'll ever be the person to bring back who he used to be, but I'm damn well going to do what I can during the time that he's under my care that's for sure."

Another moment passed before the two of them responded, Laney breaking the silence this time. "Sounds to me like you're more taken with him than you think." She winked.

Neither of them needed to know just how much I was taken with him, nursing aside. It was just one of those times where even if I wanted it to be, it cannot. When the time came I wasn't his nurse anymore, it would be back to the hospital and back to the emergency patients who'd need all the care they could get. The possibility of seeing Theon after I parted his company were slim to none, and I just had to accept that. No matter how much my mind, or my heart, said otherwise.

I shook my head, "No more than I've been with any other patient."

"Mhm, sure." Jess mused.

Laney cleared her throat, steering the conversation away from a potentially awkward place. "Anyway, we decided to do a two for one tonight. You get both of us until any one of us falls asleep, that way you don't have to worry about slipping us in this weekend if you're unable."

I couldn't help but laugh. This was something we always did as late teens/young adults, and it's a tradition of sorts none of us had ever really grown out of. I have a feeling it'll stick around for as long as one, or all three of us are friends.

"Sounds like a plan!"

In truth, I did miss these two something fierce. Being here, I didn't get to see them as much as I'd like. Only in passing would I see them in downtown Austin when I had to go and collect something, or when I'd offer to shop for both us and the main house. Other than a friendly smile and wave, there hasn't been any other chance to interact before getting on with what I was in town to do. Thankfully, they both understood this when I told them I'd accepted the temporary position, after Mara cornered me at the sandwich place.

Settling into a comfortable position on the queen-sized bed in the guest room which is my temporary home, the three of us got lost in the throes of many a conversation for the next several hours.

At some stage, I was the one who ended up falling asleep hours into our video conversation. I think. Truth is, I can't quite remember and I'm not sure I want to. With this bed quite possibly being the best one that I've ever slept in, on the inside or the out, all rational thoughts simply didn't matter.

Snuggling deeper into the bedding on top of the bed, I refused to open my eyes. It wasn't time to wake up yet to give Theon his next dose of medication, as my phone alarm would tell me when it was, therefore I didn't need to fully wake up. Sleep was a wonderful and rare thing when you could grab it at the ER, so I've more than indulged in my share during my time here. I was sure going to miss it when I no longer had it as a luxury.

The only thing that I was missing right now, were a few of my own home comforts. Not bringing more than I had to, thinking that I would be up at the main house for the entirety of my stay, I packed only what I would need. I suppose I could always head on back to my place and pick up a few things, if I really needed to. Though seeing as I'm not to be here for much longer, it would be pointless for such a short space of time.

Best just to grin and bear it, just for a little while longer.

Soon enough, I could feel the familiar pull of sleep. Tugging at my remaining consciousness to join it in deep slumber. Only too willing to let it do so, I promptly fell back asleep, straight into an all-too vivid dream

"I'm going to miss you like mad, you know. Thank God this is my last deployment." Drayce declared, bending over to pick up his duffle bag.

I would miss him too, so much. This was always the worst part of having to say goodbye to someone you loved, sending them on their way to parts unknown because it was always 'classified'. Well, second to worst thing alongside sending them off at the airport. That one was a killer, because you knew you couldn't jump the barrier for one final kiss. You stayed just before where they'd go through security, watching them until they were no longer in your sight.

"I'll miss you too, Drayce. I just wish I could…" my words caught in my mouth, unable to finish the sentence.

Drayce's hand gently came to rest on my right cheek, his thumb gently stroking the side of my face. "I know darling. I know. I wish you could too, it's just this time we're going straight from the base not the airport."

"Don't partners go to the base too?"

"Not always. Since this was a last-minute call to deploy, there wasn't time to make arrangements. Trust me, I'm as gutted as you are."

I highly doubted that. He at least would have his mind occupied while we were apart, even if he was in a dangerous, high-risk environment. I suppose the same could be said for me at the ER unit, though I had downtime and it was quite literally that. Time that I would spend feeling down, praying with all my might that no harm would come to him in whatever he was doing. My mind would often get the best of me, sending my thoughts to dark places that I spent many a night fighting being pulled back into.

Walking to the door, Drayce turned to me one last time, capturing my lips with his own in a kiss that spoke louder than words could ever say.

"Come back to me." I whispered, pressing my forehead to his.

The smile that made many things within me flutter, spread across his handsome face. "Always. I love you."

Swallowing back the tears that threatened to spill in front of him, I gave my reply. "I love you too, Drayce Anderson."

With one last smile and a cheeky wink, he was gone and out the door. His footsteps in his big boots faded with each step, silenced by the closing of his truck door before the vehicle pulled away, taking part of my heart with him.

Now that I was on my own once more, I could finally let go of the tears I didn't want Drayce to see. Not on his last deployment. Though I'm sure he knew that I was about to cry, I'm thankful that he didn't bring them up or that he didn't tell me not to cry. That always made me cry harder.

Sliding down to the floor in the spot I'd been standing in since Drayce closed the door behind him, I sat down with my head in my hands, letting free everything that had been building up inside. Probably since he first came home six months ago, somehow knowing inside that he would be taken from me at any moment, making the best of the time we'd share no matter how short or long.

It was then the dream shifted.

Months had passed since Drayce had been deployed to his next undisclosed location. As the days passed, I missed him more and more but at the same time, it was a day until he would be home and once more in my arms. Not to mention somewhere else. Only a few days remained until that day would finally roll around. Meanwhile, I was going around the house like a neurotic cleaning racoon. Everything had to be just-so for when I brought him home. The last thing he needed was to come home to a house that needed a million and one things doing to it, not after what he's been doing these long months.

No way would I become one of those women who lived to serve their men in the home, but it was the logical thing to do here. Or in any other way. I'm sure men do it for their serving wives and husbands too.

Just as I put the last cleaned item into its place, three loud rasps came from the direction of the front door. Startled by the sudden noise, I collected myself before making my way over to answer it.

It was too early and too soon to be Drayce, and I wasn't expecting anyone so…who could it be?

Opening up the door, I was met with the face of a young-ish man in full dress uniform. I couldn't quite see his face for the blinding light behind him, though in the next few moments, I wouldn't need to.

"Ma'am, are you Ms Mackenzie Bouchard?"

Oh no…no, no, no!

I've read far too many books, and watched far too many TV shows and movies to know what this was. Far too many. With his official stance, his tone and demeanour, he didn't even need to speak for me to know what he'd come to tell me. If he was speaking to me right now, I wasn't hearing it. In fact, the only thing that I could hear was the increasing beat of my heart in my ears.

Words drifted sporadically from his mouth and into my ears, the majority of them being lost by the deafening drumming of my heart. "Drayce…mission…sniper…hero… saved my life…" these intermittent words wove together as one, forming an unwritten story that would change my life forever. This time, there would be no happy ending at the end of the book. No epilogue to change the outcome.

Suddenly, the man in uniform at the door starts to scream. Yelling at the top of his lungs with the most painful sound I've ever heard, pulling me back into the moment. Why is he screaming? Why is it so loud yet…muffled? What's going on? What's happening?

As quickly as the darkness pulled me under, it catapulted me straight back into the light with a jolt. Springing into a sitting position, it dawned on me that what had just happened in that dream was more than that. It was a memory. One which came to me when my guard was down, if you could really ever be on guard when it came to your subconscious. An unlikely possibility by anyone's means, I'm sure.

No one but I knew what happened in my old house that day, not even Jess or Leary. They knew why that uniformed soldier came to my door, everyone in the damn area knew. But no one knew the series of events that happened within those four walls. That was for myself and myself alone to carry for the rest of my life. Alone.

One thing that didn't make sense which had never, ever happened before, was the screaming. Usually the dream, or rather nightmare, would end when I'd breakdown and scream-cry. Tonight was the first ever night where it ended with him screaming and my waking up in a semi-sweat. Not something I particularly like, but when you work as an ER nurse or doctor, you were bound to work up one now and then and you just rolled with it.

Brushing a few loose strands of hair behind my ears, I took a deep breath, aiming to forget about the dream and everything that came with it. Including the scream that, come to think about it, was still ringing in my ears. Exactly what doesn't usually happen when you wake up. It suddenly dawned on me as I realised exactly why I could still hear the screams of distress. It was no dream, it's Theon! Screaming from his room down the hall.

Nightmares take many forms, holding us in the darkness until we were finally able to break free. Our one freedom, was that we could move. Where our minds were bound, our limbs were free. Not Theon.

Following the screams resembling the very hounds from hell, I burst into his room expecting to see the worst. As worse as my frazzled mind was able to conjure up at this sudden outburst during the middle of the night.

Frozen in place by his casts, Theon was wrapped haphazardly by his pure white sheets, binding him to the very nightmare inside his head. His fists balled inside their restraints as sweat rolled off his skin and into the now soaked sheets.

This is no ordinary nightmare. This is a PTSD episode!

Everyone always assumes that they're triggered by things in the real world when someone was awake, which is partly true, though not entirely. They can happen equally as often when you sleep, when dreams trigger memories, or events, within your subconscious.

My limbs co-operated with my mind for once, and immediately I sprang into action. Unwrapping the sheet from his bulky body I threw it aside, ignoring the dampness meeting my touch.

"Theon." I called softly, calmly. My hand came to touch the red-hot skin of his forehead, almost recoiling at how hot it is. No response. Nothing more than his continued slumbering torment, anyway.

C'mon!

Wasting no time I ripped open Theon's night shirt, setting it on top of his groin to spare him his modesty, and removed his sleep sweats. It would cool him down gradually, rather than shocking his body with something like cold water.

Time for the main event.

Straddling his thrashing, casted body, I seated myself oh-so carefully atop him. The best thing to do here was to wake him with care. Removing my own shirt and sleep sweats, I gingerly lay flat, moderately reducing his thrashing. My skin and body would cool his body back down to a much more normal temperature, using my own body heat to match it with. Well, at least it would with the parts that weren't cast or bandaged.

Theon continued to whine in distress beneath me, his head thrashing from side to side in an attempt to shake off his nightmarish episode. "No! No! Please, no!" he cried, twisting my heart into a tight knot.

Swallowing, I shimmied up his body so my mouth came level with his head. "Here goes nothing." I muttered as I ran my lips up his throat, cheek and to his jaw, pressing a soft kiss against his ear. "Hey...shh...it's alright. Theon, you're safe." I whispered as soft as an angel's feather. "You're home. C'mon now...come back to me...I...I need you."

Reduced mobility, skin contact and a soft voice combined, Theon's moderate thrashing stilled almost immediately. His whines and groans vanished into the night, replaced by more normal calming breaths.

"K...Kenna?" Theon asked, his voice weakened and weary. "What... what are you?"

Moving my hand up from his side, I halted his worse with a finger to his full, tempting lips. "It's okay. I'll explain later." I swallowed. "Just take a moment, okay? I've got you."

With his heart racing against my chest, I felt it begin to calm with each passing moment. Inside me, I knew that this was probably the first time that anyone has simply held this man. Being there for him one human to another as he came out of an episode. He'd dealt with so much on his own not leaning on a single soul. Until now. If he had any objections or questions, he wasn't voicing them now. Perhaps later, he would. Though I wasn't betting on it. After all, people in my experience very rarely talked about an episode after it being witnessed by someone else.

After several beats, he laid his head back down into the pillow with my own resting against his stubbly cheek. A moment later, he uttered two words I never expected him to.

"Thank you." He whispered, his words genuine yet pained and tinted with a hint of...vulnerability?

Those two words would stay with me long after I would part from his side. A very long time.

Lies and deception of his military past aside, brought to light not too long ago on accident by Brett, I was glad I was here for this man tonight. He'd of course, never know that I knew. That nugget of information I'd keep to myself. Just as much as he would never know how much seeing him like this tonight, has opened many doors to memories in my mind I'd long since shut away.

He had his secrets. I have my own. Both of which would be left in the darkness alongside the stuff of nightmares. Nightmares which I planned to keep secret, and far away from Theon Brin O'Donoghue

CHAPTER FIFTEEN
Theon

Last night was probably one of the most bizarre nights I've had for a long time and believe me, I'm nowhere near short of those. Desiring time on my own, I had asked to be taken to my room where I then inevitably spent most of the rest of yesterday evening, through into the night. Seeing Brett and Kenna together as they'd appeared from the main barn really put me off dinner, putting me into one hell of a mood.

Thinking back to said dinner last night, I think I did a pretty good job at hiding what was off with me from Kenna. Though I'm sure someone as smart as her would've easily worked out that something was up. She'd just never be privy to what that exactly was. Those cards I was well and truly holding close to my chest. Metaphorically speaking, of course. If I hadn't joined the army, my skills yesterday could've made me an actor.

Pfft, sure. Me, an actor. What a laughable notion.

The only thing I've ever been good at, was being a soldier. At best, I was a second rate rancher. With it not being my heart's one true desire for a career. A lifestyle. Days had long passed since I was able to live my life how I wanted to live it, and those self-same days will never come again. Being second-rate was my life now, if I was even that still.

Not too long ago, that tiny spark of hope that I'd thought that had long since vanished, gave me the belief and confidence to believe that I could become something, again. Even if it wasn't the man I was before. I'd become the man I was now meant to be with the body that I was left with. A man that Kenna would be proud of and would be proud to call her own. Life was no longer just mine for living on my own. I'd live it with another. Someone who didn't care if a man walked on two legs, or with none.

I should've known better…

Of course she'd pick a man who can use both of his legs. It was stupid of me to ever think, consider or even hold onto that shred of hope that would let me believe otherwise. What bothered me most of all, what really rankles me about the whole thing, is that of all the people she could've chosen to see on this entire planet, she chooses Brett. My best buddy. I was closer to him than anyone else on this ranch. After all, we practically grew up as brothers from other mothers.

There was this unwritten rule, a code, if you will, that most men went by when it came to women. If it was a woman one of them was interested in who was close to another, you didn't approach her without talking it out with your buddies first. So not to step on any toes, or tread where advancements had been made. No matter how much you wanted to see where things went. If another had already beaten you to it, you steered well clear. Above all, it was about respect, and less about caveman-like principles as many often believed.

Most of last night in my room was spent trying to put these thoughts about Brett and Kenna out of my head, trying to calm myself down. It didn't work. The more I tried not to think about them, the more my thoughts went there and to scenarios I very much knew were more possible than not. Eventually, my inner raging tired me out, sending me off to sleep and to something even more horrific than my conscious thoughts.

A nightmare.

Not just any nightmare. The nightmare. It was the one that occurred every single night, sometimes worse on one night, sometimes not so much. There were nights where I would be able to break free from the horrors of my past, then there were others like last night where it would seem like I would be trapped inside my mind forever. Clawing at the darkness, doing anything at all possible to break free.

I wasn't exactly clawing at it last night. Instead, it felt as if I was weighed down by a two tonne weight. Refusing to let me up until I'd seen and been witness to every last minute of horror I'd been subjected to in reality. It's as if my mind doesn't want me to forget what my eyes saw that day. The day I watched my best friend do the most foolish, yet bravest thing he's ever done his whole life.

* * *

"Aren't you tired O'Donoghue?" I turned my head to see my best buddy, besides Brett, come up alongside me AK47 in hand. Anderson walked with that usual casual, carefree swagger about him, as if we weren't in the middle of a war zone at all. Not one ounce of cockiness about him though, he oozed confidence and pride because like myself, he was born to be a soldier. It was who we were, and what made us a perfect duo.

"Shouldn't you be addressing me as 'captain', soldier?" I smirked.

"Nah, not really."

Thank God it was just the two of us standing here next to the mess hall, or otherwise he'd have his butt whipped for talking to a superior that way. Friend or not.

We were on standby for our next mission. Details were sketchy as to when it would take place, but there were two of our teams who were on standby if we were needed, the others were currently out doing whatever they were assigned with. Some were just on guard duty. Something we all had to do at one point or another, especially when we were out on mission within our teams.

Usually before we were sent out, Anderson would be Skyping or emailing with his girlfriend. I didn't know her or her name, but he spoke about her to me on more than one occasion. Sometimes it felt as if I was in a relationship with them. Still, I didn't mind. He was happy, and it was nice to hear about something positive out here for a change.

"Not talking to the other half tonight?"

I knew he was close to popping the big question to her, he'd spoken occasionally to me about it here and there. This tour would finally be the one where he'd pay for the ring he'd designed especially for her. Which meant it wasn't cheap, not by any means.

I've been paying way too much attention to his video calls, way too much.

111

"I spoke to her on the phone earlier." He smiled, his pride in her evident. "I know we didn't have much time, so I went with that. She told me some good news though, she just passed her exams and she's officially graduating to become a nurse. She has a placement lined up at a hospital in downtown Austin for her residency."

Holy hell that was impressive!

Even though I knew college wasn't the way I wanted to go with my life, it didn't mean I wasn't impressed when someone else graduated. Hell, I was even happy for them! I'm not the type of guy to be hung up on something, especially if it was my own decision not to do something.

"Wow, congrats man! How does it feel that your girlfriend will be a nurse?"

"Fiancée."

I'm sure I heard right, but I was going to make him say it again.

Turning to him, I fought to hide the smile growing on my face. "Huh?"

This earned me a playful shove. Good thing I'm sure-footed.

"You heard me." Anderson smirked, letting his gun hang from the shoulder strap as he fished something from out of his pocket. It was a ring. Technically, it was a ring box. Small enough to fit inside a pocket but big enough for my eyes to widen as he opened it to show me the contents within. Considering I know nothing about diamonds, cuts or anything to do with rings, I was incredibly impressed at what Anderson was showing me right now.

"Damn, if you didn't already have a girlfriend to propose to, I'd be tempted right now to say yes and marry you myself." I teased, clapping him on the back. "She's going to love it. More so because YOU made it for her."

Putting the ring back into his pocket, Anderson looked prouder than he'd ever done before. "Thanks. I like to think so too."

"When are you going to ask her?"

Anderson collected his rifle back into his hands, shifting his stance back into its former state. "As soon as we're done here and back home. It's the first thing I'm going to do when I see her. Till then, the ring stays with me."

I nodded, "Fair enough. How about—"

Before I could finish, the call came for my team to deploy. We all sprang into action, with myself leading the team out to where I'd been ordered to go to, Anderson at my side in his rightful place as my second-in-command.

Around an hour later after we'd arrived at the destination location, dismounted from the armoured vehicle, took up our position, the sinking feeling I had mounting on the way here blossomed into a full-on bad feeling in the bottom of my stomach. My instincts very rarely led me wrong in these types of circumstances, and I was hoping for once, they would be now.

From what our intelligence could tell us, there was a little girl that needed rescuing from a gang of marked armed rebels. Her family managed to escape, thinking she was already out. But she wasn't. They'd found her cowering away under the couch and decided to keep her until…well…until what unfortunately happened in most circumstances like this. Hopefully, we'll get in this time before then.

Everyone was in their places, and it was almost time to get this show on the road. One, silent command from me, and we were a go. I was just about to give that self-same silent signal, when events happened all at once which would change the course of my life forever.

From somewhere around me, one of my teammates shouted 'sniper', the echo reverberating through our in-built helmet headsets. It wasn't the first time that we'd encountered a rogue sniper on a mission. They were a dime a dozen. This time though, this time would be the time to change that. My reactions were usually lightning-fast, but today, they weren't fast enough. In a split second, the life of my teammate, my best friend, was wiped from this very Earth.

I hadn't seen him coming. He just…appeared out of nowhere. Drayce's position was east of my own, where I'd assigned him to be when we'd arrived here. All of a sudden, he was no longer in his assigned position. Neither was I. In a matter of seconds, the crouch I was in was no longer the position I held. The ground came hard and fast to meet my back with a hard thud, temporarily winding me. Getting my breath back in record time, my eyes opened the split second that the sniper, who had my head as his target, took out Drayce instead.

"TAKE HIM OUT!" I barked at the men around me, knowing they'd get the job done. The rest would advance to rescue the girl from the rebels, as outlined in plan B should I or Drayce, no longer be able to lead them in.

Keeping low, I moved over to where I'd been and where Drayce had fallen. Shifting my gun to my side, I said a quick, silent prayer that he'd only sustained mild injuries that would heal with time. Apparently, no one was in to hear my prayer. What I had assumed would be a single shot, was more than one. Kneeling down and supporting Drayce's upper half as he lay almost lifeless in the dirt, I took stock of his wounds. A bullet wound to the left shoulder/pec region, one to the left side of his stomach, the leg and…my heart sank when I saw two more. You didn't need to be a doctor to know they were fatal kill shots. Right above his heart.

"Drayce! Drayce, c'mon man. Can you hear me? Drayce?" My voice was almost at a yell at this point, trying to get through to him and through the gunfire going on around us.

All noise faded away as Drayce, weak as a newborn lamb, opened his eyes up to me. "Th…Theon." His voice was as weak as he was, marred only by the slight oozing of blood from his mouth. The sight made my stomach churn as much as my mind whirred, knowing the worst was set in stone.

"Sssh, don't talk buddy. I've got you, okay? You're going to be alright."

"Liar."

The lie naturally rolled off my tongue as any other I've ever told. In these circumstances, it's what you did. When a man or woman was about to…depart, you said what needed to be said. No matter how false your words were.

"I know…what's about to happen." Drayce coughed. More blood came from his mouth as he did, which I carefully wiped away. "Just do…one thing…for me." His voice grew weaker with every word spoken, though his eyes remained determined to get this message out no matter what. With a shaky, pale hand, he reached into the pocket on his right pant side, and pulled out the ring box he'd shown to me not too long ago.

"Look…after…Macey… She's…my life. I…I-I love…her."

"I will. I'll find her, I promise."

Pressing the ring box into my hand, a smile crept onto Drayce's paling face. There wasn't an ounce of fear or sadness on my best friend's face as he breathed his last, one word alone slipped from his lips. "Macey…"

No words could even begin to describe the feelings, thoughts or emotions rushing through me. Nor would I want to even try. The man who'd become a brother to me, who'd practically been at my side and glued to my hip for as long as I could remember, died in my arms while making me promise to take care of his girlfriend. A girl who I'd have to tell about the loss of not only her boyfriend, but his last words and wishes. Perhaps the toughest mission I'll ever have to go on.

With the noise of the battle continuing to drown out around us, I slipped the now heavy-feeling ring box into my pocket, carefully closed Drayce's eyelids and brought him once more up and into my arms. We walked into this world together, this world of guns and fire, now I'd walk him out of it.

His head lolled against my chest, never again will he be able to hear the beating of my broken heart. Swallowing the big, swollen lump in my throat, I turned my back to the battlefield to carry my best friend from what was his final mission.

"I've got you, Drayce. I've got you."

* * *

"Theon. Theon. Theon!" Kenna called, snapping me back into reality and away from the memory. She sounded somewhat annoyed, having to call my name repeatedly. Little did she know what was going on inside my head, and it would stay that way too. Only I would know of Drayce's final moments, and the promise he made me agree to. One I had yet to carry out.

Looking up, Kenna did in fact have that cheesed-off look etched onto her face.

"What?"

"I've been calling you for the last five minutes." She snapped

I shrugged, "Should've tried it a bit louder then."

Well if that didn't just go and kick up her expression a notch from cheesed-off, to one smart ass remark short of a meltdown.

Still, she didn't bite. As ever, her composure rivalled that of the ice queen from The Chronicles of Narnia: The Lion, The Witch and the Wardrobe. Not that I would ever say that out loud. That little nugget was mine to laugh over alone.

"I asked if you wanted more food." Kenna snapped again. It sounded as if she was more telling me that I was finished, rather than asking me if I wanted more.

Of course, my natural go-to response would be to tease her and want more. Why wouldn't I? Truth is, I actually am rather full. After getting lost in that memory, I'd lost any remaining appetite.

"No thanks. I'm good."

"Good."

Kenna was immediately up and out of her seat taking our plates over to and placing them in the sink, busying herself with cleaning them up when we both know, it wouldn't hurt to wait a little. Guess I was right, she didn't want me to eat more.

Before I could throw up any sort of rejection, objection or anything else, the last person I wanted to see right now walked right on in the back door with a stupid ass grin on his face.

"Good morning beautiful people! How are we both today?" Brett chimed, happy as a squirrel who'd found his favourite nut after winter.

Seething didn't even begin to cover what I felt about him and Kenna, not even close. Neither of them still don't know that I knew, and I had no intention of revealing it now. There'd be a time and place for that. Until then, I'd wait patiently. After all, I've spent long enough with these damn casts on. If that didn't prove I was a patient guy, I don't know what would.

I grunted, not in the mood to give him a proper reply.

"Fine thanks, Brett!" Kenna replied, a bit too cheerily for my liking. "You?

"Couldn't be better. Ready and willing for a good day's fishin'!" He turned to face me. "Ready to go?"

Wait, what?

Kenna turned to us then, arms crossed and sporting a smug smirk. "Oh, didn't I mention it to you? I've arranged for you to spend the day with Brett and a few other guys. Fishing. I've got some arrangements to make with the hospital regarding the removal of your casts and post-cast appointments. Figured you could use a guys' day out."

Why the little…

If there was one thing on this planet that bored me more than anything else, it's fishing. I'd talked to Kenna about it a short while ago one night around the fire. The two of us were talking about our hobbies, and I'd stated just how much I didn't like fishing. I suppose this is her way of getting revenge on me somehow, and for something I don't even remember doing.

Two can play this game.

"Ready!" I said, plastering on my best fake smile for Brett. "Though, I fail to see just how much fishing I can actually do, here."

Clapping his hands together, Brett's smile got even bigger. "There's always a way around things. You know that."

Sadly, I did. If there was a way around something, it was usually Brett or I who could do it. Damn it.

"Excellent!" Kenna exclaimed, "I'll be off then. Can you handle things from here, Brett?"

Brett nodded, "You can count on me!"

Ass.

Nodding, Kenna spun on her heel after collecting her bag, and departed. Leaving us with nothing but the glorious view of her retreating behind as a memory. And what a behind it was. Not that I should be thinking about it. Yet, here I was. Doing just that.

"Shall we?" Brett said from behind me, manoeuvring me and the wheelchair from the dining table towards the back door.

I nodded.

This day was going to be a long ass one indeed. The worst part? Thanks to the damn pain meds, I couldn't have one single solitary beer.

Lord, give me strength.

CHAPTER SIXTEEN
Theon

I was right. Fishing was just as boring as I'd remembered it to be. Boring, dull, with added boring and dullness sprinkled in for good measure. For the very fact that I could do little else but direct Brett to where I wanted my fishing rod to be cast, reeled and whatnot, I was close to being the poster person for the physical representation of boredom.

We've been at this spot for just over an hour, which was one hour too many for me. Brett had yet to speak to me about anything else besides fishing, and I could tell there was something else on his mind besides fishing and where we'd come to.

This spot holds a lot of memories for us both. We'd both kissed for the first time here, though thankfully, not at the same time. It was also where we'd brought our girlfriends for our first dates. Again, not at the same time and begrudgingly to myself, it was where he'd brought me here to learn how to fish. Usually, as a result of me losing a bet of some sort. Fishing was always his go-to 'punishment', for me.

A few others joined us along the way, a few ranch hands who needed some long overdue downtime. Including Russ. At least I could count on one man being on my side, should anything go down today. There was a feeling in my gut that there would be, but just how bad it would be was lost on me.

Brett had parked my wheelchair in our usual spot where we'd be fishing from. The others were dotted sporadically along the rest of the way down the bank, mindful of each man's space needed to fish without disturbance.

Cowboys fishing…bah. Should be riding something or…roping something. Not fishing.

"Penny for your thoughts?" Brett asked, plopping himself down beside me.

I'd charge you more than just a penny, pal.

Deep down, I know Brett isn't at fault for what I'm mad at him for. Neither was Kenna, really. It's me. Me and my stupid jealousy with a woman who'd never fall for a cripple, or even someone like me if I was able bodied again.

"No, not really."

Brett's right eye squinted at me, "I don't believe you. You've been out of sorts since your dad brought you to the main house the other day. Something up?"

My so-called friend here is far too astute for his own good. If anyone would know if something was up, it was him. Cat, prepare to come out of your bag.

Looking out at the water and the rods cast out and anchored in the ground, I began to speak. "What are your intentions towards Kenna, Brett? How far do you see yourself going with her?"

With a bemused expression and a brow raised, Brett looked at me as if I'd said something crazy. A moment later, he burst out laughing with his hands holding his sides in case they'd split.

"Oh I knew it! I knew it had to be something like that which was bothering you!" after letting his laughter subside, Brett leaned back on his arms. "You're way off on this one, Theon. Way off."

"How so?"

At this point, I'm more curious than the cat to know the answer. Sitting up, Brett like myself, focused on the water in front of us as he began to speak.

"I came by the other week to bring a care package to you from your mother. When I arrived, you weren't awake. Your medication had knocked you out."

I nodded.

"After I'd fetched the package in, Kenna and I sat together out on your back porch. Though not for very long, as I had things to be getting on with."

"What did you guys talk about?"

It was worth a try, even if he didn't want to reveal what they talked about. Surprisingly to my amazement, he did.

"Not much. She somewhat remembered me from when I sprung you from the hospital, so I stopped to chat before heading back. Just to be friendly. I told her my name, and that I'm sometimes known as O'Donoghue, not O'Neil. You know why."

"Yep." Brothers by heart.

"I talked about that a little more, as well as about my folks and us growing up. Nothing deep or detailed, just surface stuff. That was pretty much it."

If that was it, then why was Kenna in such a foul mood? It didn't make sense.

"You're right. It doesn't."

Huh?

That must've come out of my mouth instead of staying inside my head. Before I could reply, Brett continued.

"To be honest, I've noticed something's been up with her lately too. Still, it's not my place to ask."

I raised a brow, "Why not, you're interested in her aren't you?"

Brett sighed and shook his head, "I'm not interested in her. Not in the way you think and certainly nothing more than a friend."

"Hmph. You looked pretty cozy coming out of the barn the other day, plucking straw off of one another like you'd showed her a good time."

Normally, this kind of thing would earn me a punch to the face if I had said it to anyone else. Not Brett. He wouldn't ever hit me no matter what I said. Instead, he started laughing his wrangler-clad ass off.

"Oh my god!" he guffawed, bending over while holding his sides.

Pinching in both of my brows, I watched him while he let out his bout of laughter. After a few moments, it looked like he was about done. "You good?"

"Yeah. Yeah, I'm good." He wiped his eyes dry of laughter-filled tears.

"Boy I knew you had it wrong. Just, not that wrong."

Dropping my left brow, I kept my right one raise. "Pray tell, how have I?"

Placing one hand on his hip, Brett half-turned to face me. "I was putting fresh hay into the stall's wall-mounted racks and she happened to come in while I was doing so. I was mid-way lifting a bale when it fell off the pitchfork while she was underneath, picking up stray pieces."

Aw, dang it.

"That still doesn't explain why you had straw on you."

Brett shrugged, "It's pretty simple. I laughed at how she looked covered in straw, so she dumped some on me to see how I'd like it."

I'd been wrong about a fair few things in my life, but this takes the cake. Not one part of Brett's words screamed 'lies', not a single word. I knew this guy through and through and not even asked to, would he lie to me. I believed him, and I believed his every word.

Swallowing back the enormous guilt lump that had been forming in my throat, I knew what had to be said to make things right. I was wise enough to apologise when I knew the occasion called for it, unlike some people.

"Brett, I…"

He held up his hand to me, halting my words mid-speech.

"Don't even say it Theon. I know you're sorry."

Jesus, I think that guilt lump is coming back…

Brett continued, "Listen, you've been through a lot. Hell, more than a lot. I know men who'd pack it in after going through what you did. You've achieved your dream by serving our country and yes, you paid the price. Does Kenna even know why you got out of the war? Have you told her yet?"

Kenna was never going to know about that. I would breathe my last before I'd even begin to tell her. It was still a miracle that she never found out from my medical records. Perhaps she doesn't have access to them? Either way, it was a miracle.

"No. She doesn't. I…I can't tell her."

Someone, somewhere down the bank whooped with muted elation, having successfully snagged a fish early on into us being here. It was a momentary distraction from a heavy subject. A moment that didn't last too long.

"That's your own business, Theon. I'd never force you to tell her, but why haven't you? You know she'll understand." Brett asked, squatting down to check his own line.

"I can't quite tell her yet. Not when I've still got to uphold my promise to Drayce. I can't make her understand or even push my intentions onto her while I've got that to carry out. I wouldn't do that to her. How would you like it if a girl came onto you, only to reveal she's promised to another?"

Brett stood up, a thoughtful look now adorning his face. "I wouldn't." he sighed. "You're right. I know where you're coming from, I do. Though I feel that maybe you should indulge her."

Indulge her? What the hell?

"I'm not seducing her!"

He smirked at me, shaking his head. "No, not that. I mean enlighten her. You won't know how she'll react to your darkest secrets if you don't try. Trust me, things are always way worse when people try to do something in the best interest of someone. Only to find that all along, the best thing to do was just tell them."

"The simple things are always the least obvious, sometimes."

"Maybe so. It doesn't mean you can't do them when you realise the obvious."

Obviously during my time spent recovering and casted up like a mummy, my friend here has become the town Buddha. A wise one, too. He raises a good point. A good yet difficult one. Soon, Kenna would be gone and back to her work. There was no point starting to open up now, not when I'm so close to being free from these casts. I wouldn't see her again once her time as my at-home nurse was over. Probably for the best, anyway. But for who?

All of this is just so messed up. My feelings for her that I shouldn't be feeling. The wrong assumption that Brett liked Kenna, and that they'd fooled around in the barn. Kenna's mood swings. All of it.

Part of me wants to tell Kenna the truth about everything. Get everything out in the open so that the only person who could ever judge me, is the good Lord himself. Hell, what am I saying? People are going to judge me anyway, no matter what I do. I could do a good deed and you bet your bottom dollar, someone will judge me to heck about it.

Demons within my mind kept pulling me back to keeping things hidden, every single time that I thought about telling Kenna the truth. About my darkest secrets. So far, they were the winning team. Burying my morality deep within me, deeper than it's been at any point in my life. And there's been some times where I've had to bury it real deep to get the job done.

"I'll talk to her about it when my casts are off." I said suddenly, trusting my mouth and head to speak before my heart woke up to protest.

Brett blinked, visibly shocked at my sudden outburst. "That's this weekend! Are you sure you want to do it so soon?"

"I don't see when I'll get the opportunity again." I shrugged, "She's going to go back to the hospital soon, back to where she's needed most. I won't have her as my at-home nurse forever. Unless…"

There's no reason as to why she can't be my nurse when my casts come off. None at all. I'll need physical therapy while I'm at home, and lord knows I more than have the money to pay for her services. If I can make a big enough case for her to stay on for a little while longer then maybe, just maybe, I could buy myself some more time to tell her everything.

Now all I had to do was come up with a case to put to Kenna for her to stay. A big undertaking considering all that I've done to her to push her away, keen for time to pass as soon as possible so we'd part company. Not to mention, my desire to be on my own.

Make up your damn mind, Theon.

Tunes weren't so easily changed, but I could feel mine changing with every passing second. Having decided on what to do next, there wasn't anything that would get in my way to change it. Not Brett, not Kenna, nothing. Having been in the army for as many years as I was before having to pack it in, when you committed your mind to something that was it. Very little would get in my way, not even an IED which luckily on the one time I happened to step upon one, didn't go off. A blessing in disguise.

"Unless, what?" Brett piped up, bringing me back into the moment.

"Let's just say that my mind is cooking up an idea right here, right now. An idea that'll get Ms Bouchard to stay with us a little longer."

Groaning, Brett ran a hand slowly down his face. "Tell me this is going to be nothing like the last idea you cooked up, because that was not a good idea. As much as you thought it was, it was as the French say, très terrible!"

"How the hell do you know French, dude?"

"When you want to please la dames, you'll do anything. Besides, don't try and side-track me, Theon old pal" He winked.

Now, it was my turn to run a hand down my face. "It was worth a shot."

It's true. The last time I did try and cook up an idea regarding a woman, it didn't end well. Let's just say, she thought I was someone else who Brett and I were trying to set her up with, and she got a little too up close and personal with me. Everyone of course got a huge laugh out of this when said friend of ours rocked up after I'd managed to get away, asking me where I'd been. Seeing no other way out of it, I explained it all. Much to everyone's enjoyment.

In hindsight, I should've said something to her and got myself out of there but…it was one of the few times when a woman had rendered me speechless. Well, how could she not when she had a hold of something I couldn't leave without?

Shaking my head, I pushed that memory far, far back into my thoughts.

"So, your plan to tell Kenna the truth?"

"Now that you brought up that time, I'm working on a new one." I muttered.

Good thing that I have the rest of the day to do it too… Hopefully Kenna will have a full and busy day where she's gone. It'll make one of us, anyway. There isn't a hope in hell that I'll achieve anything but a new plan, not while fishing is involved.

"It's just…"

Brett arched a brow at me, "Just, what?"

"We still haven't figured out what's up with Kenna. Something's buggin' her so much that whenever I'm around her, she looks at me like she wants to do me harm." I shuddered.

"Hm… Well, I suppose you have two plans to figure out. Surely you'll want to know what's up with her before you tell her the truth, right?"

"Yeah I guess so. Hey, since when did you get so smart?"

"Maybe it came with getting to know the ladies a little better." He wiggled his brows again.

Oh brother…

I was about to offer up another witty retort, when the line Brett had put into the ground for me, got a significant tug on its line.

"Holy carp!" Brett exclaimed, dashing for my line while I sat here, helpless without being able to do a thing. For once, I was glad.

"I don't know if there's carp in these waters, dude!" I smirked, biting my lip to hold back a laugh watching Brett struggle with the line.

Oh har-de-har, Mr. Comedian!" Brett said, groaning. "A little help here!"

Wiggling my hands which stuck out in either direction thanks to my casts, the laugh broke free which up until now, I'd managed to hold back.

"Now you want my help. How ironic!"

As my laughter subsided, two other men came from down the bank to help Brett, reeling in the biggest fish I've ever seen. Granted I've not been on as many fishing trips to this spot as some of the other guys, you'd have to be an idiot not to see how big that beast of a fish is. The bucket barely contained the thing once they managed to detach the hook from its mouth.

Regaining his feet, Brett ran an arm across his forehead. He looked like he'd just gone ten rounds in the rodeo arena, rather than wrestling a fish onto shore. It makes me wonder just how much work he really puts in, if he's tired out by a fish. I already knew the answer though. He always gives one-hundred and ten percent. This was just one crazy ass big fish that would tire anyone out, if they'd been the one to bring it onto dry land and into a bucket.

If anyone wasn't putting in their hundred-and-ten percent around here, it's me.

"You going to keep it, or throw it back?" I called out.

"Good question." Brett said, dusting his hands off on his pants. The two guys who'd helped him, were now walking back to their respective spots. "I might ask your old man if I can set it in the river behind the house. I can't bring myself to kill it, yet I don't want to just set it go. Not after the fight it put up."

I chuckled.

"I don't think it will interrupt any of its natural instincts or anything, by removing it from this water so…yeah. Looks like I did well."

"You? It was my rod!"

"Incorrect, buddy. You see, I set up the rod, the bait and even cast it out. Technically, all you did was sit here because we both know you don't like fishing one bit."

Aw hell.

"If you knew that already, then why drag me out here to sit around on my ass doing nothing?"

Brett shrugged, the smug smirk back on his face, "Simple. It wasn't my idea."

Immediately, my mind knew just whose idea it was, as a way of somehow getting back at me for God knows whatever I've done wrong.

"Kenna." Brett and I said in unison.

When I get back to my place later on, I'm going to find out exactly why she sent me here today, and I'm going to have two plans to go with it to boot.

Life with Ms Bouchard just reached a whole new level of interesting.

CHAPTER SEVENTEEN
Kenna

If I had stayed in that house with Theon for a moment longer, I don't think I would've been able to keep it in for much longer. Telling him I knew about his army past, at least in brief, and his PTSD nightmare were fighting to come forth from my lips. Getting out was a must and Brett was just the guy to help me do it.

While Theon was getting used to being awake after I'd woken him up this morning, I'd secretly and rather sneakily phoned Brett, informing him of my plan. It didn't take much convincing him to agree to my plan, as he too had been wanting to get Theon out and about a bit more. Though like me, he'd been unsure on just how to do it without protest from the man himself.

After Brett had arrived, I made my escape.

Once in my car, I phoned Jess to see if she was free. Luckily for me, she was. In fact, both she and Leary had the day off. It was rare for all three of us to have the day off on the same day, so while driving from the ranch, plans were made.

We'd agreed to meet at Jess' place, with Leary bringing snacks and myself bringing my DVD collection I always carried around in my car, and have ourselves a good old-fashioned girls' movie day. It's been far too long since we'd done one, and since none of us felt like going out, that's what we'd be doing today.

Thankfully, it didn't take me long to reach Jess' place. A nice little home on the outskirts of downtown Austin. Newly built along with a row of others within the last five or so years, they were built to retain the classic, traditional home exterior, while being more eco-friendly and efficient on the inside.

Jess did well to have this place all to herself, considering the wages we were both on. I was just about able to afford my apartment on it. Though I'm sure one of Jess' former relatives left her enough money to get a place in their will, not that I'd ever ask.

Stepping out and making sure I had my DVD collection safely stowed in my bag, I locked my car and quickly made my way up the path to Jess' porch.

The door to the house opened before I even made it up the path to knock on the door. Jess' beaming face smiled back at me.

"Hey! Aren't you a sight for sore eyes?" Jess laughed, pulling me in for a hug.

"Hey yourself! It's been a hot minute for sure."

Jess looked like she'd been through the mill and back. Obviously a tiring day at work yesterday, but we'll get there in a minute.

"Come on in! Leary's running a bit behind with the snacks. Not that we're running to a time, or anything. I'd like to think she's run into a nice guy at the store and they've gotten to talking a little bit."

I laughed, "Hopefully. She deserves a bit of attention."

Jess groaned, closing the door behind me after gesturing me in. "Urgh, don't we all?"

"What happened to the guy you were supposed to be going out on a date with?" I asked cautiously, not wanting to rock the boat if she wasn't ready to talk about it.

"Grayson? It didn't work out. I got there slightly before time so I could order my drink when it turned out, so did he. Only, he wasn't unoccupied when I got to the bar."

I sat down on her couch, arching a brow curiously. "He was with someone?"

"Not quite. I overheard him talking to his bit of stuff on the side... about his wife. Turns out I was on a date with a man who was already married, had a mistress on the side and kept them both from one another, and me from them."

Jesus Christ on a bike!

Pretty sure my jaw is just about on the floor from this unfortunate piece of news. "I...uh...wow."

"That's a lot more than what I had to say to him. Wow wouldn't have even come close." Jess said, plopping herself down next to me with a loud, saddening sigh.

"I can imagine. So, what happened after you told him what for?"

Jess shrugged, "Not a lot. He wasn't all too concerned that I said I was leaving. I guess having two women already on the go would do that to a man."

Not for me and...

I couldn't even dream of committing myself to someone, to then only go and play elsewhere, so to speak. When I committed to someone, it was to them and them alone. No matter what the circumstance and let's just say, the circumstance for me and my last boyfriend was an exceptionally risky one. Mostly on his part.

Tears threatened to make themselves known, but I forced them back. I didn't come here to cry. I could do that on my own time. Thoughts of a life gone by always resulted in ugly crying, to which I wouldn't ever do not even in the company of Jess or Leary.

They've seen me cry before, but not ugly cry. I had some pride and dignity left, even if it is on a microscopic scale. And I'll hold onto that for all it's worth.

"I guess we'll get all of this out in the open and then some, when Leary arrives." Jess piped up, bringing me back into the moment.

A loud, repetitive knock at the door came at just the right moment.

"Speak of the devil." I laughed, "Don't get up, I'll let her in."

When I got to the front door and opened it, there was Leary in all her glory carrying what looked like four, super heavy shopping bags laden with unhealthy, tasty goodies.

"Here, let me!"

I bent down and took two bags off of her, instantly lightening her load. "Phew! Thanks!"

Jess came and took the bags from my hands, taking them into the kitchen as Leary followed suit. I closed the door and joined them in the kitchen, leaning against the door jamb.

"Need any help with anything?"

Leary rounded on me, waving a hand dismissively, "No, not a thing. Go and sit yourself down. I'll bring in our drinks in a moment."

Reluctantly, I turned my back and headed back to my spot on the couch. Jess and Leary joined me a few moments later, drinks in hand.

"Sparkling flavoured water." Jess said, sitting beside me. "Until it's after midday, anyway." She winked, making me laugh.

What I would do without these girls, I do not know.

Though I should remember I can't drink too much when we eventually hit the harder stuff, as I have to go back to Theon's tonight. As much as my head is screaming for me to beg to stay the night with one of them.

"So!" Jess clapped her hands together, "Down to business."

Huh? Business? Oh no, I don't have a good feeling about this...

Usually when 'business' was mentioned, one of us was up for a spill session. Meaning, spilling everything on our minds until we were dried-up, relieved husks. Looks like I'm the one lined up for the chopping block.

"Business?" I asked gingerly.

Leary nodded, plopping down into the oversized 'friends'-style lazy armchair. "Tell us all about your time with the crusty cowboy of yours."

Ah, there it is. I had a feeling this would come up sooner or later. Looks like it was sooner.

I don't know what I expected when arriving, after making the call to these ladies. The subject couldn't not come up, as they knew I'd have more than a hoard's worth of non-confidential gossip to tell.

Maybe getting it all of my chest at once right here and now, would be best.

"Okay, I'll talk. But let's just get one thing straight..." I began. "He's not my cowboy. He's my patient."

Both girls held their hands up in surrender, smirks plastered across their faces. I knew they knew that I was withholding some truth there, but that could wait till hopefully, never.

"Well, you know how I got roped into it all. That's not new news. Not long after getting back to his folks' place, he wanted to move back into his own."

"Uh-oh." Leary piped up, listening intently while diving into a bag of pretzels.

As soon as the next part was out, there was no going back.

"Anyway, one day Theon's friend Brett stopped by the ranch. He'd come by to drop off a care package from Theon's mom, after which we'd got to talking. As he was about to leave, he dropped the bombshell." I paused, swallowing before continuing. "Theon was in the military..."

I didn't need to look up to know what the expressions on their faces were. I knew. Shock, pure shock, sympathy and somehow, understanding, radiated from both of them.

They knew my story. How could they not? They were there for me when my world collapsed. Without them, I wouldn't have got through that time in one piece.

I'm still picking up the pieces…

"Oh Kenna, honey…" Jess sighed.

I shrugged, "I can't be mad at Brett for it. He doesn't know what happened. Neither of them do. It's just…it brought everything back for a moment."

And then some.

I continued.

"After that, it was as if a switch had been flipped inside of me. Everything ran through my head at double speed. Why didn't I know this sooner? How could I have missed this? Was this on his paperwork and if so, why didn't I know about it?" I sighed. "Being around Theon and knowing what he must've been through…well, you know how my mind and imagination is. Wild doesn't even cover it."

They both nodded.

"On top of everything that was going through my mind, I felt…guilty."

"Guilty? Why?" Leary asked.

"I have no right to be mad at Theon or Brett for not letting me know this. After all, I'm just Theon's at-home nurse. I mean, I know I should've known from a professional standpoint but as me, I had no right to know. They weren't obligated to tell me yet, I was still mad when Brett blurted it out."

Still mourning too. After all this time.

I had no reason to tell either Theon or Brett about my former military men. My ex-boyfriends. My lovers. As me, Kenna, or as me the nurse. Besides, I wouldn't be staying with Theon for much longer, once his casts come off and he's able to live life more independently without home help. It wouldn't serve a purpose, telling them.

"Kenna, you have every right to feel the way you do." Jess said, touching her hand to my arm. "You're human and even if they don't know what happened, and might not ever know, you can't help the way you feel. Even if it means being a bit frosty with Theon."

"You're right. I know you are, but I still feel guilty. His mom came to me in that café because she wanted to help her son. I accepted her request, her plea, in the hopes that I could help her son even though I didn't know who he was."

Leary popped another pretzel into her mouth, "Then why don't you tell them? If it's bothering you that much, why not get it off your chest? Leaving or not, it might help you feel better."

Even though I'd been preaching about how my leaving soon would make it pointless to explain to them, she had a point. After spending hours beating myself up about anything and everything from not knowing about his military past, to dealing with the memories of times not too long ago, I'd only kept focused on the negative. Thinking only about why it wasn't a good idea, instead of all the possibilities of how it could be one. Once my head and my thoughts were so wrapped up within themselves, things tended to spiral and spiral fast. Which is exactly what had happened after Brett's bombshell.

And I've been taking it out on Theon ever since...

Mentally, I was kicking myself for my foolish, unprofessional, unlike myself behaviour.

Thankfully, I knew what I had to do to fix it.

The room had long since fallen into silence while I'd been thinking. Jess and Leary looked at me with expectant expressions, waiting to hear what I had to say next after consulting with my own thoughts.

Putting my drink down on the coffee table, I turned to face them both. "I've got an idea."

"Ooh, I'm all ears!" Jess beamed, eager as the fire building inside me was.

"With the next coming days, Theon's casts are due to come off. At that point, he'll be assessed for his progression or lack thereof. If he's improved enough to a suitable standard, I won't need to be his home nurse anymore."

"And if he hasn't improved?" Leary asked.

I smiled, having already thought of the answer. "Then I'll get to stay around him a bit more. It'll give me more time to think of how to explain it all to him for when I'm not his nurse. You see, when I'm not on the job, I can be personal."

Jess rubbed her temple, trying to figure it all out. "Let me get this straight. Your plan is to either way his assessment goes, is to wait until you're no longer his nurse, then tell him the truth?"

I nodded.

"Right. That way, I don't have to worry about being unprofessional or potentially, losing my job."

"Why would you lose your job?" Said Leary.

"I can't get personal with a patient. About my life or theirs, in any sort of way."

At this, Jess' eyebrows raised dramatically.

"Oh? That so?"

Without having to say it aloud, I knew exactly what she was thinking. She, and possibly Leary too, must've cottoned on by now as to my hidden... feelings, for Theon. Yet another reason why I had to wait things out before I could even begin to tell him about them. Lord knows how he'd react to his nurse coming onto him. Though I had a pretty good idea, what with my imagination.

"Yes, it's exactly as you're thinking. Both of you." I smirked.

Time had passed, albeit at a slow crawl sometimes, and not one man had captured my attention or pulled me out of my sorrow-filled thoughts. Until Theon. They knew this was a huge deal for me to even consider being with another man, let alone confess my feelings to the self-same man in question.

A second later, Leary leapt up out of her chair, pretzels falling to and on the floor, tackling me where I sat in a big bear hug.

"I'm so happy for you! It's about time!"

I had my doubts about that. Personally, I don't believe you ever stop grieving for someone you lost but instead, it's only a matter of time before you're ready to let someone else into your heart. Alongside the memory of your former love.

Right now, at this moment, I wasn't fully convinced.

After losing my former boyfriend the way I did, he occupied my thoughts more so than not, and I was finding it hard to think about someone else when they came along. Hence why I'm also being hesitant with Theon. Thoughts of a former life keep on creeping in when I'd worked so hard to contain the spiralling grief and negative thoughts, preventing me from opening my heart again.

However, Theon was the first to make my head turn towards him without looking back into the many doubts, anxieties or bad memories which held me back before.

But, would it last?

Part of me was worried that this was just a temporary infatuation, brought on by the closeness of working around and on Theon. The other part? Well, that part felt guilty. That though, was a story for another day.

Besides, we didn't gather here today to gab about me constantly.

Tucking my legs back under me, I pointed my drink towards Jess and Leary, who had regained her place in the armchair.

"Enough about me. You both agreed to meet so we can have a movie marathon. Unless…" I smirked, "You want to talk about what's going on in both of your lives since I saw you both last."

My friends exchanged a worried look between one another, before surprising me with an answer I didn't expect.

Leary shrugged, "I'm okay to talk if you are, Jess."

I looked at Jess, "It's fine with me." She said, sipping her drink with a twinkle in her eye, knowing my plan of trapping them both hadn't worked.

Damn.

Nothing could escape their minds. Not when I'm so bad at it, for starters.

"So, who wants to go first?" I asked.

With a soft sigh, Leary spoke up first. "I might as well, since y'all already know some of what's happened to me recently. You know, with the scare and all."

How could I forget? It wasn't all that long ago, and both Jess and I felt it for her. Even though we weren't going through it ourselves. Thankfully much like Leary, Jess and I attend regular screenings ourselves. Just to be on the safe side as after all, better safe than sorry.

Launching into what had happened to her since the last time we met up, Leary's voice grew lighter with every word as if a weight was slowly coming off her petite shoulders. With very few people around to confide in, I could tell this was good for her. To get it all off her mind in one go. Jess, on the other hand, is much like myself. Telling one another on a frequent basis so we're not at risk of running ourselves out of emotional and mental steam.

Somehow, Leary evaded that and I both applauded and admired her for it.

Eventually after some time had passed, both Jess and Leary had filled me in on everything that I had missed while I was up at the Big Boo-T ranch, and with Theon. It was good to hear in person everything that's happened, as there was only so much that could be said over text. Some things you just had to hear in person.

Shortly after the talks had finished, the heavier talks, we thankfully moved on to the whole reason for us meeting up tonight. The movie marathon! I'd brought in the DVD collection from my car, and we'd each chosen two movies each to watch. Luckily for them, I also carried some of their taste in movies too, just to be kind.

Thank goodness I'm more of a traditionalist. I hate not owning physical copies of things.

Digital is great for some things, but not everything.

Drinks were refilled, snacks were opened, and the three of us somehow banded together just right on the couch, snuggling together as the first of our six movies played. Up first was a movie of my choice, since I'd called the meeting and it was my collection. The titles to Fifty Shades of Grey appeared on screen, as did a wide smile on my face.

Christian Grey, here I come.

CHAPTER EIGHTEEN
Theon

"Ready?" Kenna asked, wheeling me into the hospital via the main entrance. The time had finally come for me to get these infuriating casts off, and I was more than willing to help them do it. Even though that wouldn't be physically possible, I'd give it a go anyway. It was necessary to have them on to help the broken parts of me heal, but damn was I ready to be less restricted again.

I know it'll be a lot easier on Kenna, that's for sure.

Things had once more changed between the two of us and this time, for the good. Whatever had gone down at her movie marathon night the other night with her friends, she's mellowed out. Is more friendly and receptive. There's still a bit of an...edge, to her, though. I can't quite figure it out. Still, something is better than nothing.

Perhaps this change in behaviour will make her more open to accepting an extension to her caring for me. A guy can hope.

Rolling through the main entrance, I cast my mind back to when she came back from the self-same movie marathon. Brett had just dropped me back home and after setting me up for the night, went on his way back to his ranch.

* * *

As it turned out, fishing wasn't as bad as I remembered it to be. Maybe it had to do with the fact that all I had to do was sit and watch Brett and the others fish, and fall half a dozen times. That was the cheapest day's entertainment I've ever had in a hot minute.

That said, after being asked what I wanted to do when we got back, my first answer was to be put straight into my room on my bed. I wasn't much of a movie man, unless I was in company. Tonight I just wanted to be comfortable so when we got back, Brett kindly helped me up to my room and that's where I've been for the last few hours.

Or at least, that's what it felt like. Time did always fly by when I was relaxing doing literally nothing at all.

Outside, a vehicle's low engine rumble caused me to open my eyes. It wasn't overly loud or disturbing, but I'd know that engine anywhere and the person it contained inside. Kenna.

"Huh. She's home early." I muttered.

With Kenna arranging my day out with Brett, I never got a chance to ask her what time she'd be back before she booked it out of here this morning. Yes, she wasn't accountable to me. Especially if she wasn't technically on the clock, but it's the sort of thing you say to someone else living in the same house as you. Isn't it? It's not something I'd know having only lived with my folks.

Well, there was Brett. I suppose he counted.

The front door opened and swiftly closed, confirming that the engine was in fact Kenna returning home. I half expected her to head to the kitchen to get a drink or something but instead, they were heading up the stairs, getting louder as she came closer.

Her room wasn't too far from mine, so why did the footsteps stop sooner?

I soon got my answer.

Two short rasps sounded at my bedroom door, with it opening shortly after. "Theon?" Kenna's voice drifted inside. "Are you awake?"

Turning my head to look at the clock on my nightstand, I could see that it was only 8:30pm. Not a time I'd be asleep as even with medication.

"Yes." I answered. "Come in."

With my invitation, she slipped inside my room.

My eyes roamed her body from head to toe as she closed the door behind her. Good God. There wasn't much time to notice what she'd dressed in this morning, but holy cow! How someone could make jeans and a plaid shirt look good, I don't know. Kenna though, did it and made it beautiful. Thank God it was only a girls' day today.

Looking back up to her face, I recomposed myself. She'd come in here for a reason, and I was more than curious to find out as to what it was.

"I bet you're wondering what I'm doing here."

I'm also wondering if you're a mind reader.

I nodded at her, "Yes. I am. What brings you by?"

Kenna walked closer until her knees met the end of my bed. She played with her hands where I couldn't quite see, almost as if she was nervous to talk to me. I couldn't think why, I haven't seen her all day.

"I know you're not one for late night chats, so I'll keep this brief." She paused, collecting herself. "You might have noticed that lately I've…well, not been me, around you. I just want to apologise for being short and snappy. It's not me and I wanted to say sorry."

Using my left hand as best as I could within its confines, I patted the vacant space beside me. "Come sit."

Surprisingly, she took my cue and joined me on the bed, sitting in the vacant space.

"Listen, I did notice something was up with you. I figured you'd tell me when you were ready or if you wanted to. Still, it wasn't my place to ever ask. Now…" I shifted as best as I could into a new position. "I wasn't exactly nice to you in the beginning, was I?"

Kenna's face softened as she laughed, shaking her head. "No, you weren't. You were more bear than man. I'm pretty sure."

I laughed too. She was right, after all. Mind you, a bear would've probably been easier to deal with regarding medication. Just shoot a dart at it and it's done. Might have been easier to do the same with me, come to think of it. Perhaps I'm more bear than I thought…

"I'm sorry, Kenna. For everything I've put you through until now. Truly." I said.

Kenna did a double take at my words, looking as dumbfounded as I felt inside that they slipped free from my lips. In truth, I don't think either of us expected to be apologising to one another tonight. More so myself, as I'm not really one to admit my mistakes. Let alone apologise. The old me would, I'm sure. The new me is ...well, prideful. Especially if I was wrong.

A second later, a small, soft hand touched mine. My eyes looked up to meet Kenna's as she spoke, "Apology accepted."

I swallowed, "Y-yes. You too. Even though you have nothing to be sorry about."

She gently nudged my side, rolling her eyes heavenward, "Jesus O'Donoghue, can't you just accept an apology without being stubborn?"

"Where's the fun in that? I wouldn't be me if I wasn't somewhat stubborn."

"True, true."

We shared another laugh, which helped ease any remaining awkwardness between us. It certainly made me feel better, I don't know about Kenna. By the looks of her face, it seemed it worked on her also. Which I'm most glad about.

It was only after our combined laughter ended, that I realised Kenna still had her hand over mine. Though now it was slightly wrapped around my exposed fingers. As much as I'd love to have it there all night, I needed to spare her cheeks which right now, were blushing a deep crimson.

Gently, I cleared my throat. "May I have my hand back?"

"Hm?"

It took her a moment to realise what I meant. Looking down at our hands, she sprung back as if my touch was hotter than the sun. "Oh! Sorry!"

I couldn't hold back the smirk fighting to break free, she was just too adorable when flustered. Which wasn't often. Part of me was proud that so far, I was the only one who has been able to do this to her and if I had my way, I'd continue to be. If I decided to pursue something with her.

Soon, I'd know my answer.

"Anyway, I better leave you to your thoughts. I've intruded and made a fool of myself for long enough already." Kenna said, sliding off the bed and straightening out her clothes.

"Never."

She half-turned back towards me, a smile tugging on the corner of her mouth. "Smooth-talker."

"If only you knew." I muttered.

There was so much more I wish I could say to her, do with her. Holding back while being restricted has never made me feel more confused and infuriated in my whole life. Just when I wanted to take a risk and let old demons lie dormant, they would wrestle my remaining sane thoughts. Flooding into every corner of my mind as to why I shouldn't. One of these days, one of us would win. And I was determined it was going to be me.

"What was that?" She asked, turning to face me.

I shook my head. "Nothing. Thank you uh…thanks for stopping by tonight. I hope you had a good day with your friends."

Kenna smiled, nodding her head, "I did, thanks. It was good to see them again." She rocked back and forth on her feet. "How was fishing with Brett?"

Now it was my turn to groan, "As entertaining as watching paint dry. Whose idea was that, by the way? Yours or his?"

"Oh, that was all mine!" she grinned, not bothering to attempt even dismissing the fact. "To be honest, it was kind of a low ball on my part. I organised it knowing you'd detest every moment of it."

Usually this sort of thing would get me all riled up. Not now. Not tonight. If anything, I'm amused at her tenacity and boldness in admitting it. Plus since Brett fessed up that it was Kenna's idea, I was more than keen to hear it come from her mouth. Willingly or otherwise.

Just this once, I'll let this slide.

"Well played, Miss Bouchard. You got me good as for the most part, it was as boring as I remembered it to be."

At this, Kenna winked and made her way to the door, pausing and turning back with her hand on the knob. "I aim to please, my dear patient."

Oh sweet Jesus.

She continued before I could comment, "Anyway, I really must leave you be. Unless you need something?"

I shook my head, "No, I'm good. Thank you. Brett saw to me before he left."

"Alrighty then, sounds good!"

Not as good as something else I'd rather be suggesting to you right now, though that will have to wait till another time.

"Yes. Goodnight, Kenna. Sleep well."

"Goodnight, Theon. You too…" Kenna said, slipping out the door a moment later. I could tell she wanted to say more but like me, she was holding back.

There would be another time and hopefully another day for us to get whatever was on our tongues, out there. Well, there will be if she accepts the extension. Which I plan to put to her when I get my casts off in a few days' time.

For now, both of us for once in what has felt like forever, can go to bed content. Mostly. She was still able to move around into her go-to sleeping position, whatever that was. How I was looking forward to the day where I'll be on my front again. It'll be a long day coming that I'll ever consider sleeping on my back. Unless…

Nope! Don't even go there boy!

Sighing, I closed my eyes and settled in for the night as best as I could. Pushing thoughts of the temptress far, far away.

Just before I felt myself drifting off to sleep, I swore I could feel something tickle my foot.

Wait…what?

* * *

A ding sound pulled me out of my thoughts. In the time I'd spent thinking about that night, we'd cleared the main entrance and the lobby. Kenna was now wheeling me out of the elevator onto an unknown floor.

"What happens now?" I asked, curious.

Turning the wheelchair and us right, she brought us into a unit of the hospital I haven't been into before.

"A doctor will take your vitals before I take you down to get your casts off. How are you feeling?"

I could tell she was nervous to ask me that last part but in truth, I'm less negative about the whole thing than when I was first casted six weeks ago. Between the talks with Kenna about what I could potentially do when out of the casts, and the treatments I could seek depending on the results, I would almost go so far as to say I'm optimistic.

Almost.

A few nights ago, I swore I felt something tickling my foot. Or maybe it was my foot feeling the sheets over my body? I wasn't sure. The feeling was alien to me and without tests, I can't confirm or deny what I felt. It just gave me the spark back inside of me to hope that maybe, just maybe, it was something telling me I could someday walk again.

God willing.

"Good. I'm feeling good." For now, I'll leave it at that. If all goes well, she'll be the first to know the truth to my thoughts.

After getting my vitals checked and overall health assessed, it was time to head down to the room where my casts would be taken off. X-rays were scheduled for afterwards, which the doctor said would check the healing of my broken bones which after six weeks, should be well on their way to being fully healed. If they weren't already.

Kenna had been outside the room during my assessment. Or so I thought.

"Where did you go off to just now?" I asked as she pushed me back down the hall towards the elevators we'd come up in.

"I just quickly dashed up to the ER unit. You know, just to see how things are. I'm not usually away from it for this long."

I asked, "Do you miss it?"

There was a longer than expected pause before she continued. We'd arrived and were in the elevator going down before she did.

"I'm…not sure. I miss the feeling of helping more than one person. No offence."

I shrugged, "None taken. Go on, please."

"Well long story short, I don't miss some of the things I thought I would while at the same time, missing the things I wouldn't. It took a lot of hard effort and hours to work towards my degree and position as an ER nurse, I just guess I wasn't ever expecting to be away from the unit once I had it."

That, I can understand.

There was so much that missed about being out and about in the field. Leading men and women to help those who couldn't help themselves. When you're born to do something and it's all you've ever known or wanted to do, a sense of loss lingered within you that really would never go away.

It was hard to deal with at times, so I could understand her state of mixed feelings.

"I understand."

Soon, we'd long-abandoned the elevator and were at the unit where my casts would be taken off. There weren't many people here, so I assume I'd be called in pretty quickly. Only a few kids with their parents, and the odd adult were dotted around the room, all with varying casts on waiting to come off.

Kenna and I chatted quietly in the meantime, passing various comments about those also in the waiting room by guessing how they'd hurt themselves. Not that we'd ever find out, but it was a fun pastime.

"Theon O'Donoghue?" a voice from across the room called out.

"Here." I replied, feeling like I was back in elementary school, answering my name in the homeroom.

Thank God those days are behind me...

Swiftly like nothing on earth, Kenna rose to her feet and briskly wheeled me into the room. Its walls were as starched white as the waiting rooms were, only this time it had a few child-friendly posters and stickers on them. Just to make it friendlier and less frightening to the kids who might be nervous about cast removal.

If any kids were like me when I was younger, they'd appreciate the distraction from worrying your arm might be cut off when the cast was being removed. Those damn scissors were bigger than necessary and scary to boot. Who wouldn't be afraid of them coming at you, cutting ferociously?

Kenna put the break on the wheelchair and plopped herself down in the seat against the wall. "Still okay?"

I nodded. "Yep. Still good. How long does it take?"

"For normal cast removal? Minutes."

"What about me?"

"An hour? It depends. The doctor will have to go carefully as we've yet to x-ray you."

Great. Fabulous, even. I knew today would be a long day, though I didn't imagine it would take all that long to hack off these casts with those cruel cutters.

Any protest or comment I was about to make, was halted by the arrival of the doctor who would be taking the self-same casts off. He looked to be around his late thirties, early forties, with a kindly face and an air of experience about him.

"Good morning, Mr O'Donoghue, Nurse Bouchard." He nodded to us. "I'm Doctor Zolotov. How are we today?"

Fantastic...

"Great. Can't wait to be free, if you know what I mean."

136

He chuckled, "That I do. So, shall we get down to it then? No waiting around?"

"That's the idea."

"Alright then!" he clapped his hands together. Walking around the large table/bed in the middle of the room, he wheeled a smaller table around to its side. On it laid something I've never seen before. "Nurse, will you help Mr O'Donoghue up onto the table, please?"

Without missing a beat, she leapt into action by doing just that. Albeit with a tiny bit of a struggle.

Situated on the table, I eyed up the tool I couldn't quite see fully before. My eyes widened in horror at the sight before them. "W-what's that?"

Doctor Zolotov looked up at me, knowing exactly what I was referring to. "That's to take your casts off."

"What happened to the scissors?"

Behind me, I could hear Kenna low-level chuckling as the doctor answered me.

"Times have changed since you probably had a cast off last, Mr O'Donoghue. This is how we do things now. Much easier and less messy."

I swallowed.

The scissors were one thing but this? This torture device, which resembled a handyman's DIY tool cutter, was a whole new level of hell-to-the-no.

Yep, I'm having a stiff one when we get out of here. No matter what Kenna says. I'm going to need it.

CHAPTER NINETEEN
Theon

The hour spent getting my casts removed couldn't go by fast enough. If I thought the scissors were bad as a child, this was worse. Way, way worse. This time around, it felt like I was in a horror movie and quite literally, couldn't move a muscle.

My eyes never opened for one moment and if Kenna's hand wasn't broken by the time we were finished, with my grip, I'll be amazed. Which is exactly how I found myself now, being wheeled down on a portable bed to the x-ray department.

Not to mention the noise of the damn tool Doctor Zolotov used brought me right back to one memory in particular, making my forehead profusely sweat. Due to the fact I was holding it in, keeping it from Kenna. I'm sure if I was to get it off my chest, I would've felt better. Now just wasn't the time to open up to her about it.

Once when we were on a mission in an area I still can't bring myself to even think about, we came across two young children. They'd been left behind as a result of a sudden ruckus in the area, and had obviously ran away from the danger while getting lost in the process. Unfortunately, they had taken shelter in an abandoned home which as a result of a bomb drop, had collapsed on top of them.

Thankfully, we always had a selection of tools on hand should we ever have needed them. Including a saw that could cut through large stones and rubble, clearing small areas which helped free people from tight spaces. Which is exactly what we tried to do for those precious, innocent children.

Tried. Oh how we tried.

Not long after cutting away at the rubble which once was what we assumed was the doorway, shifting rocks and piling them to one side, we found the remains of the children. Huddled in one another's arms, a girl around eight years old, held her baby brother close in what sadly were their final moments.

Our hearts collectively dropped at the sight. All hope rested on a small chance that they'd managed to find a pocket of space and air where they could lay safe until we were able to get to them. Sadly, this was not the case. No matter how much we all wished it to be different. The sight before us was enough to put the strongest man off his rations. It was simply devastating and horrific.

The sound of the saw was one I would never, ever forget. Failing to get to those children in time was one of my biggest failings, no matter how many times I was told it wasn't. I was free of my trappings, but those children… well it doesn't even bear thinking about. At least when I was on the ranch, I could disguise a bubbling PTSD attack. Here, not so much.

Down in the x-ray department, they were ready for us when we arrived. Kenna and another hospital staff member, the radiologist most likely, helped her bring me in under the huge x-ray machine in the centre of the room.

Kenna stopped beside me, "I have to step outside until you're done. Okay?"

I nodded, "Yeah. See you on the other side."

I was rewarded with her signature smile, followed by a view of her retreating back and...oh sweet lord above, something else.

Not now, O'Donoghue.

Soon after Kenna left with the door closing behind her, the radiologist went to work. Various x-rays were taken up and down my body, corresponding to the various injuries caused by the fall from Spirit, the now named horse who threw me. Kenna had named her as such as after meeting the said beast for the first time, she deemed it to have spirit.

I wasn't going to argue with its name. It was appropriate. Though it would be a cold day in hell before I had enough spirit to ride her again.

All of a sudden, a thought dawned on me. Hard.

By taking x-rays of pretty much all of my body that means...oh god. That means they're going to check up on my pre-existing injury too. I swallowed at the thought. Bringing it up would raise questions as to how I got it, and I wasn't going to divulge that piece of information to Kenna just yet.

I'd obtained shrapnel would to my back after carrying Drayce out of the field. Somewhere close to us, an IED went off and somehow, I ended up with a gash across my back. I was damned lucky that Kenna hadn't seen it yet. Which was a miracle in itself, considering she did practically everything from dressing me, to washing me and then some. I always managed to keep my back as flat as possible, with what little movement I still had and made sure she was always in front of me.

Someday, she would find out about it but by then, I would be ready to tell her the story of it and along with it, about Drayce.

I sent up a quick prayer that I would be lucky today, too. Hopefully, it will be heard.

"Alright, Mr O'Donoghue. You're all done." The radiologist said, coming around the protective 'barrier' on the other side of the room.

During the whole thing, I kept painfully still. Not that I had much choice to do otherwise. Ever since my casts had come off not too long ago, the temptation was there to try and move the parts of me that were able to. Minus one appendage, of course. He was as silent as the night right now and would remain so.

The only reason I have resisted the temptation up until now, was the underlying fear I've been holding onto these last six weeks. Even if I didn't say it aloud, it was there. If at the end of the six weeks when the casts came off, nothing worked that I was hoping it would, I knew how I'd feel. In all honesty, I knew exactly what I was doing and why. Putting off the truth and pushing back the reality of my situation.

Yet, the small inkling of hope was there that my legs would move again. Despite the truth staring at me in the face.

The truth always hurts the most.

For now, still is where I'd remain.

"Great. Thanks." I replied.

In a day full of going back and forth, I was once more wheeled out to Kenna who was waiting for me in the corridor. Next, physical therapy.

A short trip later, that's exactly where we were.

Kenna could stay with me for this next bit, which was a blessing. Without saying so, I knew I needed her here for at least moral support. Afterwards, we'd head up to the doctor who saw me when I first came in six weeks ago. He would tell me from all the tests today, what my overall prognosis would now be.

The PT room looked much like the old sports hall from my middle school. 70's style wood panelling lined the walls and the floors were almost the same. If I was in a better mood, I would almost joke as if to say this was more of a sauna room, than therapy. But I didn't.

Pulling the wheelchair I'd been transferred to before leaving the x-ray unit to a stop, Kenna crouched in front of me, her right hand gripping the armrest. "You doing okay?"

"As okay as can be expected." I said, offering up the honest truth.

"Personally, I think you're doing great."

I arched a brow, "Yeah? You're not just saying that because you're my nurse?"

Even though part of me wishes you were more than that.

She stared at me with a deadpan, nonplussed expression. "I'm going to pretend I didn't hear that. You know damn well that it isn't the case, mister."

Well damn if that didn't make me feel like I was being scolded by my mother.

Before I could apologise, the physical therapist who'd been working with a young boy when we arrived, made his way over to us with a bright smile on his face. Clapping his hands together, he stopped in front of us.

"Theon O'Donoghue, I presume?"

I nodded, "Yes, that's me."

"Nice to meet you." he turned to Kenna next, "You too, Nurse Bouchard. Long-time no see."

Sweet holy moly of somewhere north-poley. Does everyone know her?

Reaching her hand out, Kenna shook his hand. "Good to see you Frank. It's been a while. Ready to start work with Theon here?"

She clearly detected the rising tension with me at Frank's boldness towards her, moving the conversation along to what we were both here for today.

"Ready and willing! Shall we begin?" this time, Frank was addressing me. His patient.

Choosing not to reply with a snarky comment, I simply nodded. I was more than ready, for the most part.

"Great! Okay, from what I've read on your charts, you've got quite the resume of areas we'll be working on today and on any necessary follow-up appointments. Let's start on your upper half, and work from there."

Which is exactly what we did. All three of us.

Going through the list of things to test on my torso, arms and neck areas, Frank was surprisingly professional and thorough in his examinations. Much to my relief, I was able to move my arms, hands and shoulder joints with little to no difficulty. Only a few twinges here and there let me know I was still somewhat healing. Nothing that a few occasional painkillers couldn't deal with.

My chest and collarbone too only protested with a dull, mild-like pain. From breaking them or fracturing them in the past, I knew they'd heal up pretty quick and with the right care, wouldn't give me much trouble. Next however, was the real test.

My legs.

The problem was not even anywhere within my legs, but my spine. Having landed right on the wrong spot after coming off the horse was what caused the loss of use. Or so I'd been told.

Frank had moved away for a moment to the doors to the PT hall, after someone had called him over. I was too distracted by my own thoughts to notice that Kenna had once more crouched down in front of me. Only when she started to speak did I look at her, with my eyes meeting hers.

"Penny for your thoughts?" she asked.

For you, I'd charge nothing.

Looking over to see that Frank was still speaking to the person who had called him over, I turned back to Kenna and replied.

"I'm…tense. Nervous, sort of." I balled my hands in and out of a fist, "What if…what if I…" I trailed off, unable to complete the sentence.

Tingling radiated through my hand and up my arm as Kenna placed her hand over mine. It was a familiar sensation whenever our skin met, one I wouldn't forget in a hurry. "Theon, listen to me." Her voice was soft. "I've been with you long enough to get a rough idea of who you are and what you're like, without diving into unprofessional and personal territory. You're not a man to give up even when it seems like you're beaten. I may not know much about you from before your mother asked me to take you on as a patient, but I don't need to. The man you are now and the man I know now is more than enough to work through anything that comes his way no matter how bad the card is from the deck of life."

I opened my mouth to reply, but she held up a hand, cutting off any words about to come out.

"Today doesn't mark the start of the end. Not at all. I can tell that's what has been worrying you in that today is judgement day in your mind. It's not. Today is the day when we can literally figure out the next step to take. Question is, are you willing to take the next step, even if it's not one you imagined?" she asked, watching me for my answer.

She was right, again. Every word she uttered is true.

Fear did often get the better of me sometimes, especially when I'm down and out of luck. Still, that meant that there was some luck left over. I wasn't down and out for good. At least not get. I had my answer.

"Yes. Yes, I'm ready."

Hopefully I sounded as determined as I felt inside, because the last thing I wanted was to sound uncertain.

"That's my man."

Huh?

I arched a brow at her, "What was that?"

There was no need for her to repeat it. I'd heard exactly what she'd said. She called me her man. Now I just wanted to know exactly what she meant by that. No way was that a simple slip of the tongue. I knew Kenna. When she said something she meant it with both her head and her heart.

Her cheeks went that adorable crimson again, as she tried to come up with an answer to my question.

"N-nothing!" she cleared her throat, standing up to her full 5"9 height. "I mean, nothing."

"Oh really?" my lip twitched. "Because it sounded like you called me your man just then. Or are my ears in need of testing too?"

Go on, take the bait.

She never did. Much to my chagrin. Ever composed, she simply dismissed my challenge as if I'd never said it.

Unfortunately, neither of us got to spar with one another, as Frank walked briskly back over to us. Done with his conversation with whoever had taken him away in the first place. Putting his hands on his thighs when on his knees in front of me, he exhaled. "Sorry about that folks. Someone had to cancel their session last minute." He looked up at me, "Ready to continue?"

With one last quick look at Kenna, I nodded. "Ready."

My shoes had been taken off when we'd arrived earlier before we got out of Kenna's car. I wouldn't be needing them once we got here, so we just removed them before entering the hospital.

Frank went straight in for the kill. I watched as his hands moved towards my left foot, my heart beating faster with each passing second. I closed my eyes, eagerly awaiting the moment of sensory contact.

"Theon? Can you feel that?"

Huh? Hasn't he grabbed my foot yet?

Cracking open my eyes, I looked down. Oh.

I was seeing exactly what my darkest fear had been telling me inside all along. Frank did in fact have my foot in his hand, gently manipulating it and the joint. Only, I didn't feel it. Of course I couldn't. How idiotic of me to think otherwise.

Despite the pep talk from Kenna, I could feel myself shutting everything out after this result. For once I'd decided to hang onto the slither of impossible hope that might give me a sign that walking again was possible. Clearly, I'd chosen the wrong path yet again. Chosen the wrong person on my shoulder to listen to. A colossal mistake.

You fool. You utter, utter fool.

Of course you'll never walk again.

Game. Officially. Over.

CHAPTER TWENTY
Kenna

Watching Theon's face fall from his hopeful expression, I knew the answer to Frank's question. My heart is dropping with it for Theon. All hopes had been riding on this one moment, to add to the already glowing spark. Suddenly, water was thrown right over it and put it out in his eyes. Which were now sad and vacant.

I'd meant what I said to him a moment ago. This wasn't the end. Instead, it was merely a stepping stone to a better place. Every word I had spoken was the truth. Though I secretly had hoped for a more positive outcome for Theon's sake. And for mine.

Night after night as I laid in my bed, I sent up a silent prayer to whoever was up there, that they'd give Theon back the use of his legs again. Evidently, no one was in whenever I sent one up to be heard.

Considering I'd seen everything from minor concussions to limbs being detached due to whatever reason, it's surprising me just how much this is feeling like a knife to my stomach. Perhaps due to the fact that I've been staying with Theon these last six weeks, getting closer and sometimes up close and personal with him, it feels like it's hitting closer to home. More so than usual.

If Theon wasn't going to be needing my services for much longer, which I'm not even sure is true right now, I knew for sure he'd need to see a therapist. For his own sake. There was nothing wrong with his mind or his behaviour, but I can see him even now, regressing inside and shutting down. If I as a nurse can't bring him out of this again, then there would be no choice.

I'd do anything for you, Theon. I wish you could know that.

Plans were already whizzing through my head on how to help him but for now, getting him mentally through the next twenty four hours is key. If I could get him through the next twenty four hours with at least a glimmer of hope back in his eye, I knew he would get back to a good place in the end. I know it in my gut.

Theon has a strong will about him, on the inside. Not to mention, there's something about him that tells me he's been through some rough stuff before, so I have no doubt in my mind that he'll get through this We'll get through this.

After finishing the appointment up with Frank, I took Theon up to see his assigned doctor. The final stop for the day. Frank had really worked out Theon's muscles, limbs, joints, just about everything he hasn't used in six weeks, to the point where I'm sure under his shroud of sadness, he was hurting from a different kind of pain. It was almost strange to see Theon in a normal way, for once. The only times I've seen him were when he was on the table in the ER unit when he first came in, and casted up like a starfish.

Seeing him sitting here like this while we waited for the doctor to come in, was almost surreal. I'd gotten used to seeing him casted, as weird as it probably would sound if I said it to him aloud. He probably wouldn't see it that way, though. I could tell he was itching to be out of the casts more than anything.

I guess he won't take well to my surprise now... not after this.

My thoughts were interrupted when the doctor walked in, closing the door behind him before holding his hand out to me. "Nurse Bouchard, thank you for bringing Theon in today. It's been a while."

I nodded, returning the handshake, "You're welcome, doctor. Yes, it has. Six weeks, to be exact."

The doctor turned to face Theon next, slipping his pen into his top pocket. "Good to see you again, Mr O'Donoghue. Out of the casts now, I see. How are you feeling?"

No response.

As I suspected, Theon had gone radio silent. No doubt lost in his own set of spiralling thoughts. There was only one thing I could do. Clearing my throat, I stepped up next to the doctor.

"Excuse me. If I may, doctor. Can I speak to you outside for a moment, please?"

A fleeting moment of confusion passed over his face before he nodded. "Of course. After you, nurse."

After we left the room, I slowly turned to face the doctor. "Thank you for agreeing to this. I just feel it's better off said here first."

"Of course. What did you want to speak to me about?"

The matter was delicate, so I had to proceed with both delicacy and caution.

"You've probably read from his file, that not too long ago down in PT, he failed his sensitivity test. Frank, the PT assigned to him, tested the feeling throughout his hips, thighs, legs and feet and...nothing. There was no feeling there. I could see on his face that he was expecting to feel something, even in the smallest way but, that wasn't the case. The news didn't exactly hit him well, as you'd expect. I'm going to see about getting him some therapy, to help him cope with the struggles going on inside of his head right now. I just thought you needed to know before you did any further...assessments, on him. Tell him the truth, I know he'll value that. I just think both of us should be tactful." I swallowed. "I hope I'm not being too forward with this, doctor. I suppose after working closely with him for six weeks, I've grown to have a certain...fondness, for him. For his care, I mean." I was quick to clarify.

The doctor, who I now recognise as Doctor Vaughn, even without his name-tag that should be pinned to his uniform, stayed respectfully quiet while I spoke. Letting me finish before he spoke up.

"I fully understand what you're trying to say to me, Nurse Bouchard." He said, his tone soft.

"Kenna, please." I insisted.

"Kenna. In that case, call me Nathanial. Nate, for short if you wish." He smiled. "I'm glad you've told me this out here. Personally, I think it was the right thing to do. Not all people put their patients as first as you have, it's admirable and shows you have their best interests at heart."

Huh? He's praising me?

Before I could ask why this was, because all I was really doing was my job, Nate continued. "I remember the day he was brought in. Such a state he was in." he shook his head. "I know you're not going to be assigned to him forever, so let's get this done and treat him right. Okay? Get you back on our unit with us to help those, like Theon, who need it."

But, was the ER where I wanted to be anymore?

I'd worked long and hard to be a nurse, to be placed here. Did I really want to give that all up for…what?

Ever since I started working for Theon, well, technically for his mother, I'd developed a love for working one-on-one with a patient who needs long-term care and attention. It was a different feeling of self-satisfaction, knowing you were doing your bit to make a difference in someone's life. I would almost go so far as to say, refreshing.

In the ER, so much was going on at any one given time, you never had the time to get familiar, so to speak, with a patient. You saw to them, assessed them and got them to where they needed to be within the unit. If you were lucky enough, you'd be assigned a patient to care for if they had to stay for any long periods of time. Like I was with Mr. Rodriguez, then Theon.

What was worrying me most about my change of thought, rather than heart, was, would it be a waste? Would my time at college and working in my residency be a waste if I simply gave it up to pursue another career within nursing? Normally, I would know the answer. Right now? Not so much. There was just so much going on, not necessarily with myself, which is of higher priority.

I don't need to decide right here and now what I wanted to do, I still had some time left before returning to the ER, where I would have to make a decision and sharpish. Plus, there is Jess and Leary to consider. Their opinions often help me decide on important events in my life. Even just talking to them helps so, no need to rush. Yet.

Anyway, I've stood here thinking about myself for far too long. Time to direct the attention back to Theon.

Finishing up my conversation with Nate, we both entered back into the room where upon walking inside, it was clear to us both that Theon hadn't moved an inch. Which didn't surprise me much. As I stepped back to his side, Nate was the first to break the silence in the room.

"Alright, Theon…" his voice trailed off as I noted that he'd changed how he addressed Theon, making things less formal. Obviously as a result of our talk outside about tactfulness. "Shall we proceed with this assessment?"

From the corner of my eye, I saw Theon nod. At least that was better than nothing. It showed some part of his consciousness was listening to us.

With one last subtle nod to me, Nate began his assessment.

Having worked in the ER unit for long enough, I'd seen and done this a million times. Where every patient had different injuries, the method and routine of assessment remained the same. Just as Frank had done earlier, Nate ran through the list of injuries Theon had come in with. I noticed that he skipped the part about the PT results, not needing to add fuel to the fire. After reading through the rest of the papers within his file, Nate looked at Theon.

"Well, I've got some good news for you today, Theon. The results from your x-rays look fantastic. Your breaks, bruises and fractures have all healed into the 90-99% range. There won't be any need for you to have any more casts on your upper half."

My breath caught in my throat, meeting my heart which also felt trapped there.

Even though he didn't say it, I could hear the words left unsaid. About Theon's lower half. His legs. Hopefully what Nate would say next, would ease the blow a little more than the explosion that has already occurred.

Thankfully, that's exactly what he did.

"Now, I know what is running through your head right now and believe me, I've seen enough patients to know without asking. I won't go there, it's not necessary. What is, is moving forward. Specifically, what we can do to get you up and about again because I'm one-hundred percent sure when I speak for both myself and Kenna here, this isn't the end of the road for you. I see you walking again and I'm going to use every possible resource to hand to make it happen. In fact, I'm willing to stake my reputation as a long-serving doctor at this hospital on it."

Being careful not to let it show on the outside, I inwardly swallowed at Nate's words.

He was right.

I couldn't put my finger on it, but something within me to, told me that Theon would walk again. And I'll be damned sure to watch it happen, come hell or high water.

My eyes flicked down to Theon, waiting to see what his response would be. If there was one. To my surprise, that is exactly what I saw. At least, a hint of something.

Theon's right brow was raised ever so slightly, as if he was considering Nate's words. Or possibly, thinking the man was a fool for suggesting something that he had suddenly lost faith in believing. We'd soon find out which it was.

Nate went on to explain a few treatments which he thought would be beneficial for Theon, which would hopefully spark the signs of potential progress. We both knew there was no sure-fire, go-to treatment to instantly cure immobility, as each patient responded differently or not at all, to each one. Though as Nate said, we'd try everything humanly possible.

My decision on whether to stay on as Theon's at-home nurse or not, was made.

I was fooling myself if ever I thought there was another one. He needed me and that was that. It was the decision on whether or not I'd be returning to the ER after leaving his side, which was still up in the air.

Air which was getting thicker by the second.

Eventually after an almost-response from Theon, his lips looking like something was about to spring forth, I knew this was the time for a less than divine touch of intervention.

Giving a nod to Nate, he thankfully read my silent cue to leave Theon and me alone. Clearing his throat, he grabbed the file he came in with. "Yes, well, I'll leave you with Kenna for a short while to decide on what you want to do next, so we can proceed as soon as possible. As soon as you reach a decision, we'll go from there. Theon, Kenna." He nodded to us both, then swiftly left.

It was now or never. Do or die. Well, maybe not the last part…

Crouching in front of Theon, I took both of his hands carefully within my own. "Theon O'Donoghue, look at me." I said with a semi-authoritative tone.

Amazingly, it worked. Theon's eyes snapped up to mine in an instant.

Time to work my magic. Let's hope there's enough to save the soul inside this man.

"Yes or no answers only, you hear me?"

He nodded, slowly.

"Good. Answer me within two seconds, no more no less." I swallowed. "Understand?"

Another nod. *Good. He's listening.*

"Did you understand everything Doctor Vaughn said to you, yes or no?"

"Yes." He whispered.

Good, Theon. Come on, keep going.

I gripped his hands just a little more, still encased within my own. Making me feel somewhat like they were too small to do the job, compared to the size of his. "Do you want to give up here, in this room, right now?"

"N-no."

"Do you want to continue until you find a treatment that works?" Please say yes…please.

"Yes." His voice raised above a whisper this time.

"Do you, Theon O'Donoghue of Big Boo-T ranch, want to prove to the world and to all those who love and hold you dear, that you have it within you to prove Mother Nature herself wrong, and show every doubt, fear and demon that those legs that have carried you through many things your entire life, will once more carry you again and walk you into your future?"

His hands slowly pulled out of mine, turning the tables by taking them on his own. His eyes with every word I spoke, looked like they were bringing that spark inside of him back into life and if I didn't know any better, I would say that across his face showed a look of hidden determination. Just below the surface, but it was there.

Straightening his back and his shoulders wide, his eyes locked onto mine and didn't leave as he gave his final answer.

"Yes. If you'll be right there with me for me to walk to."

At this moment, I knew that we were no longer speaking as nurse and patient, but as Theon and Kenna. Two unknowns with a whole lot more unknowns ahead. One thing I do know is my answer to his request.

"There's no place I'd rather be, Theon. Yes, I'll be right there with you. Every single step of the way."

No matter how many steps it takes. I'll be there.

CHAPTER TWENTY-ONE
Theon

"Yes, Mara. I promise to update you, or Theon will, as soon as we're back. See you soon." Kenna said over her in-car phone, finishing the call to my mother. The two of them had been on the phone for the last five minutes, though I can't tell you what they were talking about. I tuned out around one minute into their conversation.

After leaving the doctor's office minus my casts, that's where it was lost on me. Well, mostly. I remember talking to Kenna about wanting to try and walk again, with her help. After that, it was hit and miss as to what my mind chose to remember my ears hearing.

Parts of Kenna speaking somehow managed to stay within my befuddled, confused mind. Once she'd manoeuvred me into her car, asking me questions about this and that once we got back on the road. I'd managed to reply with the occasional grunt or 'yeah', when being asked on what we should do today and if I was okay with it.

To be honest, I didn't really care. I told myself no matter what the results would be today that I would fight to walk again but…I never expected for the news to hit me as hard as it has done. Kenna did her best to reassure me that everything would be alright and that we would fight this together, but it wasn't enough to keep the demons at bay. Those irritating, nagging demons that prayed on the slightest worry or insecurity.

Demons I thought I'd long-seen off since my days out on the battlefield.

Clearly, they were more stubborn than I thought because it seemed like they were back and here to stay.

If Drayce were here, he'd knock some sense into me.. And I'd welcome it.

Lost in my thoughts, I'd failed to notice that Kenna had driven us to my folks' ranch where she'd parked next to my dad's truck. "Why are we here?"

"I've made arrangements with your mom and dad."

"What sort of arrangements?" I arched a brow, "They're not my keepers, you know. I'm old enough to look after myself?"

It was her turn to arch a brow at me, "Who said anything about them looking after you? Besides, it's clear that you do. Hence why I'm here in the first place."

Yeah, because my mother approached a total stranger in a sandwich shop. That's totally normal.

Before I had a chance to protest, people from left, right and centre appeared. Milling around the car doing God knows what. Kenna was well out of the car by now, I could see her flitting back and forth in the rear-view mirror. Doors were opened, bags deposited and familiar faces gave me a friendly smile and wave on their way back to wherever they needed to be.

Meanwhile, I sat getting more confused by the second.

Next thing I knew, the passenger door swung open and my mother's face and body filled the space, crouched down at my side. "Hello darling." Her eyes swept over my outwardly-normal body. "How are you doing? How are you feeling?"

"Good." I swallowed, "Glad to get the casts off."

She nodded, a soft smile on her face. "Who wouldn't?"

"True." I exhaled. "What's going on mom? What's with all of the people?" I asked, gesturing my head to the last people leaving the area.

A shrug was all I got in response.

"You don't know? What's Kenna up to?"

It was clear that she was up to something, something concerning us, this car and God only knows what. I wasn't the type of guy to ask a million and one questions, but I had just the one buzzing around my head right now.

"Well…maybe I do. Yes. Yes I do." She nodded, firmly. "Though I'm not going to tell you what. That's up to Kenna, it was her idea after all."

What was?!

Irritation slowly crept into my bones, with my blood just starting to boil at the lack of answers I wasn't getting. As much as I was feeling irritated, I held it back. No way was I talking it out on my mother. She wasn't the one accountable for all of this, even if she played a part. Which I still can't be sure of because I don't have answers!

"Right, let's go!" Kenna said, hopping back into the car's driver's seat.

"Um, go where, exactly?" I asked.

My mom closed the door and the window was wound down, enough for her to lean on the open window. "Jesus, you're so impatient. You get that from your father, you know."

Beside me, I heard Kenna chuckle. I'm glad she was laughing quite literally at my expense, here.

"Thanks again for the quick turnaround, Mara. I really think this will do Theon some good. Not to mention improve his chances of progress."

Turnaround? Do me some good? Progress?

What is going on?!

Looking back and forth between my mother and Kenna, I had hoped that one of them would come forth with an answer. Alas, they didn't. At least, not to the question I wanted to know about.

"I agree. His father thought so too. Not to mention Brett and the others." My mother added.

Brett is in on this? I should've known. That man has his fingers in all sorts of pies, when it comes to me and what's best for me. He means well, I know. I'm just grouchy over…well…everything. Perhaps whatever these two, and the others were up to, won't be as bad as I'm currently thinking it will be.

Maybe they're right, and I just need to suck it up and take it like an adult.

The engine cut off all conversation as Kenna belted herself again, turning her head back to my mother, "I'll let you know when we're there."

"Of course. Take care, both of you!" my mother beamed. Turning to me, she cupped my cheek with her soft, slightly wrinkled hand, "You're looking so good, Theon. So healthy. Your father and I are so proud of you for carrying on. Don't give up now, okay?"

Damn. There was that lump in my throat again.

Whenever my mother or father would pull the 'pride' card on me, I always got choked up. The two of them had as much pride in and of me, as both their son and the secret soldier I was now. On top of everything I've ever done before joining the army. If they said they were proud of me, they meant it. Really, meant it.

"Thank you, ma."

With a nod and a final kiss on my cheek, she retreated back and stood on the front porch, ready to wave us off. She did that with anyone, anytime they went out. It was her thing, and was really sweet. Not to mention a tradition of sorts, for her.

I waited until Kenna had backed us out of the ranch drive, and had gotten us on the road to quiz her about what's going on.

"Where are we going? What's going on?" I asked, softly.

"We're spending the next two weeks out of town. I contacted your mother on the way back from the hospital to see if they had a place for us to stay and thankfully, they did. Well, sort of. They have friends in Dripping Springs who remodel houses and rent them out. We've worked out a deal for us to stay for two weeks, so I can do some intense physio with you and get you walking again."

That's right. My folks just about knew everyone in and around Austin, but I remember the people Kenna is currently talking about. Cassie and Joe Jenkins had known my parents for around thirty years or so, give or take a year. They'd met when my father went on a trip to Dripping Springs years ago, where he'd bumped into and made a quick friend in Joe. Since then, they'd done business whenever a new horse, cow, bull etc, was needed on our ranch. Until now, I'd forgotten that little nugget of information, as I didn't directly deal with Joe. That I left up to my father, since they were good friends.

"Why couldn't we do that back at my place? Or my folks' ranch?" I asked, curious.

Kenna shrugged, "Since you don't want to go into town and have everyone see you, I thought a change of pace and scenery would make you happier, more open to wanting to try to walk again where you won't have every eye in town watching you."

For the second time in less than half an hour, the lump was back in my throat, forcing me to swallow it back. She was doing something nice for me, of her own will, and I was being an ass. Again.

Being mindful not to move too suddenly, I looked at Kenna. "I…um… thank you." I managed to say. Genuinely thankful for her thoughtful thinking.

Guessing by the expression on her face, I don't think she was expecting me to apologise, and so easily, too. "Y-you're welcome." She cleared her throat, quickly composing herself. "Now let's not draw on the negatives, or anything else. Let's just get there and see where this next step takes us. More so, you. Okay?"

"Okay." I nodded.

Maybe things were turning for the better, after all.

CHAPTER TWENTY-TWO
Kenna

Thanks to Theon tuning out after we'd left the hospital, I'd managed to make arrangements to stay in a house in which Theon's parents knew the owners. With luck only known to the few, the house wasn't being used and was open for us to rent out for two weeks. Plenty of time to begin Theon's recovery and road to walking again.

If I had told Theon what I was up to, for sure he would've tried to stop me. Which made me twice as glad I took the initiative to strike while he was stuck inside his own head. Mara had only been too happy to agree and help me, with the added confirmation from Theon's father. Both of them were more than happy to help me, if it meant helping their son.

Now, we were just a few miles from Dripping Springs. At least that's what the sign said. I'd never actually been before, but after some googling and GPS input, it wasn't a long drive to the town.

Theon had long-since dozed off in the passenger seat, which was something I was glad about. On top of the mental exhaustion he'd been through these last six weeks, he was about to be physically exhausted and would need all the sleep for the strength needed to begin his recovery. Physio was not easy. Not when we had as much to do as Theon needed done.

I just hoped with all that I had, that when it comes to the tough, he doesn't get going.

A short while later and thankfully, an uneventful drive later, we arrived in the town of Dripping Springs. It was a quaint little place, from what I could see en route to the place I'd booked for us. As we got closer, I just knew this was the place to get Theon back on his feet. No pun intended.

The man in question, still silently slumbered beside me. Totally unaware of our arrival into the town. Soon though, I'd have to wake him up. Glancing at him out of the corner of my eye and seeing how peaceful he looked, that was the last thing I wanted to do. But it had to be done.

"Theon." I called, gently.

Nothing. No movement.

God this man can sleep.

A fact I've learned once too often. The man was the very definition of a deep sleeper. Often I had to resort to less than conventional methods to wake him, not wanting to hurt him while he was in his casts. I must say, I got pretty creative. Jess and Leary would've been so proud.

After a few more futile attempts, I gave up on trying to wake Theon and proceeded to the address on the GPS. Thankfully, the drive wasn't long at all as not fifteen or so minutes later, I pulled up in front of the house. A fifty-something year old man already waiting for us, sitting casually on the front porch of the one-floor property.

He gave me a friendly wave as I killed the engine, which I returned. Silently wishing I had woken Theon up before we got here, not knowing we would be having a visitor. Unbuckling my belt, I turned away from the man who I assumed thinking twice about it must be Joe Jenkins, and faced Theon.

There was no time to waste in waking him, as Joe was waiting for us.

"Right, here we go." I whispered.

Leaning in, I carefully clamped my right hand over his mouth and my fingers of my left hand over his nose, carefully cutting off just the right amount of air so he wouldn't be in any sort of danger.

I got my answer pretty darn quickly.

His eyes sprang open and I sprang back into my seat, gripping the steering wheel while pretending to look concerned, as if wasn't the one to make him cough himself awake. Coughing and spluttering, he looked around a little confused before his eyes settled on me. "W..what…" he coughed again, "What happened?"

"I don't know. You must've swallowed something the wrong way while sleeping, or something." I shrugged, turning the keys again to make out like I'd just turned off the engine.

"Is that even possible?"

"I should know. I am a nurse, aren't I?"

Impressively as I waited for his reply, Theon seems to have got over his sudden pull from slumber. "Hmph."

A knock on my window pulled me thankfully from having to make up any more excuses to Theon. I carefully opened my door so as not to knock the man back, "Hi, can I help you?"

"Yes. Well, actually, it's I who is here to help you." he offered his hand out to me, "The name's Joe Jenkins, I believe I spoke to you on the phone, Ms Bouchard."

So this is Joe!

I returned Joe's shake with a beaming smile, pleased to finally be meeting him in person. "Yes, that's right. We did. It's lovely to finally meet you, Mr Jenkins."

He returned his hand to his side, before waving off my formalities. "Call me Joe, please. And this must be the gentleman in question who you were bringing with you."

Theon sat up in his seat, "Yes sir. Theon O'Donoghue." Carefully, Theon reached a hand across me to shake Joe's. "This was sprung on me this morning."

Brief shock appeared on Joe's face, before quickly vanishing again.

I'd filled him in on as much as I could regarding who Theon was, what my plans were and what I would need when we arrived to stay for the two weeks, so it must just be coming back to him.

"I see. Well, nonetheless, I hope that your impromptu stay at this home will prove to be fruitful for you both." He said, his hands clapping together. "What say we all get inside so my son and I can give you a tour of the place?"

I blinked, "Your son?"

Joe nodded, "Yes. Well, one of them." He chuckled. "My wife and I have five in total. My eldest, Ralph, just got married and is expecting his first child with his new wife, Robinne."

Beside me, I swear I felt Theon's body tense up.

Why would that be?

"Yes, we'd love to get inside. Thank you." Theon piped up, quick to change the conversation away from talk of marriage and babies. I'd quiz him on that at a later date. Something had to be up for him to change the subject so quickly.

With a little help from Joe, Theon and his wheelchair were both now inside the charming, one-floor home.

Front door closed and all of us now in the front hallway, I turned to face the boys, "Thank you for the help, Joe. I appreciate it."

"Happy to help. Now, I'm sure you'll want to have a look around this place. But you two look more than capable and I don't want to intrude so, I'll just cover the basics." He turned and pointed to his left, "On that side of the house at the front you have the main living space, kitchen and washroom. Complete with a washer-dryer and storage. Behind me..." he half-turned, pointing at the door behind him, "Back there is a home gym we've tailored for physical therapy specifically. And finally..." he completed the turn to the other side of the house. "Bedroom, bathroom/wet room en-suite and access to the wheelchair friendly back porch and garden."

Woah. My mind was blown away at it all. The simplicity yet functionality of the place was simply astounding.

There was just enough for us here to use, without feeling overwhelmed with what we have at our fingertips. Besides, sometimes the simple things in life are what end up becoming of the most use to us.

Theon, however, was yet to say a word about any of this as he sat watching our exchange in his wheelchair. An unreadable expression on his face.

"Wow, Joe. Whoever designed this place really put a lot of thought into it!"

"Why, thank you!" a voice said, coming from behind Joe.

Coming from the bedroom/bathroom side of the house, a tall, dark-brown haired man who had to be in his mid-to-late twenties, with an enchanting smile on his face. I would go so far as to say he was incredibly handsome-looking, but that title goes to Theon.

Wait...what?!

"Ah, Ralph. Didn't know you were planning to stop on by here today, son." Joe said, embracing the former stranger as his son, whom he'd mentioned not too long ago outside before helping me in with Theon.

Ralph shrugged and stepped back, "I wasn't, but Robinne wanted me to deliver this to the people who'd be staying here." He said, lifting a foil-covered dish in his hands. "Didn't want them to arrive without having something to eat after the journey."

A proud look crossed over Joe's face, "How thoughtful of her. Speaking of, allow me to introduce Theon O'Donoghue and Kenna Bouchard. They'll be the ones staying here for the next two weeks." He took the dish from his son's hands, placing it gently on the table in the hall off to the side.

I stepped forward and held out my hand, which Ralph immediately shook. "It's nice to meet you, Ralph. Thank you for the food! Or rather, please thank who I assume is your wife? Girlfriend?"

Ralph chuckled, stepping back from our shake to hold up his hand complete with a silver or platinum ring on his ring finger, "My wife, Robinne. We've been back from our honeymoon for about a month, and she's been itching to learn something new so, my mother has been teaching her a few of her own recipes. Don't worry, I've tested a bite from the same batch of casserole she left for us and it's not all bad."

This earned him a gentle smack upside the head from his father.

"Okay…" he chuckled, "It's pretty darn good."

"That's better." Joe nodded.

Ralph turned away from me and shifted his attention to Theon, holding out his hand. "Nice to meet you. Theon, right? I think I remember you and your folks."

Surprisingly and considering he'd been quiet this whole time, Theon raised his hand and shook it with Ralph's. "That's me. It's been a minute, hasn't it?"

"Fifteen years or so at least, I'd say." Ralph nodded. "How are your parents doing these days?"

Theon sat back in his wheelchair, "They're doing good, thanks. Mom's active as ever, and dad…well…let's just say he's not the type to slow down until he falls down." he chuckled.

Ralph tipped his head back and laughed heartily, "I know how that is…" he joked, giving Joe a friendly nudge in his side, "Right, pa?"

I watched as Joe turned and gave Ralph a gentle-ish smack upside the head, "You may be married with a child on the way, boy, but you just wait. Someday you'll reach my age and realise nothing will stop you from a good hard day's work. Nothing at all."

The platonic love between the two was hard to miss. There was no trace of malice or upset as Joe smacked Ralph, who now wore a smirk on his face. I could only hope that someday, even many years from now if I ever had a son, they'd be as close as Joe and Ralph. Or even Theon and his father. The two were completely different in how they showed their affections towards their sons, but affection is still shown in some form.

When we lived closer, I was the same with my mom and dad. Public displays of our love for one another was something we were never afraid to do, unlike some. Some people I once knew wouldn't even let their moms hug them in public. That I couldn't and still don't fully understand. Maybe that's just me, I don't know. Hugging either my mom or dad, no matter where it would happen, would be something I'll always want to do. Period.

Clapping his hands together, Ralph brought me back into the now and out of my own thoughts, "Well I must be going. Robinne and I are heading out to our first scan this afternoon."

"Ooh, how exciting!" I beamed.

"Right?" Ralph smiled, "Pa, you want a ride back to the ranch?"

Joe shook his head, "No thanks, son. I drove here. My truck's around back. I pulled up there to check on the back fence. You go home and take Robinne to that scan, and let myself and your mother know how it goes, a little later on. In fact…" he turned to Theon and myself, "Why don't the two of you join us for dinner tonight? Just for your first night here. We won't get in your way after that, I promise."

Come to think of it, there wasn't anything that I had set in stone for Theon and me tonight. Everything I have semi-planned for us officially started tomorrow. Or the day after, depending on if I could get him motivated mentally enough to start sooner, rather than later.

I wasn't even sure if I had made plans for tonight, if Theon would be up for it. Turning to ask him, I found his eyes were already watching me, waiting for my question. "W-would you…" I cleared my throat. "Would you be up for that?"

He shrugged his shoulders, "I wouldn't mind." He looked over to Joe, "Only if we wouldn't be intruding, that is."

Joe waved his hand, "Of course not. In fact, I'm sure my wife would've beaten my hide if I hadn't invited ya'll. Kenna, you have our address, is seven okay for you both?"

"Seven is perfect, thank you, Joe." I smiled, "And thanks again for the food, Ralph. Thank your wife for us, if that's not too much trouble."

"None at all. Y'all have a good day and enjoy ma's meal tonight, you'll enjoy it." he winked, shook his dad's hand and swiftly departed, with Joe himself bidding us a temporary farewell, leaving not long after.

It was only after the two of them had left, that I realised that I was alone with Theon again. It's not like it's the first time the two of us had ever been alone, though it was the first time in a place that wasn't either my workplace, or his home. I could feel a blush starting to creep its way up my cheek at the many inappropriate thoughts running through my mind, thoughts in which Theon wouldn't be privy to, God willing.

Thank God it's only me who was having them. Or is it?

"Kenna? Kenna? Hello, can you hear me?"

Huh?

Looking down, Theon wore a half-concerned expression. "You're miles away there. You okay?"

No! I'm thinking about things about you that I shouldn't!

Mentally giving myself a shake, I nodded. "Y-yeah. Yes. Yes I'm fine."

To be honest, I'm stunned he's even asking me that. In all the time we've known one another, this is the first. By no means was Theon an emotionless husk, he had times where he showed raw emotion and humility, but not normally towards me. I think our open and honest talk earlier in the hospital must've opened him up, just a little.

Progress is progress.

I looked at our bags sitting in the hallway. They really needed to be carried through to our rooms, and put away. Since we were staying for two weeks, there would be no living out of our suitcases. Not that I'd do that, anyway. I hated living out of a suitcase. Never could understand why people did it, especially if they were staying somewhere for a week or more. It takes ten minutes to unpack and pack up again, just do it!

"C'mon, let's get unpacked and get you ready for tonight." I said.

Theon arched a brow, "I thought it was women who were the ones who usually took longer to get ready?"

I squinted at him, trying my best to look somewhat not amused, "I don't know where you've heard that, but I can promise you that it doesn't take me long to do anything."

"Duly noted." He snickered, amused by his own retort.

"Not in that way! I can assure you I can last longer tha—" I cut myself off, realising where my mouth was heading way, way head of my brain. "N-nevermind! Let's just get this done."

Placing our cases gently on his lap and minding his delicacy, I pushed his wheelchair through towards where Joe had said our bedrooms were. Only, when we got there a moment later, I must've misheard what he said.

"Uh…Kenna. I see a bedroom. Singular."

Oh sweet Lord! Please tell me it's not what I think it is!

Alas, it was.

What lay before us was indeed a bedroom. One, bedroom. Not two. One.

When I booked this place for us, I was sure as sure can be that I'd booked a place with two bedrooms. Unless… No, it couldn't be possible. Joe wouldn't book us into this one on purpose, thinking we might be a couple. The chances of that were slim to none. No. This was all on me. I was the one who booked the place for us through Theon's mother.

THEON'S MOTHER!

I didn't want to think she would do anything sneaky when it came to Theon and me. Well, besides the fact that she sneakily hired me behind his back in the hopes of getting him to want to walk again. That was the very definition of sneaky.

Judging by the look on Theon's face, he'd also thought and came to the same conclusion as me. And he didn't look too pleased about it.

Oh hell.

The next two weeks were certainly going to be a lot more personal, and up-close than I'd expected.

Let's just hope, if there is a God, that I can last two weeks in the same house, the same bed, the same space night after night. Because if being in the same bed as him was anything like when I had to be close to him the last time, I was going to need all the prayers I can muster.

Fast.

CHAPTER TWENTY-THREE
Theon

The second that my eyes caught the singular, double-bed in the only bedroom within this place, I was both celebrating and screaming inside. Both parts of my rationale were fighting against one another as I sit here, and I have no clue which side would emerge victorious. Would it be the side to me that was secretly giddy about it? Or would my nervous, flighty side kick one of us out quite literally, into a new bed?

Whichever side won…well…they would still have to deal with Kenna and how she would react.

So far, there hasn't been a single tell on how she feels about it. And I have no clue on how to break the awkward silence between us, in order to move on.

Who would think something as simple as a bed would have me tied up in knots?

Having been on several missions, there were times that I had to bunk with my fellow army buddies. That, I had no problem with as on many of those occasions, no one had a choice about hardly anything, and even the higher ups hunkered down with those whom they led into the field.

This though? Well this is a whole different kettle of fish. Kenna wasn't in service with me, and we certainly did have other options to choose from. If only either of us could think of those options right now rather than staring at the bed, that would be great.

Guess it's going to be me…

"Hey, why—"

"Theon I—"

We spoke at the same time, obviously thinking on the same wavelength. I cleared my throat, "Go ahead."

"I…uh, yes. Thank you. Why don't we get you ready for dinner over at Joe's? I'm sure his wife would appreciate two handsome men turned out nicely. Don't you?"

Okay, not what I was expecting. At all.

"Besides." She continued, "We can squeeze in your first therapy session before we have to go. Does that sound good to you?"

Inwardly, I raised a brow.

So this is how she wants to play it, huh?

Two can play this game, baby.

Straightening my back, I half-turned my head to face Kenna, "No time like the present."

Based on the look she now sported, I'm guessing she wasn't expecting me to agree to her about-face statement. Which was clearly an obvious diversion away from the bedroom scenario. To be honest, I even surprised myself yet, here we are.

This was going to go really good, or really bad.

Time to find out which it's going to be.

At six o'clock, Kenna and I left the house to head on over to Joe's place for dinner. Based on the address she'd put into the GPS, it wouldn't take an hour to get there. Not that I was going to argue with her about it. Especially after what we've been doing up until leaving just now.

We'd both carried on as if neither of us had seen the bed in the first place. An impressive feat on both of our parts.

Kenna had carried out her plan of first starting my physical therapy, which hurt like hell. I'd expected to struggle a little having had most of me in casts for the past six weeks, but never did I imagine feeling as weak as a mouse lifting up a tonne of bricks using my arms properly for the first time.

If my old army buddies could see me now, for sure they'd shake their heads in shame.

As for my legs, well, no news is usually good news. Not in my case. The things were as useless as ever and despite Kenna's constant optimism, the sinking feeling remained within my gut. Telling me I'd never walk again.

Damn that horse!

It had been an unnerving feeling to be using my arms again, but I was determined as hell to get them back to their former selves, as it were. Not that I'd ever admit that to Kenna. No. I wasn't ever going to admit to her that she and her blinding optimism was one of the things fuelling my inner fire to gain my strength back. That nugget of information was staying with me.

After we'd done enough physical therapy to make me ache for the next eight-thousand years, we moved on to getting ready for dinner. An interesting series of events in anyone's books.

Somehow, by the grace of God, I managed to convince Kenna to let me dress myself. Mostly. There was no way in hell I'd be able to dress my lower half. Not yet. But my upper half, I could. It was also the part of me that was thankfully shielded away from her for the last six weeks and if she only knew what was underneath, my cover would be well and truly blown and the jig most certainly up.

Once I was dressed, both my upper and lower half, I had the pleasure of watching Kenna get herself ready. Something I never thought in my life I'd be glad to witness. A woman dressing. It's never interested me before. Only getting them out of clothes, not in. For some reason, watching Kenna as she'd dressed for this evening fascinated me.

She'd ended up wearing some comfortable-looking jeans, flowy, flowery blouse and cowboy boots. Her hair was up in the most captivating ponytail I'd ever seen. As I sat here while she drove along, I felt my eyes drifting frequently back to it. Followed by my eyes roaming down the rest of her, taking note of everything several times over.

Jesus Christ, what's happening to me? Get a grip, O'Donoghue!

Thankfully, my wandering thoughts were shut away once I noticed Kenna was pulling into the start of a long road leading up to what would be Joe's home he shared with his wife whose name keeps escaping me.

"Are we almost there?" I asked.

Kenna nodded, "Yep."

"Why didn't you tell me?"

She looked over at me, before quickly returning her eyes to the road, "You were in your own world over there. I couldn't bring myself to take you away from your own thoughts. You looked so peaceful with whatever you were thinking about."

Thank goodness she couldn't actually read what I was thinking of, because those thoughts were anything but peaceful. They were downright sinful. Not to mention, thoughts I shouldn't be thinking but couldn't help it for the life of me. There was just something about Kenna that kept drawing me back to her, and I was sure as hell going to find out exactly what that is.

The car pulling to a stop once more brought me out of my own thoughts, and had me reaching—albeit carefully—for my seatbelt, which clicked open with ease.

Kenna was quickly out of her seat to come around and help me back out of the car. Meanwhile, I looked up and spotted two figures waiting for us on the porch. Watching our every move.

"Looks like they're waitin' on us." Kenna said as she opened the door, the wheelchair already waiting at her side for me to be shifted into. Like a sack of useless potatoes.

"Mhm. Country folk do that sort of thing. Unlike in the big cities."

As soon as I'd said it, I regretted my words.

I knew Kenna was a city girl, born and bred. Yet, I'd still let those stupid words slip from my lips. Why am I such an ass?

If that was my best attempt at trying not to think about Kenna by saying something callously mean, these next two weeks were going to be a lot tougher and longer.

"True. City folk, depending on if they're born there or have moved, treat others differently. If you're city born and bred, you're still welcoming as country folk would be. Only, country folk who believe that we are not as welcoming clearly don't know us as well as they think they have us pegged down as."

Well damn. If she didn't just go and feed me a slice of humble pie…

Laced with a spicy, fiery cinnamon undertone.

"Listen, I—"

"Hey kids!" Joe's voice interrupted me. Breaking off what would've been an apology. "Glad you could make it! Need some help there?" He said, nodding towards where I still sat in the passenger seat.

On a dime, Kenna spun around to face Joe. A pleasant, friendly smile on her face. "Thank you! That's kind of you to offer. If you'd kindly help get him into the wheelchair, I'll go introduce myself to your lovely wife!"

Before I had a chance to object, off she went. Striding up to the porch in a leisurely stride, right on into the arms of Joe's wife. They immediately started chatting to one another and for once in my life, I wish I knew what the hell two women could be nattering on about with one another.

You're getting nosy in your old age, boy.

Joe made swift work lifting me out of the car and into the wheelchair, leaving me wondering how he was able to still lift someone as big as me at his age.

"Don't even go there, son."

I blinked. "Huh?"

"I might not be as young as I used to be, but I still muck in where I can and thanks to my lovely wife over there, I'm still in good shape from her taking good care of me. In more ways than one." he winked.

Where I was somewhat mildly bemused of his declaration into his... marital rights...I admired his passion for work. A passion I missed and hoped as hell to carry on with in the near future.

I chuckled, nodding, "Yes, sir."

Next thing I knew, he was pushing me up to the front porch where we joined Kenna and Joe's wife. I couldn't help but notice a plastic, foldable ramp had been set in place so I could get inside. How thoughtful.

After pulling me up said ramp, I was turned to face the two beautiful ladies before me.

"Theon O'Donoghue, this is my wife and the love of my life, Cassie." The affection pouring from Joe's words were hard to miss.

"It's an honour to meet you, ma'am." I said, gingerly raising my arm to gently kiss the back of her hand. "I'd tip you my hat, if I could. Except, I don't have it with me."

Cassie laughed, walking over to her husband's side, "If I didn't know any better, I'd say you've been taking lessons from this charmer here. Anything is possible after knowing him for even a minute."

"That's all it took for me to know you were the one I was meant to be with, darlin'" Joe said, kissing her on the cheek.

Much like my own parents, Joe and Cassie weren't afraid to share their affections for one another in front of two...well, one, stranger. This was old school love right in front of my eyes, a love I couldn't help but see Kenna noticing too. Her eyes crinkled at the corners. Out of sadness, or admiration?

"Well...I don't know about that." I laughed, steering Kenna's attention away from them.

Cassie clapped her hands together, "Let's get y'all inside so you can get some food inside of you. I'm sure you've both worked up an appetite today."

Yes, but not in the way I'd like...

As we made our way inside, Kenna pushing my wheelchair through the front door, I couldn't ignore the feeling in my gut. A feeling that was telling me tonight wasn't going to go as I'd expected it to.

Much to my surprise, the dinner—a very delicious one—passed without anything bad happening.

Maybe that feeling in my gut wasn't about something bad, but instead was nerves.

Pfft, no.

Dinner with two lovely people was nothing to be nervous about. Even if they did know me as a little kid, or had previous acquaintance with my folks with the potential of throwing up the occasional embarrassing story I'm sure was buried somewhere within their memories. No. The nerves, if there had been any, would be from keeping myself doing something ass-like to Kenna while in their house.

The last thing I wanted to do was be an ass to her, let alone under someone else's roof when they were being so hospitable.

I'd managed to have my fill of Cassie's delicious cooking which surprised me greatly. Having only started to use my arms properly earlier today, I'd expected to struggle more than I did. It was only within the last ten minutes or so after finishing my last spoonful of mouth-watering trifle, that the beginnings of a dull ache made itself known.

"Joe, Cassie, dinner was delicious. You've got to tell me how to make that sometime before we leave, so I can cook it for Theon and me." Kenna said, smiling.

Kenna. Cooking. Kenna cooking in shorts. Bare legs. No socks. A warm glow on her cheeks…

What in the blue blazes...

My mind skipped ten chapters ahead in the story of 'Oh Hell No', there. Where did that come from?

She'd cooked for us several times…technically, every day, since we'd come to my place. So why in the merry love of God did my mind wander off so fast? And to a scenario like that of all things.

Actually, I did know why.

I couldn't remember the last time I was with a woman. Weeks, perhaps even months at this stage, of no female attention with my downstairs brain had me going goo-goo over a girl who'd never be mine, or with me, in a million years. For more than one reason.

No girl wants a man like me. Not one.

Besides, Kenna deserved better. Which is exactly why I had to shelve these wandering thoughts, and fast.

I cleared my throat, "Yes, thank you both. I would go so far as to say it was on par with my mama's cooking, but don't tell her I said that." I winked at Cassie.

With my secret confession promised to be kept as such, we soon disbanded from the table, with Cassie insisting Kenna's help in washing up not being necessary. Usually the rule went if the host cooked, the guests would offer to clean. Not today.

Having an itching for something to do, Joe took up the task and ambled away into the kitchen. Leaving Kenna, Cassie and myself to retire out onto the back porch where we could catch the start of the beautiful Texas sunset. One of my favourite things in the entire world. Nothing could beat it.

Other than Kenna's beauty.

There goes my damn brain again…

Eventually after doing the washing up, Joe joined us out on the back porch where the four of us sat and enjoyed the sunset together, tossing around various subjects as we drank some sweet tea. Which I'd been relegated to once I was handed pain meds. No alcohol for me until I'm off them.

Overall, I'd say the two of us were having a better time than we'd expected to have. Given our earlier awkwardness at the bed situation which thankfully, didn't come up as a topic either by Kenna or Joe.

A short while later, the sound of a closing door from somewhere within the house halted any and all talking.

"Ma? Pa? You guys here?" a male voice called out.

"Out here, son!"

Son? That voice didn't sound like Ralph...

The owner of the voice stepped out of the back porch door, coming to a stop as soon as he saw Kenna and I sitting out here. "Ah, sorry! I didn't know you had guests."

Joe smiled, "Nonsense. Reed, this is Kenna Bouchard and Theon O'Donoghue. They're in the one-story easy-living place we fixed up. Kenna, Theon, this is one of my other boys, Reed."

"One of five, but best of the bunch!" Reed smiled proudly. His eyes cast over to Kenna and instead of shaking her outstretched hand, he kissed the back of it. "Pleasure to meet you, Kenna. I hope you enjoyed my mother's delicious cooking. I'm kind of sad I missed out on it."

How the hell did he know we were here for dinner? Smooth jerk.

Okay, so maybe that was a little...a lot...mean of me, but is kissing Kenna's hand really necessary? What's wrong with a good old-fashioned handshake? Nothing!

I have to cut this off, and fast.

Clearing my throat loud enough, Reed's eyes snapped off of Kenna and onto me as did hers. Their hands thankfully parted ways. "Pleasure to meet you too, Reed." I said, making my presence known. Which he'd clearly forgotten about as quickly as his father made me known to him, his focus having gone to a prettier place.

As he made his way over to shake my hand, I could feel Kenna's eyes shooting me daggers. Even though I wasn't looking at her, I knew she was doing it. I shook Reed's hand, giving it a firmer squeeze before letting go. Quickly making him retreat to the safe zone of his parents where he shook Joe's hand, and gave Cassie a peck on her cheek.

"Sweetheart, I've left some leftovers in the fridge. I had a feeling one of you would be round tonight, so I stored some there just in case." Cassie said, tapping her hand on his shoulder.

"E-excellent, Ma! I'll uh...I'll just go grab myself some."

Retreating inside, Reed made a quick exit.

Speaking of...

"Joe, Cassie…" Kenna said, speaking up just as I was about to open my mouth. "You both have been the kindest hosts, and it's been a pleasure to meet you Cassie and talk with you both this evening, but I'm afraid Theon and I are going to have to make a move."

Exactly what I was about to say…

"Oh? Is everything alright?" Cassie asked, sounding slightly concerned.

Kenna nodded, "Yes! It's just…" she looked at the watch on her left wrist, "It's almost time for me to give Theon his medication and I stupidly didn't bring it with me. I'm so sorry to be so rude, especially after the delicious meal and wonderful company."

I knew Kenna was hamming this up so it didn't look like we were escaping to avoid anything hostile now that Reed had shown up, especially with how I reacted, but her efforts were worthy of an A+.

Not to mention, she did pack my medication. It's in the glove compartment of the car. Though I wasn't going to divulge that bit of information.

"Not a problem." Cassie smiled, "I understand. And don't you go worrying that you've upset either myself or Joe, because you haven't. Keeping up to date—or rather, time—of medication is important."

Joe nodded, agreeing with his wife, "Indeed. Plus, I think I can speak for both of us in returning how much we've also enjoyed tonight."

To be honest, so have I. At least, for the most part. Right up until Reed started getting bit too flirty, with Kenna. Okay, I knew I was overreacting. But still, was a kiss really necessary?

Cassie stood as did Kenna, the two of them embracing in a warm hug, "We'd love to have you two back again before you leave. If you'd like to come back, that is."

"Of course!"

Hopefully without interruption…

Reed was just coming back out the doors as Kenna and I were heading in, Joe and Cassie on our heels to show us out like the hospitable hosts they'd been all evening. We made short, yet polite work, of saying both our thanks and final goodbyes, heading back to the car now encased in the dark of the night.

Once inside, we waved goodbye to our hosts. Finally alone.

Immediately, the awkwardness was replaced by the radiating frustration coming from Kenna in the driver's seat.

She'd remained unusually tight-lipped about my response to Reed's appearance and kiss. Usually she'd be all over me and giving me a lashing from her fiery tongue. Not tonight. I suspect the fact that Joe and Cassie being there played a part, as she probably didn't want to be rude in their presence. Mostly though, I'm ninety-nine percent sure it was because she was waiting for the prime opportunity to chew me out.

And it was looking like the drive back to the house was going to be the perfect opportunity for her to do so.

CHAPTER TWENTY-FOUR
Kenna

I swear if I had stayed in that house a moment longer with Theon, something at some point would've made me snap. At him!

Everything was fine with him until Reed turned up. As soon as he did and he'd kissed my hand...Theon changed. His words became clipped, and his tone snippy. I wasn't fully sure as to why this was, though I was starting to get an idea.

He's jealous!

Wait, hold up. Jealous?!

Theon O'Donoghue hasn't been jealous of anything when it came to me. Not even the fact that I was able to walk, while he is left sitting around. So, why be jealous now? It's not like Reed is the first guy to talk to me I mean, look at the whole Brett debacle. He'd handled that better than this. Just.

The man in question sat quietly beside me, thinking about God only knows what. Hopefully he was thinking up what he'd say to apologise to me, but I knew that was a long shot.

Why would Reed kissing me make Theon jealous?

What made him act like an ass?

When did Theon care about another man touching me?

Could he possibly...no! No he can't! There's no possibility that he could...that he does...that he has...

Does...does Theon have feelings for me? The self-same feelings I've been fighting off practically since I first became his at-home nurse. No, that's impossible.

Isn't it?

Or am I interpreting his reaction wrong? Could it just be that he's jealous to see another man be kind to me, because he and I have been each other's own company, minus a few visitors, for almost two months now?

Yeah, that has to be it! It has to be.

I gripped the wheel as I continued to drive back down the long ass drive, which would lead back to the way we came earlier. The journey home wasn't a long one, but it would give me enough time to quiz him now. Before I lose my confidence and chicken out.

Game face, on.

"Okay, what in the hell was all that about back there, hm? What's the matter with you?"

I'm guessing he was expecting me to snap, because he didn't as much as twitch at my harsh tone.

"What do you mean?"

"What do you mean, 'what do I mean'? You totally acted out on poor Reed just as he arrived to see his folks! He didn't even know we were there, Theon. Why did you start on him like that?"

Theon tensed, leaving a good pause before he replied, "He was getting too personal with you, Kenna."

"Too personal?!" I laughed, "Theon, he didn't do anything remotely too personal with me. Were you seeing what you think you were? Or were you seeing what your mind was envisioning instead?"

His head snapped my way, "He kissed you hand! What kind of a guy does that to someone he's just met? What in the hell is wrong with a simple handshake?"

AHA! So it *was* the kiss, after all!

Theon O'Donoghue was jealous of a stranger kissing my hand. If I wasn't so appalled at his behaviour, I'd be laughing right now.

"You've got no right in being upset if someone kisses my hand. I'm an adult, I'm single and if someone wants to kiss my hand they can damn well do so! I don't need your permission for that."

"Yes I have! I have every right!" he said, his voice growing louder.

I scoffed, "Oh? Do tell!"

He shifted in his seat, snapping his head back away from and out onto the road ahead, "You are MY nurse, which means you are in MY care and in the employ of my parents. While you are working for us and looking after me, it is my job to look after you. Which includes if need be, warning off any potential...suitors. If anything were to happen to you, at the hands of anyone else while under our...my, care, I wouldn't forgive myself."

For the first time in my life, I'm genuinely speechless.

Where on Earth did that come from?

Does he really mean it? Of course he does, it's Theon.

Under the tough exterior, he has a heart of genuine kindness.

Despite his true, kind intentions, there were parts of what he'd just said that were downright out of order.

I was employed to look after him. No matter what he thinks, it does not work the other way around. As for warning off potential suitors—a very medieval name—that wasn't his or his parents' decision. I was free to date, or see, anyone whom I so desired to. Despite being here with him for two weeks, on my normal days off when back at his place, I could easily go out on a date or two.

So, why didn't I?

I already knew the answer to that, and it was sitting right beside me.

Damn him.

Still, his last words were what was getting to me most right now. Out of everything, I knew he meant those words with no malice, but out of the kindness of his heart. Maybe he didn't realise how it sounded to me, but I did. He cares about me. Genuinely cares. And that's something no man has done for a long time. Not since...

No! I chide myself, shaking my head to rid me of those thoughts.

I wasn't ready to go back there just yet.

When we'd started out from Joe & Cassie's place, I had every intention of ripping into Theon, asking him what he was playing at and why. Now though. Well, maybe I didn't need to anymore. Perhaps this requires a calmer approach, after all.

"Listen…" I sighed, "We're both tired and it doesn't matter who did what or why. Let's just get back to the house and relax. Okay?"

Theon turned back to me, his mouth half-open and poised to speak. No words came out. After a couple of beats, his mouth closed and he slowly nodded. Looking as surprised at my words as I felt inside. "Okay."

That one word was all I needed to put this behind me. Looking back at the road, the tension eased. Allowing us to get back to the house in a thankfully comfortable silence.

A few hours have passed since we came back from Joe and Cassie's place, and we were just about to head to bed. Something the two of us had been putting off these last two hours. We managed to avoid talking about it earlier, but there was no way we would be able to do that now. Not when we both were tired and in need of a good night's sleep.

Sleeping on the same bed truly was the only option.

I wasn't so reluctant to relegate Theon to the couch, and I was heavily tempted by the cozy bedding so, sleeping in the same bed it is.

Theon had been wheeled into the bedroom and to his chosen side of the bed before I went off to wash in the bathroom and dress in my more moderate pyjamas, where he remained as I walked back in. His eyes followed me as I came around to him, to help him into bed.

Not something I thought I'd be doing. At least, not getting in with him afterwards.

"D-do…do you…" I cleared my throat. "Do you want any help getting in?" I sighed at my voice breaking. Damn my nerves!

Theon had made good progress starting physical therapy with me earlier today, using his arms again for the first time. But there was no need to push him too early, or too soon.

His eyes snapped away from my face to the bed, then back to me. "Please."

Carefully, I shifted him from the wheelchair and onto the bed, having already pulled back the cover before going into the bathroom.

"I'm going to slowly lay you back. Okay?"

Another nod.

I took that as my cue, gently lowering his upper half with one hand supporting the back of his head and the other at the back of his shoulder. Swiftly followed by lifting up his legs and placing them inside the bed before laying the duvet on top of him.

Silently, I made my way around the bed and without looking at him, slipped into my side. Immediately enjoying my decision to have chosen here instead of the couch.

I wonder what Theon thinks of this.

He'd yet to say anything on the matter, much to my chagrin.

The only indicator that he was in bed with me, was the sounds of breathing coming from the other side. Theon O'Donoghue was a loud breather. Lungs like a horse, given the build he sported. Oh, and also the heat. Body heat. Texas was hot enough on a good day, but add to that the warmth of my full-body pyjamas and his body heat…boy howdy was it toasty.

One night down, thirteen to go.

Thirteen long, long nights.

Turning onto my left side, my go-to sleeping side, I exhaled. "Goodnight, Theon."

I wasn't expecting a reply. Usually when I laid him down to sleep, he was out before I'd even reached his bedroom door to leave his room.

Not tonight.

"Sweet dreams, Kenna." He said, his voice a low, velvety rumble.

Sweet dreams? No. Not with you in bed with me, Theon.

There was a high chance that my dreams would be anything but sweet tonight.

CHAPTER TWENTY-FIVE
Theon

I knew the exact moment Kenna had fallen asleep. Her breathing changed from undercover erratic, to a steady, slow pattern. She thought I was the one who had fallen asleep, waiting for me to do so before she could relax after being tense for so long. Not that she knew I knew that.

After years of training my body and my breathing, fine-tuning it to appear one way on the surface, as often in the field we'd need to be literally as quiet as the dead, I was able to fool her into thinking I was asleep. It didn't take her long to drift off afterwards, exhausted both mentally and physically by the day's events.

To be honest, I wasn't far behind. Though I had a lot more on my mind than she did, which was keeping me awake while she sleeps peacefully beside me.

When we were in the car ride home earlier, with her laying down how she felt about my reaction to Reed kissing her hand, it made me wise the hell up. I already knew I was acting somewhat...okay...fully childish, but she would never have understood me if I had told her the real reason why. I think.

It's a constant battle inside of me to tell her the truth. To tell her that what I feared in the beginning, the feelings for her, were now no longer feared. Instead, I celebrated and welcomed them. So, if that's the case, why can't I just man the hell up? Oh wait, I know why.

Reason number one—a reason I've come back to so often—she's my nurse. I knew all about that patient-nurse clap trap that she can't do anything about. As long as she's my nurse, it can't be anything more than that.

Reason number two, she might not feel the same. Even though every now and then, I thought I've seen something in her eyes, or felt a connection when we touched, there is still every possibility that it's just purely a biological reaction. Person to person, rather than her having a genuine response to me.

Reason number three and probably the biggest holding me back...the promise. The promise I made to my best buddy, Drayce, on his last mission out in the field, to find and take care of his girl. A promise as each day passed, failed to be kept.

I'm sorry I keep letting you down, Drayce. I'm so darn sorry.

Deep down, I knew that Drayce wouldn't be mad at me for failing to carry it out yet. He didn't have a mean bone in his body. If anything, he'd be cheering me on to walk again if I had been blown up and he still alive. The thought made me swallow back a thick lump of emotion in my throat.

Someday, somehow, I will find that girl His Macey.

Now that I'm out of my casts, arms more so than legs, I can finally get to work in hopefully tracking her down. My progress so far...well...it was one ration short of pathetic.

Once I find her, it then begs the question on what the hell I'm going to do with her. I can't once I find her, demand that she lives with me or I with her, just so that I can keep an eye on her. No, that would be going too far.

There was also Kenna to think about. How would she react to my bringing Macey into my life? Would she see her as someone I'm taking care of? Or as a rival?

Stupid question, I know. Nonetheless, one again I feel myself coming back to often.

Sighing, I closed my eyes, taking in the quietness of the night.

Night wasn't usually a time where I felt fully relaxed. For so long, it meant night missions and hours awake at a time, watching your back with both sets of eyes. The ones in the front and back of your head. Even when I was at home, pre-horse accident, I found myself to be up at odd hours of the night doing odd jobs. Just to make myself tired again so I could sleep. It wasn't like work at the ranch wasn't making me tired enough during the day. Some habits were just harder to break than others. Sleeping at night was one of them. Oh, and throw in nightmares too. Those suckers when I did get the odd good night's sleep in, would make sure as hell I wouldn't have a good fighting chance.

I wasn't sure as to how much time had passed since I closed my eyes, attempting to let any and all thoughts drift away. What I was sure of, was how much warmer I was than when I first got into bed, and I knew it had nothing to do with what I was wearing, or the covers that laid on top of me. Kenna. It had to be.

There was no resisting it, I had to look. Just to see for...ah hell, I just wanted to be nosy. No point hiding it.

Turning my head, my nose almost brushed against Kenna's. Woah! No way was she that close to me when we first got into bed.

Ah hell...she's a spooner.

That had to be the only explanation for her legs brushing up against mine right now. I mean...

Wait...what?

Her...h-her legs?!

It wouldn't take Sherlock Holmes to figure out she'd moved closer to me in her sleep with the motive of spooning, albeit unconsciously, but how... No, I had to be imagining this. It was a simple deduction. If her top half had moved closer to me, her legs would have too! Right?

Even if they had, which is highly likely, I wouldn't have been able to feel them. They would have just laid there like my own are doing, except for I wouldn't be able to tell that they were there, deduction or no deduction. Swallowing back the next lump in my throat, I knew there was only one way for sure to find out.

Lifting the covers—gently so I didn't wake Kenna—I looked down into the bed, down our bodies, and down to where our legs were. My eyes widening at the sight before my disbelieving eyes.

Her legs! They...they're touching mine!

Technically, one of her legs was half-thrown over my left leg, but I didn't care about the semantics. The mere fact that I thought I had imagined a feeling in my leg not too long ago, was no longer a figment of my imagination. I had felt something then, just like I had felt her leg right now.

As I continued to stare down at our legs, the feeling had fled as fast as it had come. Ever so slowly, the feeling of her slender leg against mine became nothing but something of sight, not sight and touch.

The fact that this had happened twice now should've reassured me that this wasn't just a freak thing. My nerves playing tricks on me, tricking me into hoping that the feeling would return in full. Sadly, my old demons wouldn't let me have hope without a fight. Did they ever?

No, they didn't.

Rationality had been drummed into me by many a person in that I shouldn't be too optimistic, just in case things wouldn't work out and I'd go too hard on myself. Potentially dragging my focus away from whatever I was doing. That same rationale was kicking in now. Big time.

More of me than ever before hoped that this feeling wouldn't stop here, and that it would occur again. However, there was the other side to me that was fighting that freeing feeling, telling me that I shouldn't get my hopes up. That it could be my nerves acting up and I was only feeling the sensation of that, thinking I was feeling something in my legs again.

All the more reason like before, I would be keeping this to myself.

Kenna...she didn't have to know. *Wouldn't*, know.

I knew she would kill me if she ever found out that I'd kept these... happenings, from her. After all, it was her job to fix up and heal people as best as she could.

Well, almost everyone.

There were people in this world that sadly when they were damaged, weren't meant to be fixed. No matter how anyone tried.

Looks like I'm one of those people.

CHAPTER TWENTY-SIX
Kenna

Almost two weeks had passed since our dinner with Joe and his wife, Cassie. Technically, twelve days, six hours and thirty minutes. Not that I was counting. Much. Time had just simply flown by, faster than I've ever known it to.

Maybe it was down to me trying to cram as much into each day as possible, without tiring Theon out too much. All while knowing that in two short days, my extension period as his nurse would be up, and I would have no choice but to leave his side and return to the hospital.

But, is that where I want to be?

The question is one I've been asking myself for weeks now, and I was still no closer to coming to a decision, than I was back then.

Two more days. I had two more days to find it.

Back to Theon, he has come on in leaps and bounds since our first physical therapy session. The strength in his arms was improving with each day that passed, and I could see how much happier he was for it. Even if he didn't want to admit it, and thought that he was hiding it from me well enough.

Even his PTSD attacks had lessened. They no longer occurred at night, though he still mumbled the odd intelligible word or sentence. I knew it would take some time—for whatever had caused them—for the attacks to stop completely so for now whenever it looked like he was on the verge of having one, I intervened.

It was only in his legs that still held the problem. The one we all avoided physically saying out loud, though knew was still the most cause for concern. I had hoped by now that there would have been some sign, or indication, that his legs were receptive to touch and would begin to feel sensations again. Hopefully leading to them being strong enough to walk on but sadly—for Theon more so than me—it wasn't the case. His legs refused to work or to feel anything.

Still, there was something deep down inside of me that was telling me not to give up. Not after all the false hopes or let downs. And I was determined to listen to that feeling.

During the times that I was working out his muscles, nightly calls from either one of Theon's parents, cooking us dinner or chatting with Leary and Jess on the phone or Skype calls with my parents, we went out and explored the charming little town of Dripping Springs.

I found that Theon was more open to exploring around the area, due to the fact that no one knew him here. No one knew what exactly had happened to him, therefore they didn't reserve the right to judge him like folks back in Austin would. Not that anyone has the right to judge anyone in the first place, regardless of if they are familiar or strangers.

Our first stop was the main street in town, in order to scope out what Dripping Springs had to offer in terms of shops and rather surprisingly, it had more than we'd bargained for, considering it was a small town. It had a cute clothing shop, a bakery, a small bar, food store and the cutest little bed and breakfast! That place ended up surprising us even more when Cassie walked out of it, laying to rest our curiosities by informing us that she actually owned and ran the place! How we didn't find this out when we had dinner with them, I don't know.

I even did a little bit of research and found a small, community gym just on the outskirts of town and managed to get Theon in there for a quick workout with one of the staff members! Lucky for me, he turned out to be someone who'd worked with paraplegics before, so was able to get a one-on-one session with Theon, while I went off for an hour around the little park across the street.

We'd even been out earlier today for lunch! The lady in the bakery recommended to us that we should check out this English-style pub, which had been built fairly recently. I'm glad that we did. The place served the most delicious food I've ever eaten in my life. So much so, I'm half-tempted to move to England to eat more delicious food!

Even Theon liked it, and he was a massive lover of classic American food as a rule. It wasn't often we ate, or I cooked something non-American. The change of food was welcome to us both.

The man in question right now happily resided on the couch in the living space. Since we'd had a good day and got some exercise earlier, I decided to forgo any physical therapy tonight and let him…us, have a relaxing night in doing whatever he…we, felt like doing.

He chose a movie marathon.

Fine with me. It's been forever since I had a good old-fashioned movie marathon. That is, not counting anything I've binge-watched on Netflix. I don't count the digital stuff as real movie-marathon, but that's just me. Others, I know, would disagree.

In the meantime, I was here in the kitchen cooking us up something to eat while watching the movies. Theon had requested an all-American burger and fries—of course—with all the trimmings. Typical Theon. Meanwhile, I didn't crave a burger. Instead I craved my simple, yet legendary, cheese pasta.

Boiled, lightly salted water, cooked pasta shells, a little butter and cheese and boom…instant deliciousness.

It was a food cooked for me by my mom's mom, my Nana, when I was a child. Whenever I used to go and visit with her over in England every summer, she would cook it at least once for me. Huh… Maybe that's why I loved the food at the pub earlier today. I never thought of that at the time as we ate though.

I finished cooking our food, plating it and bringing it to where Theon still sat in the front room. "Here you go. Want a cushion for that?" I asked, sitting down beside him.

He nodded, "Please."

I usually ask that question at dinner, since he still can't feel anything from the waist down. Don't want him burning anything...uh...vital.

Cushion and plate on his lap, I turned my attention back to the TV, the remote now in my hand. "What do you want to watch?"

He shrugged, "I don't mind. You pick."

Well, this is new.

None of the men I've ever been with--not that I'm with Theon--have ever let me pick a movie before. God forbid! My tastes were never theirs and as a result, I was always subjected to countless action, shoot-em-up, gory and zombie-esque movies. Yeah, not exactly my type of movie. Not that it mattered. As long as they didn't watch my type of movies, that's what mattered.

"You sure? There's nothing you want to watch?" I asked.

"Not really. Well...anything that's not war-themed, I'm good with."

That makes two of us...

Thankfully the TV in this place came with Netflix, which we have been using to the fullest. I selected an old BBC series called Merlin, starting back at episode one of the first series. I've watched this series countless times, and yet I still found myself coming back to watch it after finishing the last episode.

"What's Merlin?" Theon asked, taking a massive bite out of his burger.

I shook my head quickly, "You'll make fun of me if I tell you how I got into this series."

"Aww c'mon, I won't. Tell me." he begged.

Goodbye dignity my old friend.

"Okay. Well...um...after my first boyfriend broke up with me many years ago, I went the typical route of feeling sorry for myself, crying endless tears and eating absolutely everything in sight no matter if I was hungry for it or not." Theon chuckled, and I continued, "So, I went and stayed with my grandmother over in England for a while, hoping to forget him. While I was there, she let me use her laptop and I was able to watch some shows there. Merlin was one of them. I'd just missed the end episode of the last series, so I binge-watched the whole thing from start to finish on something called BBC iPlayer. It's like catch-up TV, of sorts. I was hooked from the first episode, and every now and then I just click and re-watch it. In a way, because it second-hand comforted me back then, I watch it to feel the same. Even when I'm not sad. Does that make sense?"

For a moment, Theon stopped eating his burger to listen to me. "Huh. I never knew you had an English grandmother."

"That's what you got from all of that?" I blinked.

He shrugged, "Sure. I mean, why dwell on what made you upset? Okay, he broke up with you. Do you know the reason why?"

"No. I don't."

"See, there you go." he said, taking another bite of his burger. "That's why I mentioned your grandmother. Far more interesting and I'm sure something you'd rather talk about, than your ex."

I really hate it when he's right...

He's been right one too many times lately.

"Hmph."

I heard him chuckle from the other side of the couch, but I chose to ignore it. Taking a fork full of my cheesy pasta instead.

We sat in a comfortable silence as the first episode continued to play, both of us eating our respective foods. Theon though, well, he was done eating his a lot faster than I was with mine. I swear the man never even stops to chew his food, he just hoovers it in!

"So, tell me more about yourself." Theon said, breaking the silence.

He wants to know more about me?

Why now?

The only people I've ever really spoken to about any of my ex boyfriends, were Jess and Leary. I guess I'm not opposed to talking about them to him, I'm just lost as to why he's chosen now to ask. We've had so much time together already. I suppose our impending separation has a part in his asking.

Only one way to find out.

"What do you want to know?"

"Whatever you want to throw out there. Lord knows people keep poking and prodding for information I don't want to talk about, so just tell me something about you that I don't already know." He said, inclining his head.

I suppose...it wouldn't hurt to say something about my exes. He won't ever meet them. Or know them. They're in the past so it can't hurt. Right?

"I have a habit of picking men in the military. Not on purpose, I mean. Whenever I've been so lucky to have had a boyfriend, it's just worked out that they've been in some area of service. My first boyfriend had just joined the Marines, fresh out of when we left high school. My next boyfriend--a little later in life--was in the British Navy, and my third and last boyfriend he..." I swallowed hard, thinking of him. "He never made it home from his last tour of duty in the army."

Beside me, I swear I could feel Theon tensing up. I looked at him, only to find a mixed look between sympathy and agony on his face. "I'm...sorry. Not that sorry helps but...I am."

I sighed, "Thank you. People think that saying sorry doesn't help, and that they know it's something probably everyone has said but...it does. More than they know."

He nodded, "It does."

"You've lost someone too?"

It took him a short minute, but he nodded his head. "Y-yes…" he swallowed, "My best friend. Other than Brett, I mean. He....he lost his life, not too long ago."

His voice is laced with pain as every word passed his lips, twisting at my heart.

"Do you want to talk about it?" I asked.

Much to my surprise, he gave me another nod. He continued, "The two of us went out with some of our other friends, as we did regularly. Nothing usually happened. Well, nothing out of the ordinary. Only that night, something did happen." he paused, moving the food off his lap. "We were set upon. I saw he was in trouble and I…I went to help. By the time I got to him he...it was too late. He'd been hurt, badly hurt. Beyond the point of medical assistance."

As he spoke, I inched closer until I was sitting right beside him, my hand now gently placed on his forearm. Hoping in some way, it was comforting him. He carried on.

"The rest of our group managed to get away, they were safe. My best friend, he...he…." I gave his arm a gentle squeeze, "He died. In my arms. I was powerless to save him. His injuries were too severe, too far advanced for me to even temporarily do something until we got him medical assistance."

Sweet Lord Jesus.

"His last wish to me, was to take care of someone precious to him. His girlfriend, whom I've never met. I made him a promise as he lay dying in my arms, that I would find her and watch over her for him. That promise has been broken, it hasn't even been made."

Until now, I kept quiet and let him talk. "I doubt that."

His eyes snapped to look at me, "What makes you say that? I have. I've failed him by not carrying out the promise I made."

"There has to be a reason, and not one that is your fault. Theon, since I've known you I've gotten to know you pretty well, I'd like to say that there's nothing within your character in which you'd willingly or knowingly not carry out a promise."

Something in his eyes changed then. All traces of anger had vanished and was replaced by something much softer.

I half expected Theon to say something back to be, but no words came. He continued to look down into my eyes, searching for something that was clearly running through his mind right now.

Speak, Theon. Please. Speak.

As I willed him to speak, I failed to notice his face getting closer to mine. Inching slowly forward until I could feel his breath escaping through the small gap between his top and bottom lip. His lips?

The prior conversation had all been forgotten for what was happening right here, right now.

Days and nights have both long since passed where I dreamed of this moment, knowing very well that I had no right to. Convincing myself that it couldn't happen for one reason or another but right now, all reason be damned.

My eyes closed, waiting for the moment to happen.

Just as our lips were about to meet, a shriek which could only have come from the devil himself, cried out from the TV beside us. Immediately, I jumped back away from Theon to my original place on the couch. The timing could not have been more inappropriate if someone had orchestrated this.

Obviously, fate had other plans for us and kissing wasn't it.

I dared to glance over to Theon, curiosity at a major high. He rubbed his hand on the back of his neck, eyes looking everywhere but at me. Awkward.

Great. Just great. Now he's not going to want to do that again any time soon. I don't even know what made him want to do that in the first place! I sure as heck won't get the chance to ask now, not with him acting as if that was the most embarrassing thing he's ever been caught doing.

"So...uh...want to watch the rest of this series? It looks fun!"

Hold up. What?

He's not going to address our almost kiss?

He wants to watch the rest of this series?

My mind couldn't catch up fast enough. Actually, it could and it is. I'm just...stunned. Theon isn't one to shy away from confrontation, as I have found out one too many times, so why is he staying quiet now?

I'm too tired to even begin to ask, so it looks like he'll be getting a free pass this one time.

Try and tell my mind that.

I'll be thinking about this over and over, for hours yet.

With my heart beating away like an African drum, I settled back into my place on the couch, "Sure." Preparing for what would be now a silent yet awkward, rest of the evening.

Much as I predicted, it had been one of the most awkward, silent evenings of my life. Theon and I watched the remaining series one episode of Merlin, before getting ready for and getting into bed.

Theon had pretty much gone to sleep as soon as I laid him down with his head on his pillow. Lucky. I wish I had that ability. Instead, I've been laying here for God knows how many hours, replaying our almost kiss.

How many times do I have to think about it, before it decides it's had enough? Clearly, not enough.

"Kenna..." Theon's deep voice groaned from beside me.

I turned to look at him, "Yes? You okay?"

I didn't even realise he'd woken up, my thoughts had distracted me that much.

He looked somewhat pained, his brows pulled in tightly, "Pain. Need painkillers. Please." he groaned.

Pain is often worse at night, as I discovered from treating patients when doing a night shift. Theon must be in agony. He never asks for painkillers, not even at his worst. I wasted no time in jumping up out of bed, rounding the bed to his side and grabbing the rarely-used set of painkillers Theon had been using long before I met him.

Reaching into the nightstand's cupboard, I pulled out the pill bottle. Knocking a few things out in the process. Worry about those later! Quickly I made my way to the bathroom, filling a glass semi with water before dashing back to Theon's side, placing the pills and water on the nightstand.

"Do you want me to sit you up?" I asked, panting from dashing about.

He shook his head, "No."

Waiting no longer, I handed him two tablets and the water. I watched as he successfully swallowed them, keeping an eye on him to make sure he didn't choke on the pills. He didn't. Much to my relief.

Swiftly, I took the water away from him again as I knew in just a few moments, he would be out like a light. Always was after he took any pill of any kind. Placing the glass on the nightstand, I caught that very moment with my own eyes. Head back on the pillow, all pain drifted from his face as the pills slowly took effect.

He always looks so sweet when he's asleep.

I stepped back, planning on picking up the things I had spilled when suddenly, a spike of pain shot up through my leg from my foot. Ow! What the hell? Thankfully as I bent down to check my foot, it wasn't bleeding. Just sore and imprinted with a...circle-shaped something. What had I stepped on?

Crouching down, I immediately found the cause of the pain. My brows pinched together as I picked up a platinum ring, sporting the most beautiful of diamonds on its top. It was truly the most captivating ring I have ever seen, and I hadn't seen a lot. Well, other than rings I've bought for myself over the years, anyway..

Staring at the ring, I couldn't help but think why Theon would have it. And why I haven't seen this until now. It was in with his pills and considering I've spent so long with him, I should've stumbled on this sooner. Right?

Thoughts flooded my mind as I remained rooted to the spot.

Is this an ex's ring?

Does he have a girlfriend?

Why is he carrying a ring around?

None of these did I know the answer to.

Twisting the ring between my index and middle finger, the light from the nightstand lamp caught something on the inside circle of the ring. Is that...an inscription?

I've always loved when men and women inscribed rings! Something about it fascinated me and always gives me warm fuzzies.

Squinting my eyes, I tilted the ring round and whisper-read aloud the inscription:

Macey, My always & forever. Love, Drayce.

My whole body went cold. Numb. My legs wobbled and from my crouched position, I felt myself collapse to the floor, shaking while tightly gripping the ring.

No one has used that name for me for weeks...no, months. And there was only one person who ever called me by that name. So why the hell does Theon have a ring in his possession, inscribed with the phrase quoted to me every morning when I woke up, from my deceased boyfriend?

The pieces did not slot slowly into place, they came in like a tsunami. Wiping away all the fog that had been surrounding me until now. Theon's promise. The girl he hasn't found, but swore to watch over. His best friend--Drayce--dying in his arms. His past. His military past. Everything. Every last little bit of confusing, mysterious nugget of information made the most sense it has ever made. And they were slowly slicing away at me, making me bleed inside.

Glancing between Theon and the ring, I knew what my next move was.

Stuffing everything back into its place, I rose to my feet. Come morning, it wasn't going to be me who would be waking up next to Theon O'Donoghue.

CHAPTER TWENTY-SEVEN
Theon

"C'mon Theon, you're not giving it your all! Give me more!" Brett said, holding the other side of the red punching bag.

He's been screaming at me for almost two hours now. Two long, gruelling hours spent trying to get me worked out. Well, my muscles. I had already worked out and had been for the past three weeks. Ever since I woke up to one angry bed, and one even angrier mother.

I don't remember or even know what had happened that night, not after taking the painkiller. All I did know was that when I woke up the following morning…I was alone. Kenna had vanished without a trace or so much as a goodbye. Nothing of her remained within the house. It was like she hadn't even been there. Or even existed.

She must have contacted someone—namely, my mother—to come and collect me. We weren't due to leave for another day at that point. A whole day in which I had planned to reveal everything to her that I had been holding in for far too long. That last day was well…it was going to be something special. Now I would never get the chance to tell her.

I went back home with my mother with not one, but two, tails between my legs. Lost. Confused. Alone.

Since then, life went back and settled into the new 'normal'. I started working on areas of the ranch that I could do sitting down. I did the paperwork from my dad's office. I also started searching for Drayce's girlfriend. Anything to take my mind off of Kenna's unannounced disappearance, I did it.

"Sorry, man. My head isn't in it today." I sighed.

Brett had been more than patient with me since I came back to the ranch. He started a daily workout routine with me in between his own work. Who put him up to that, I don't know. I didn't want to know. What I did know was that I wasn't feeling up to today's workout.

"You don't say. What's on your mind?" He asked.

The usual. Kenna.

Brett nodded, "Ah, I see. Theon, buddy, you can't keep doing this to yourself."

"Doing what?"

"Beating yourself up about Kenna. It's not good for you or your head. You've got two options. One, forget about her and try and make life as good as it can be for yourself or two, seek her out."

I cocked my head, "Seek her out? You mean, go snooping around until I find her again. Ask her why the hell she left me alone that night? No, I can't."

"Then what do you want me to say, Theon?"

"I don't know!" I shouted. "I'm sorry. I didn't mean to yell at you."

Coming over to me, he clapped his hand on my shoulder, "I think my friend, you already have your answer."

I did? Huh. Maybe, just maybe, I do.

"C'mon, let's get you out of here and out for some fresh air." Brett smiled, guiding my wheelchair out of the makeshift gym, which used to be an abandoned storage shed many years ago.

Outside, the sun shone a little brighter today. A stark contrast to how I felt on the inside.

Brett wheeled us over to the corral where we turned out horses, trained them up and got a feel for what they could do. It also was the self-same corral in which I had my accident with the horse, now named Cináed. It means 'born of fire'. It also happens to be Gaelic for 'Kenna'. It was only fitting I named the horse after the very woman it eventually brought me to. Even if I had got hurt during the process.

It was a day I will never forget.

"Stop thinking so hard." Brett said, leaning up against the fence.

"You know what happened here. How could I not think?" I sighed.

He turned to face me then, a nervous look crossed his face.

"Spit it out, Brett. Whatever it is that you want to say. Go on, it's okay." I added, softly.

After a little pacing, he began, "Okay...well...do you remember that day you saw Kenna and I coming out of the main barn, and you thought we were...up to things?"

I nodded.

"Well...we were..."

My fists clenched, as did my jaw, "Explain. Before I junk-punch you."

Brett held both hands up, "Easy there, partner. I can do one better. Let me show you."

Show me? How would that explain what he wants to say?

Before I could say another word, he spun on his heels and headed for the aforementioned barn. My eyes widened as he emerged, reins in hand, with Cináed walking behind him.

She never let anyone come near her but me. Ever. Even after my accident, she kicked up a fuss with anyone who remotely got close to her. Various ranch hands had to take it in turns to groom her, clean out her stall and generally be around her. So I was told. I hadn't even talked myself into being around her since the accident.

Truth be told, I'd be up and away if I had the chance. Most of me was screaming to bolt, even under impossible circumstances.

Brett brought Cináed to a halt a few feet in front of me. "This is what we were up to."

I arched a brow, "You two were doing it on a horse?"

God I hope not.

With a laugh, he shook his head, "No. You'd rip my plums off if I even so much as touched Kenna."

"Damn right." Without a second thought.

"Anyway…" Brett stroked Cináed's neck, "Kenna had been working on a little surprise for you. All those times she had a spare moment and you thought she was doing something with me? Well, she was. Sort of. I've been working around horses long enough to know how to train one up. Only, you were the one training this beauty here before your accident. Kenna knew how much it was cutting you up that you both got hurt, and didn't get to finish breaking her in so…she decided that's what she would do. Especially since our girl here would only let Kenna near her." He laughed, "She asked me to step in and tell her what to do so she not only didn't hurt your horse, but knew she wouldn't get hurt herself."

Son of a sainted mother… Kenna, you amazing woman.

With every word, my throat grew tighter. Guilt piled up on top of guilt, as night after night did I curse Brett out. Thinking he had been doing something with Kenna behind my back when she…when they…she was doing something out of the kindness of her heart for me.

"Kenna…" I whispered.

It was then that Cináed knickered, bobbing her head before slowly making her way over to me, her reins slipping out of Brett's hand. He didn't bother to stop her as I gripped the arms of the wheelchair, doing my best not to freak out or make her nervous.

Holding my breath, I waited to see what she would do. Hoping to hell that it wouldn't be something bad. Unlikely, considering what Brett had just told me about Kenna breaking her in and training her to surprise me. Well, consider me surprised.

Cináed lowered her head once she reached me, and butted her snout against my hand as if urging me to stroke her. Slowly and swallowing back my nerves, I complied.

"Hey girl." I said softly, "It's been a while, huh?"

She blew through her nose, as if she was answering 'yes'.

Woah.

Behind her, Brett chuckled. "Yeah, we discovered she's smart too. Well, Kenna did. I can't take any credit for that. She's the one who spoke to this girl as if she were speaking to one of her friends."

I couldn't help but laugh. It sounded like something Kenna would do.

For a moment, I just sat here stroking Cináed's nose. Both of us staring at one another, with me not saying a word. Her eyes spoke the words she physically couldn't say, and the message was coming across loud and clear.

She was sorry.

There was no way I could know or confirm that for sure, but something within me knew that is what she was trying to show me with this gesture.

Looking up, our eyes met one more time and I exhaled. "I forgive you." And I did. No matter what happened that day, I had come to terms with it and in my heart I knew Cináed didn't do it on purpose.

"You forgive her?" Brett said, coming to collect the reins. I nodded, "Yeah." I gave her snout one more stroke before bringing it to my forehead. "I do."

Knowing Kenna had worked so hard to do this for me, to write this one wrong which brought about the most major change in my life, there wasn't any doubt in my mind to forgive the beautiful beast in front of me. Lost in my thoughts, I failed to notice Brett take Cináed back to the barn and return on his own. Once more leaning against the corral fence. "You alright?"

I flicked my eyes to look at him, "Y-yeah. Yes." I nodded, "Surprisingly, yes."

He nodded, "Good. Because...there's one more thing you should know. Something I've taken the time to look into something you started."

Oh?

"I've found your mystery girl. Drayce's girlfriend." He said, sounding somewhat nervous.

Now this *is* a surprise.

I wasn't mad that he looked into this without my permission, as I trusted him implicitly, I'm just dumbfounded that he was able to find someone that I had tried and failed to do.

"So, who is she? What's her name?"

A beat passed before he answered, "Mackenzie Kenna Bouchard. It's Kenna."

Mackenzie?

Kenna?

Mackenzie Kenna Bouchard? My Kenna?

For once, my world didn't collapse under me. It completely shattered into a million, confusing pieces. How could this be...is it even...possible?

"K-Kenna? How...is she...ARGH!" Pain like no other shot through my right leg, as if someone had impaled a spike within it.

I shot up out of the chair, gripping my leg as tight as I could to try and dispel the feeling. Only when I did so, did I realise what I was currently doing. As soon as that happened, the adrenaline left as quick as it came and I dropped to the floor with a loud thud.

"THEON!" Brett shouted, rushing over to my side. He supported my weight and slung an arm around his shoulders, "Did you just...how did you...what happened?"

Sweat coated every part of me as I tried to form the words, but none were able to form a sentence. I knew exactly what had happened. Sort of. Medically I had no clue. But I didn't need a doctor to confirm what had slowly been happening these last three weeks.

Hot damn. Hot, hot damn!

The tingles had been growing stronger and stronger, but I continued to deny what was happening. Thinking it was just something to do with nerves and my own imagination. Not allowing my hopes to get too high, before they were dashed again.

No more would that be the case.

Grunting, Brett manoeuvred me back into the wheelchair, sitting me where I'd sprang up from.

I had no idea how or why the hell this was happening here, now, but sure as horse dung was horse dung, I wasn't letting this escape from me this time.

I knew exactly what I was doing next. And it involved my legs, and one miss Mackenzie Kenna Bouchard.

CHAPTER TWENTY-EIGHT
Kenna

Fate was laughing her big fat ass off at me right now. Big time. How have I ended up here of all places? Never in my wildest dreams did I think that I would be back here, almost three months on from when I first set foot inside.

Had it really been that long since I first filled in for Jess? It must have. It was deja vu all over again, being back here.

Jess had called me again not too long ago, much like she had back then, and called in sick. Being the sucker I am, I offered to fill in for her. Not knowing where she was supposed to be working tonight.

Why didn't I ask where it was before accepting?

Because you'd help her out no matter what. That's why.

The building that I couldn't take my eyes off, that I would be stepping into shortly, was the self-same building in which I had an encounter with the rude, self-obsessed party guest. Theon.

I didn't know it was him at the time, but this is where we first met. Where it all began. Where it all should have ended.

With a sigh, I headed inside. Intent on putting those thoughts behind me.

Unlike three months ago, there was no chance of meeting Theon here tonight. The thought relaxed me some. Yet…it also made me somewhat sad. I guess a part of me was hoping for a repeat of way back then, only with a much happier outcome. The chances of that happening were less than slim to none. There was no chance.

Stepping inside, I greeted a few familiar faces who called out 'hello' as they dashed about. Not having time to stop for a proper conversation. Whatever this was about tonight, there were plenty of people attending. The whole main room was full of people, packed from wall to wall.

"Kenna!" A familiar voice called out.

I turned to see Maeve, one of the senior servers I spoke to three months ago, coming over to me with a jug of something balancing on a tray. "Fancy seeing you here! Let me guess, Jess called in sick didn't she?"

I laughed, nodding, "Yes. Only a half an hour ago, in fact. Luckily I wasn't doing anything."

"Not working the shift at the ER today?"

"Not tonight, no. It was my day off." I chuckled, "You know how rare those are for me."

It's true. I very rarely had spare days off. Especially since I picked up every available shift I was legally allowed to work. Just to keep my mind occupied away from anything that would remind me from what I ran away from.

A look of sympathy crossed her face, "And now you're stuck here for the night."

I shrugged my shoulders, "It's not so bad. After all, I have you to keep me company and to talk to. Right?" I smiled.

Maeve returned my smile, "Right! Well, why don't you go on ba
—" it was at that moment, another server slipped and collided against her back, and everything went into slow motion.

I reached forward to steady Maeve as she lost her footing, but failed to notice the jug that was once on her tray was now hurtling towards me. The next thing I knew, red-coloured liquid—wine, I assume—went down my entire front, turning everything that was white to red.

Thankfully the server who had collided with Maeve had caught her, saving her from what would've been a nasty fall thanks to the spilled wine. Lucky me for getting in the way of that one.

"Oh no! Kenna, I'm so sorry!" Gasped Maeve, stepping away from the server who profusely apologised before scampering away.

Great, just great.

"No, it's alright. It's not your—"

She immediately grabbed my shoulders, halting my words. Spinning me around, she turned and began walking me in the direction of and into one of the changing rooms. "We can chit chat and apologise later. There should be something spare in here for you to change into. Come out when you're done!" She said before swiftly turning on the light and shutting the door, leaving me all alone.

"This could only happen to me…" I said to absolutely nobody.

A sigh escaped my lips as I looked around for something to change into. Considering this was a changing room used by guests, I'm going to say now that there wouldn't be much—if anything—to change into.

Specifically, something in my size. It wasn't often I fit into things on the fly.

Looking around, my prior thoughts were confirmed swiftly. There was literally nothing in here. Nothing other than a few mothballs and a dress bag.

Dress bag?!

The last thing I wanted to do was to borrow someone's dress without asking first. Especially if it was an expensive one which at a function held here, wasn't an unusual thing. That said, what choice do I have? My outfit is ruined and I didn't think I would need to bring a spare, not for one night's work. This would have to do.

"Let's just hope this thing fits…" I muttered.

Opening up the bag, I was left speechless at the beautiful dress within.

Holy Moses! Sweet. Holy. Moses!

My mouth gaped at such a dress being left here on its own. Surely someone would have worn this? It couldn't be left here in a bag!

The dress—a strapless gown—started off with a sparkling silver glitter corset bodice, slowly turning into a dark, azure blue further down to the skirt of the dress. The gems got fewer and fewer until you reached the long, poofy, tulle skirt where now it looked less like a crystal ball, and more like romantic stars that shone on a clear, Texas night.

This dress...this beautiful, stunning dress was the exact replica of the dream prom dress I'd described to Theon on night we were in Dripping Springs over dinner. Right down to the pattern of the tulle used on the final layer of the dress skirt.

I continued to stare at the dress until a knock on the door caused me to jump, "Kenna? How are you getting on?"

Maeve! Sweet niblets!

"A-almost done!" I said, hoping to sound convincing enough.

Looking back and forth between the dress and the door, I could see that there was no other choice. Looks like I'm putting on this gorgeous dress.

"And make a quick and hasty exit afterwards." I muttered.

Quickly shedding my clothes until I stood in nothing but the bra and panties I'd donned earlier today, I thanked my lucky stars that the bra came with a strapless option. A sheer bit of luck if there ever was one. I detached the straps and buried them in with the pile of my ruined clothes.

Time to see if I say yes to this dress...

I carefully removed it from the dress bag, placing the shoes from the bottom onto the floor, unzipped the zipper and with the utmost delicacy, laid it on the floor with an opening for me to step into. Please don't let me ruin this dress, Lord. Please.

Stepping into the opening, I took a deep breath and prayed. The fabric felt amazing as I glided the dress slowly up and onto my body. The silk —or whatever the material was—felt as smooth as sheets when I've freshly shaved my legs and as every woman knows, that's one of the best feelings in the world.

I stopped at intervals to zip up the back of the dress so I didn't need to struggle holding the dress up, leaving me only needing to zip it up my upper back. Which was a cinch. Next was the shoes. No way will those fit me! Much to my surprise, they did. If this wasn't a Cinderella moment then I don't know what is!

Turning to the mirror, I couldn't believe the image before my eyes. No way could this be me. No way was I this glamorous even when I dolled up for a night out! No, this was all the dress. One hundred percent.

It's just a shame that my hair was the only thing letting me down. I suppose it wasn't too bad though, especially since this is only going to help me get the hell out of dodge. No one will care if my hair is slightly out of place. No one except for me, anyway.

Another knock on the door interrupted my stare, "Kenna? You alright?"

"Y-yes! I'm ready!" I called back.

Time to face the music. Big girl panties...on!

Sucking in a calming breath, I rounded on myself and opened the door with one big pull of my arm, surprising Maeve on the other side.

"Oh my! How stunning you are! And look, you fit into it all!" Surprisingly...

"Thank you...but I have to...I-I'm sorry I can't sta—"

Before I could tell her I wasn't able to stay, she had grabbed hold of my hand and was proceeding to pull me in the direction of the main room where I had seen the guests gathering when I first came in.

"Maeve, no! I can't go out there in this! This is someone's dress, I need to leave!" I whisper-shouted. Sadly, it fell on deaf ears.

Faces whizzed past me as Maeve manoeuvred us through the throng of people. What is she up to? What's going on?

Just as I was about to throw up another objection, she stopped us just in front of the stage at the front of the room.

"I need you to stay here for me, okay? Don't move!"

Now I couldn't care about the people around me, or if they were even watching our interaction, I just wanted to know what the hell was going on!

"Don't move? Maeve, what's going on?"

Before the last words left my lips, she had already up and dashed away. Back through the throng of people.

A second later, the room was plunged into pitch blackness. Strangely, no one screamed. Which is what I was fully expecting if no one was expecting something to happen. That means...

Footsteps shuffled, hushed voices whispered around me and a moment later, a bright, white light turned on at the other end of the room as it did over me, temporarily blinding my vision.

Lowering my hands, I squinted my eyes trying to adjust to the sudden intrusion of light from being plunged into the dark. Is that? No...no, it can't be!

Sitting in a wheelchair was the main person who had been occupying my thoughts every night since I ran out on him back in Dripping Springs. Theon O'Donoghue was here and he's...in uniform?

Of course he was in uniform. He was a former soldier who had served in the army. A fact I had willed myself to forget after Brett had blurted it out one night weeks ago.

The people that had occupied the room had all moved into groups either side of the large space, all who were staring at me while giving Theon and I enough room to do...what?

What is going on?!

I was willing myself to move, to march on over to him or to even leave the room but alas, my legs did not comply with my head. I remained frozen in place as I watched Theon roll himself closer until he was about ten feet away.

"Hello, Kenna."

My heart began to pound at the mere sound of his voice, after being denied it of my own cause. Holy cow. Not to mention, my mouth had gone completely dry. Taken aback at this sudden turn of events. Wait a minute! It's all making sense now! Jess calling in sick...Maeve spilling the wine...the dress...everything!

Theon did this. But, how? Why?

190

That is exactly what I intend to find out!

Straightening my back, I finally found my voice, "Theon. What's going on?"

Thanks to the lighting, I got a chance to look him up and down since he'd rolled forward. After I ran away from him, I did a little digging after finding the ring in his nightstand. My digging confirmed that Theon was the buddy that Drayce, my deceased boyfriend, had been going on about. Though he never mentioned him by name, which I thought was always odd.

Theon had served with Drayce in the military, and had been on the final tour. The tour in which Drayce lost his life.

Since discovering that fact, I decided not to look any further and that burying everything for now just to forget, was best. I was wrong. So, so wrong.

Apparently, Theon didn't get the memo.

"Well, you kind of took off on me. So I had to chase you down."

"Chase me down? Theon, even if that's what I wanted you to do, why did it take you weeks to do it?" My voice wobbled, betraying my tough front.

He looked at the people on either side of the room before casting his eyes back to me, "Because of this…" uniformed men came from either side of him from behind, each laying a hand on his wheelchair as he slowly but surely rose from it.

ROSE FROM IT?!

Someone behind me used a hand on my back to steady me, as once more my traitorous legs decided to go wobbly on me. Can I really be seeing what I think I'm seeing? How is this even possible? There wasn't any chance of…of this happening again!

Standing proud and sure, I watched as the impossible did in fact happen. Theon, albeit with a slight limp in his gait, walked right on up to me. Stopping at arm's length. "We meet again, Miss Bouchard. Minus a milkshake thrown at me this time, I hope." He chuckled, and I couldn't help but help a small one escaping myself.

It's true. The last time the both of us were here as I was thinking about earlier, the night ended with me tossing my drink all over him for his rudeness. I doubt that's going to happen this time.

I had forgotten how tall he was when standing. Yes, I had a good idea of what it was when he was laying down, but you always got the real full effect while standing up. He had to be six foot, if not just over. And all six foot of him was watching me, wondering what I was going to say next.

"How is this…when did you…how is this…"

He chuckled again, the sound vibrating through my whole body, "Well, that part is a long story. The short version is…one day I decided to act upon this feeling I was too scared of before. I decided on what I was going to do. I was going to fight, Kenna. I was going to fight for something I know two people, among many, would be kicking my ass to do if they knew I had the chance to walk again. One of them was you."

I swallowed, "And the other?"

The smile that spread across his face reached all the way to his eyes, crinkling at the corners ever so slightly, "You know who."

"Drayce…" I whispered.

"Yes. He would've handed me my ass if he was here, making sure I would walk again even if I didn't want to."

That was Drayce, alright. Always was a positive pusher for those in need of someone to be there for them.

"How did you…how did you know who I was? That I was his…"

I jumped at the contact of his hand on my upper right arm, "I started searching after you left, but Brett was the one who finished it for me. He wanted me to find Drayce's mystery girl as much I wanted to know where the hell you had gone. Little did either of us know, we were searching for the same person."

Theon…

His hand continued to travel down until it reached mine, cupping my hand in his, "That's just one of the reasons why I'm here tonight. Among many"

"W-what are the others?"

"There's only one that matters right now, the rest can wait until after we've made up."

I laughed as happy tears threatened to form in my eyes, "You sound sure about that."   "Oh I am. Kenna, for the longest time I've been walking through the darkness. Stumbling around with no clue how to break out back into the light. I went into the military because that's what I thought I always wanted to do, following in my father's footsteps."

I blinked, "The party…that was for your father."

"Yes." He nodded, "During the course of my service, it never even occurred to me to want to have a relationship outside of a sexual one, no emotions or intentions of furthering it attached. Not even when I was honourably discharged did it enter into my mind."

"Why?" I asked.

He shrugged, "I guess I was too afraid of opening my heart. Cheesy, I know. But true. Since I lost the person closest to me at the time, I couldn't bring myself to get close to someone, for fear of losing them as well. I wouldn't have been able to bounce back from another loss. So, who you met all those months ago was the man I had moulded myself into. An ass."

"That's putting it mildly." I scoffed, rolling my eyes heavenward.

"True, but all that changed when I met you."

I swallowed again, "Me?"

"You. Ever since I first set eyes upon you when I woke up in that hospital room, I knew there was something special about you that would tie you to me forever. Only, I was too scared to act on it when we met again thanks to my mother."

Mara.

My head started to feel dizzy with all of the information that it was receiving, but I kept my eyes on Theon's handsome face as he continued, determined to hear him out as his once closed gates were now wide open.

"I denied myself, and my feelings for you, for so long. Deciding that you were better off with a man who was whole. A man who could give you so much more than a broken man who couldn't even walk. I should've let you decide that for yourself, but my own foolish thoughts got in the way of that. I'm sorry."

It was then that the tears broke free, slowly streaming down both of my cheeks before the thumb of Theon's other hand wiped them away. "I-it's okay."

"No, it's not. I was wrong about that and a lot of things, including how I treated you for so long. Kenna, there's something I've come here today to ask of you. It's a pretty big ask."

Oh my God!

I knew it wasn't a proposal, as neither of us were remotely ready for that. But whatever it was had my heart beating a mile a minute in anticipation.

"Kenna, you were the woman who brought me back to life. The woman who gave me a second chance, who made me feel again, faced my fears and gave me hope for the future, and gave me a purpose to walk again. To walk alongside you in life in whatever capacity you'd have me. I've made you wait three months for this, and I can't wait a second longer."

His hands slowly came off their respective places and cupped either side of my face, preparing me for what I finally knew was about to happen. The same thing he had just been talking about which I had been dreaming of for far too long. Our first kiss.

The second that his lips touched mine and our bodies stood flush against one another, everything before this moment in time slipped away. All the anger, the sadness, the bad memories and tough days that brought us to where we both stood, wrapped in one another, faded away into memory. Replaced only by the love and warmth of his kiss.

I couldn't care that our first kiss was being witnessed by dozens of people. Fate had decided that this was our moment and this was how it was meant to happen and for once, I agreed with fate.

For the first time in my life, I felt complete. And it was Theon O'Donoghue who was finally completing me.

Eventually, Theon broke our kiss while continuing to hold onto me as if I was his anchor to this world, "Mackenzie Kenna Bouchard, this is me. This is who I am and this is my other uniform. I was meant to find and be with you all along. Would you accept this former soldier-turned-cowboy for all that he is, flaws and all, and let him love you like he knew he was destined to do, thanks to one amazing man who brought us together?"

Reaching up, I cupped his cheek in my hand, "Only if you do the same for me, Theon O'Donoghue."

He winked at me, strengthening his hold around me, "Deal."

I know now after all this time, that life has a way of surprising me when I least expected it. Its latest surprise was Theon O'Donoghue. Former soldier turned cowboy, now the man who I could only ever see at my side until the end of forever.

Just as I was about to lean in to seal the deal with another kiss, Theon halted me by stepping back out of our embrace. "There's one more thing…" he said, reaching into his pocket and bringing out the self-same ring I had stumbled upon in the nightstand. This time, attached to a silver necklace chain. "Carry us both, Kenna. He was going to be your forever at one point, and he was my best friend in the entire world. I won't ask for your whole heart, as I know he will always have a part of it. So what I'm asking is, will you give us both a shot? Me as your boyfriend, and him as our guardian angel, guiding us through life as one?"

Swiping at my eyes, I nodded. "Yes. Yes with all my heart."

I bowed my head as Theon slipped the necklace over it, completing the mission Drayce had set out on long ago. Now I would have the opportunity to carry him in my heart forever as I begin this new stage of my life with Theon. My guardian angels both in heaven, and on Earth.

Thank you, Drayce. I'll always love you. Thank you for guiding me back to Theon, I'll take care of him for you from this day forward.

No longer was Theon O'Donoghue the secret soldier. He was my past, present and my future. And I sealed that future with another warm, wholesome and completing kiss to the claps, cheers and celebration of all of those around us.

Our story was just beginning, and I couldn't wait to see where it was taking us. Both of us, together. As one.

THE END

Below is a sneak peak from Book Two in my Always Alone Series, Texas Eire. Enjoy!

CHAPTER ONE

Ryder.

If days got any better than this, then I sure as hell wasn't aware of it. Living in the here and now, well, I'm more than happy to stay right where I was. Pulling my six-year-old American Quarter horse, Whiskey, to a stop, I removed my cowboy 'cutter' hat, wiping my brow to remove the sweat before sliding the hat back on.

Today was up there with the hottest of days, that's for sure. June in Texas was always a shirt-drencher, usually peaking in July and August. Though today it was unusually—and swelteringly—hot.

I usually avoided solo rides around my folk's ranch on days like this, but I decided to go for it and like a fool, I was paying for it with in this heat.

Should have just stayed home and hosed myself off...

More fool me for wanting to escape the madness of the main house, even for a little while. What with five men and two women coming in and out all day, it was hard to find a moment's peace. Still, I wouldn't change it for the world. I craved the chaos. The noise.

A lot had changed in the last six months, since my brother married his now wife, Robinne. Ralph came to me one day to hatch a really haphazard plan on how he planned to ask Robinne to marry him. Thankfully with myself being the brains of the bunch, fine-tuned his plan and she had ended up saying 'yes' to him, right in front of the whole town.

They got married on Christmas Eve last year, to which I was made Ralph's best man. *Which went down with the rest of my brothers...as you can imagine.* I said yes to being his best man because I know out of all of my brothers— no matter how close we all are—Ralph would be the one I would go to to ask the same question.

Not that I plan on marrying any time soon...or ever.

That was a story for another day.

Two weeks after Robinne and Ralph's wedding, they returned from their modest honeymoon in Castlewellan, County Down in Ireland. Robinne had been speaking on and off about how she'd always wanted to go there someday, so my brother being my brother, he made it happen. Of course. He would do anything for her, including letting her decide where they would honeymoon. The love-sick puppy.

Still, that doesn't come close to a 'bombshell' which none of us saw coming. Back in March, and around the time which things were finally starting to calm down, Robinne and Ralph announced that they were expecting their first child together. They were at the 'safe' twelve weeks mark to be able to tell others, apparently.

This is something we all really should have seen, as looking back on it the signs were all there. We were just all clueless to them all. Robinne never drank with us at dinner, she'd stopped eating her favourite deli meats and the poor girl was throwing up here and there. To be honest, there was a mini sickness going around at the time, so we wouldn't have guessed it was pregnancy that was making her throw up.

Delightful.

At least the upside of all the puking, I would someday soon be an uncle. An *uncle*. Me, an uncle! I knew one day one of my many brothers would settle down and pop out a kid or two, though I didn't expect it to happen so soon. Especially with the twins being as precocious as they are, I half expected one of them to announce it first. Still, I'm only twenty-six. Not a bad age at all to be an uncle, all things considered. At least I'd be the coolest uncle this kid is ever going to have. No matter what my brothers think, I'm going to be the coolest of us all. Let them wait and see.

Removing my cowboy hat, I wiped my drenched brow.

Hot damn. There's got to be some way to cool off in this heat!

My thoughts immediately went to Robinne. What with her being six months pregnant, she would be feeling this heat more than the rest of us, the poor thing.

Looking around, I spotted the perfect way to cool down on this hot, Texas day. Up ahead and mere metres away was a river my brothers and I would often play in as kids. Having not been up this way in a while, I'd gone and forgotten about it.

With a soft click of my tongue, I rode Whiskey right on over to the river, hopping off his back. "Go on, buddy. Wander for a bit, while I take a dip." At my words, Whiskey nonchalantly walked away a short distance, his head dipping to nibble at the grass at his hooves.

Whiskey had been my horse ever since he was a young colt. Since he wasn't going to be ridden for barrel racing or roping, I'd taken Whiskey off the hands of a buddy of mine to work on our family ranch. As soon as he was ready to leave his mother, he was mine.

Of course when I went college, my father took over the caretaker role. Damn horse was spoiled rotten. Not that the beast minded, he relished the extra pampering and attention. As soon as I was back home though, the reins were quite literally back in my hands and I raised him the rest of the way.

At his own pace, the horse in question ambled off down the side of the modest riverbank, nibbling at the slightly longer grass away from the water's edge.

Looking around, I made sure one last time that there was no one around to watch the show that was about to start. In no way am I ashamed of my body as in fact, I'm quite proud of it. I just don't believe in being an accidental exhibitionist. I did have some principles, after all.

Making short work of stripping off my clothes, I wasted no time in getting into the cool water of the river. The sensation causing tingles from the tips of my toes to my head as I waded in, the water level reaching my belly button. Reaching the middle of the river, that level happily settled at my chest.

The coolness of the water was exactly the perfect thing to cool down my overheated body, having been on horseback under the sun for most of the day already. Good thing I decided on stopping for a dip. Going back to the main house would've only made me hotter. At least this way I can cool down before heading back.

On the upside, at least the fence had been mended before this dip. All morning, I've been riding up and down the many fence lines across our sprawling property. Why? To check that none of the animals had gotten in or out, or that anyone had broken through on four-wheelers. Damn kids. Summer was their peak time for troublemaking, and it was our job to keep up with it.

I'd been tasked with more fence-checking, since Ralph had insisted Robinne stop the task at three months pregnant. Not that it bothered me, I loved being outdoors. Just me and my horse, exactly how I like it.

Robinne had taken on lesser taxing tasks at the request of my brother, much to our relief. The last thing we wanted was for anything to happen to her and the baby. She's happy doing all of the ranch's paperwork and admin until her maternity leave finishes, after the baby is born.

Putting all thoughts of horses, brothers and babies out of my mind, I swiftly dunked the rest of not touched by the water, under the water. The coolness of the water fully coated every part of my skin, the feeling was deliciously relaxing. I might have to get a pool installed at my place after this.

Everything else that could have possibly been lingering in my thoughts and in my mind, melted away. Naturally, my body floated up out of the water, bobbing me gently at the surface. Thankfully this river wasn't fast-flowing, so there was not a great worry of being carried too far down stream.

Relaxing in the most contented state I've eve been in for a long time, I had no idea how much time had passed since first getting in. What I *did* know—or rather feel—was the sensation of someone's eyes watching me. It couldn't be Whiskey, as he'd be too far down the bank to see me so...who or what could it be?

Opening my eyes to the blinding sun, I shifted into a standing position with my feet now firmly planted on the riverbed. Droplets of water cascaded down over my eyes, head and body, returning back to the river. Wiping my eyes free of water, my eyes caught sight of what had been watching me. A woman.

Correction, a stunningly beautiful woman.

The dark-haired beauty stood on the opposite riverbank to where I'd first entered the river earlier, staring at me with her mouth agog. For some reason, I found myself doing the exact same, minus the gaping mouth. I knew I should be asking her what she was doing here, but words failed to make an appearance as I took her in from top to toe.

Brain and mouth, any time you want to engage would be nice, thanks.

Rising up on my toes, I stood up higher in order to hopefully speak to the woman. If my brain was now working, that is. Only, I would if the woman in question didn't spring back in…what, shock?

What is wrong with her? Has she never seen a man taking a dip befo—

Oh no…

"Woah!" I said, cupping myself to protect what little—or rather, big, modesty—I had left. "I-I can explain!" I called out, hoping to clarify what I was doing standing stark naked in a river during the middle of the day.

Before that chance even came, the wide-eyed, raven-haired beauty fled. Scarpering away back up the bank and away from me, while I stood here holding all that I held dear.

"Wait, hang on!" I yelled louder. Scrambling up the side of the river bank after the mystery woman, I slid my discarded clothes on as best as I could and in record time too. Never mind the fact I was wet, I have to tell this woman about what was going on.

By the time I'd slipped on my boots and hat, jumping the river in order to follow her, it was too late. She had vanished.

Damn it!

Now I was never going to clarify my intentions, and she—whoever she was—is going to think the worst about me. Fantastic. Not to mention, I'd be stuck thinking for the longest time about who she was.

The mystery woman would remain just that, a mystery.

THANK YOU

I have so many people to thank this time around, compared to when I released my debut book. So allow me to address you all with a message which covers each and every one of you.

Thank you for being so amazing by supporting me through making my literary debut, and for being so encouraging ever since. This next book has been so long in the making, and has truly been only possible thanks to the drive you all have given to me to write it.

I hope you enjoy this story as I did writing it. Until next time!

-Philippa x

ABOUT THE AUTHOR

Philippa is an introverted writer, come pet-shop worker, living in the West Midlands, UK. She currently has the support of her parents, grandmother, wider/non-biological family and her eight-year-old cat, Bell, who just loves to sit in front of Philippa's laptop so she can't get any writing done. She is planning to continue to write, while looking to complete online editing courses later this year, in order to become a part-time fiction editor. Her only other work to date is her debut novel, Solivagant.

When Philippa is not on her laptop writing, she can be found diving into one of her many paperbacks from her favourite author, Kelly Elliott. As well as watching tons of anime, posting to her Instagram accounts, spending time with her amazing grandmother, enjoying a healthy dose of her favourite Jameson's whiskey, and cuddling her cat Bell like she was a baby instead of a cat. She dreams of becoming a 'proper' author someday, and has high hopes of achieving the dreams she thought were once impossible.

PHILIPPA'S OTHER WORKS

Always Alone Series:

Solivagant (Book One)

Printed in Poland
by Amazon Fulfillment
Poland Sp. z o.o., Wrocław

58418165R00120